BLOOD VENGEANCE

MATT BANNISTER WESTERN 9

KEN PRATT

Published in the United States by Wolfpack Publishing, Las Vegas

CKN Christian Publishing
An Imprint of Wolfpack Publishing
6032 Wheat Penny Avenue
Las Vegas, NV 89122

christiankindlenews.com

Paperback ISBN: 978-1-64734-200-5
Kindle ISBN: 978-1-64734-199-2
Library of Congress Control Number: 2020947566

BLOOD VENGEANCE

Author's Note

One of the saddest parts of American history is the lack of attention given to the massacres of American Indians. There have been many, but only a few are commonly known such as Wounded Knee, Sand Creek and others which are pretty well documented. The Bear River Massacre of 1863 in southeastern Idaho was overlooked by the news happening during the Civil War at the time. If you ask, most people have never heard of the Massacre of Bear River. The number of those killed was listed by the army at 250. However, it is believed many more lives were lost that day with estimates between four hundred to five hundred Shoshone slaughtered by the 2nd California Volunteer Cavalry, on the morning of January 23rd, 1863. The Shoshone were not given a chance to talk peace or a chance to surrender, they were attacked and killed. It is one of the largest, if not the largest massacre of Native Americans in American history and still today sadly remains largely unknown.

My own native blood is of the Madesi band of the Pit River Tribe in Northern California. Again, the history of our tribe is bloody and victims of another seldomly known piece of history that is mentioned in this book, the State of California put cash bounties on Indian scalps and many California Indians lost their lives and the proof needed to be paid was their hair.

In this story, I wanted three viewpoints, the proud soldier, the haunted and regretful soldier, and the victim. I can tell you right now the character of Wes Wasson was hard to write and may be the most hated character that I have ever written. I hope you despise him as much I do.

This book is dedicated to the memory of our American Indian ancestors from all tribes, bands, clans, and nations around this country.

Ken Pratt

Chapter 1

Matt Bannister climbed the steps of the Branson City Hall, which was also the Jessup County Courthouse at the end of Main Street and opened the heavy door. He pulled the hood of his buffalo coat back and made eye contact with the attractive, Debra Slater, who was waiting for him. She was the daughter of William R. Slater, the Branson Mayor and President of the W. R, Slater Mining Company.

"It's nice to see you again, Matt. How are you?" she asked with a pretty smile. She was in her mid-twenties, with blonde hair and pretty blue eyes on her triangular face. She stood about five-foot and four inches tall, but she was already involved in city and county politics. She was the City Recorder and active in most meetings, groups and activities. She was a small lady, but her attractive face wasn't to be trusted any further than her father or brother's were.

"I'm good. Do you know why I was asked to be at

this meeting?" He had been summoned to be at the City Council Meeting at seven o'clock.

Debra frowned. "No, I don't. All I know is it's a meeting with the business owners tonight."

"The Elite Seven, huh?" he asked sarcastically.

She chuckled. "Well, I've heard them called worse. So you're courting Christine Knapp, now. I am glad she has recovered from being shot. She's a nice lady from what I hear," she said as she led Matt down a hall. She paused outside of a door and turned to look at him. "I hope it works out well for you."

He nodded. "Thank you. Christine is still recovering; she isn't healed yet."

"Hopefully, she will. They're waiting." She opened the door to let him enter first into a room with dark mahogany paneled walls. There was an American flag hanging from a wall and a portrait of George Washington along the back wall. Seven men sat in their assigned seats in front of their nameplates around a long curved semi-circle table. They all sat in comfortable leather padded chairs and had a cup of coffee sitting in front of them. A smaller table with a single chair was set near the center front of the half-circle.

"Have a seat, Matt," William R. Slater said. He was a man in his sixties with short gray hair combed neatly with a gray beard about six inches long.. William had a long, thin face and a hooked nose that made him look like a hawk. His gray eyes showed the cold and heartless determination that had made him the silver king of Oregon, William

Slater wore an expensive suit and casually glanced at Matt as he opened a file in front of him.

Matt smiled at his brothers Lee and Albert, who sat at each side of the curved table. Josh Slater, the Vice President of Slater Silver Mine, sat beside his father, William. Roald Chalkalski, the owner of Seven Timber Harvester Company, Louis Sorenson, was the owner, editor of the Branson Gazette Newspaper, and James T. Hatfield was the President and founder of the Branson Savings and Loans Bank. The seven men were the wealthiest and most influential men in Branson. Debra sat at a desk off to the side of Matt. She opened a folder and grabbed a pen to keep notes of the meeting.

After some friendly greetings, William took his wooden gavel and knocked it on the table three times. "Let's get this moving." He looked at Matt intently. "Marshal Bannister, it has come to our attention that the recent tragedy at Bella's Dance Hall may have been avoidable if you had not of recommended to the Sheriff, Tim Wright, that he hire Martin Ballenger. Can you…"

"What?" Matt asked, with a questionable narrowing of his eyes. "I never recommended Martin to anyone."

William Slater looked at him over his silver-rimmed spectacles. "You deny you recommended him to the Sheriff, Tim Wright?"

"We all know Tim's the Sheriff, so you don't need to keep emphasizing it. The only thing I ever told Tim was that he needed to fire Martin after he followed Paul Johnson and Sam Troyer home and threatened them. You can ask both of those fellas about that. That happened the day before the shooting of Edith Williams, Phil Mears and Christine Knapp as a matter of fact. I had nothing to do with Tim hiring Martin."

Josh Slater leaned forward and pointed a finger casually at Matt as he asked pointedly, "Didn't you meet Martin before Tim did? Didn't you suggest to Martin to apply for a job as a deputy? Is that not true?"

"It is. Martin asked if I was hiring and I said no. In jest, I told him to go ask Tim for a job." He chuckled lightly. "I never thought Tim would hire him."

William spoke with no humor in his voice, "There's nothing funny about this, Marshal Bannister. Sheriff Wright has come under heavy condemnation over this shooting. The fact is, it goes back to your unwillingness to work with or to even get along with, our Sheriff. Tim has been good for our community and you continue to refuse to get along with him. Isn't it true that you have struck Tim a few times and threatened him repeatedly to do your best to rig the next election to go against him? Can you tell us if that's true or not?"

Matt shook his head slowly, growing frustrated with the questioning. "I can't rig the election; you're the only ones that can do that. But I can and will support whoever runs against him if they are suitable to do the job. I do not share your feelings about the Sheriff."

"So, you're not denying laying your hands on

him?"

"No, I'm not denying it. Would you like to know why?"

"No. That's not relevant."

Lee Bannister stated, "I think it is."

"No," William argued sharply, "as Mayor and President of this board, I don't believe we have time to listen to the mute details that do not excuse abusive treatment of one of our elected officials by anyone. I believe we have proven that Marshal Bannister doesn't like our Sheriff and has a personal conflict with him and is, therefore, trying to undermine and humiliate him with every opportunity he has. Isn't it true that you attacked the Sheriff, Tim Wright, Travis McKnight and my son, Josh, in the Monarch Hotel this past August? Is it not true that in that unprovoked attack that you broke the Sheriff, Tim Wright's nose and busted Travis's head open, leaving a nasty scar on his forehead and physically beat and intimidated my son as well?" he asked in a rising voice.

Matt took a breath and looked at William Slater irritably. "Are you sure you want to go there? Maybe your son's wife would like to know why I went there. Do these other men know why you were there, Josh? Let's talk about it and see how great your Sheriff is then, shall we? Listen, if you want to try to kick some dust on my boots, that's fine. But do know, your pig pen's going to be blown wide open in the meantime, and there's a lot of crap in there that you probably don't want your voters knowing about. Am I right?"

Josh Slater stared at Matt for a moment as his face flushed. William Slater's cold eyes narrowed as he changed the subject, "We'll move on, for now, to come back to that at a later time, if necessary. It's also come to my attention upon reading the death certificates that two of my employees have died of strange occurrences and the investigations are still pending on both? Why are they still pending?"

Matt laughed sarcastically and shook his head in frustration. "I haven't finished investigating yet."

"Do you have a suspect? We've all read the autopsy reports," William motioned around the room. "So, have you, I'm sure. Do I need to reread those autopsy reports here in the chamber to be sure we're all on the same page? We're talking about two of my finest employees, Leroy Haywood and Roger Lavigne. And the intentional destruction of one of my cottages by burning it down. Why are their investigations not completed? You've had ample time."

Matt grinned slowly. "I think we all understand what you're asking. To answer your question and end this quickly, I'm still in the process of investigating their deaths."

"Why are you grinning? Do you think this is funny?" William asked accusingly.

Matt shook his head. "No. I find it needless. Is this really why you asked me here without any notice at seven o'clock on a Thursday night? Do you read every employee's death certificate or just these two in particular? Because if it is just these two, then I have questions for Josh pertaining to the law. Questions like, 'why did he have your amazing employee, Leroy Haywood, come to his office and ask him to take two more of your finest employees and go harm three Chinese men employed by my Uncle Luther?' My follow up question would be, 'why were they paid their wages for taking the day off?' That's one of the questions I'd ask because two of those Chinese men are dead; they were thrown over the edge of the quarry pit. The third was scourged by a whip laced with stones, teeth, and glass that I found in Leroy's cabin. He was at home sleeping when he was apparently on the clock at work according to his paysheet. The same is true with the other two men. I find that kind of suspicious, myself."

"Marshal, that is complete nonsense!" William shouted while pointing the gavel at Matt. "Let me remind you that each one of us in here invested our time, energy and money to get you here in town. We built your office to your likings and we reached out and used our influence to get you a United States Marshal position. We are the reason you are here and the reason you have that badge! You would never have earned your way up to a U.S. Marshal without our investment in you. And now you're paying us back by laying your hands on my son and breaking our Sheriff's nose? You bust Roald's manager's head open with a rifle and you've arrested my employees multiple times and now when two of them are dead, you can't find a suspect!" he shouted angrily. "Can I ask why you're failing to do your job?"

Matt looked at William Slater evenly. "I am doing my job. Mister Slater, if you think I'm going to get down on my hands and knees and spit-shine your shoes and scrub your bedpan because you all invested in me and my office, you're dead wrong. Tim is your pawn; I am not. Your employees murdered two men and I arrested them for that. That is my job. Your employee's deaths are strange, I do agree, but there is not an ounce of evidence to prove it is one person responsible or another. As stated on the death certificates and you can read it right there in front of you, the investigation is pending. I don't know how hard that is to figure out without asking me to explain it to you again."

Light snickers sounded from both sides of the room from several of the men. William Slater glared at Matt angrily. "I don't appreciate your attitude, Marshal. Do you have a suspect?"

"I do."

"And who is that?"

"I'm not saying who at this time. May I suggest you just let me do my job?"

William folded his hands in front of him and spoke calmly, "I suggest you start working with us and not against us. I had hoped when you came here that you would be sitting up here with us behind closed doors, helping to design the future of this county and town. I'm beginning to think we have the wrong man. Leave the Sheriff be and I want an arrest made and these crimes solved. Do remember we made you and we can destroy you just as easily. That is all. You can go."

Matt stood up and smiled slightly. "Can I say something real quick?"

William Slater looked at him despitefully. "You may."

"First of all, I'm not a businessman; I'm a lawman. In the middle of the dirt and grit with some blood on my hands is where I belong, not sitting in here around a half-round table, thinking I'm big enough to play a game of chess with the people of this community. But do not think for a minute that I'm a pawn that you can move around or sacrifice because I'll bring my world into yours and I don't believe you'll stand tall and arrogant for long if I did. My guess, William, is you'd piss your pants like your son did that night at the Monarch Hotel. In short, don't threaten me because I'll call you on it."

William's eyes burned into Matt. "You're walking on thin ice, Marshal. We had the power to get you that badge and office, and we certainly have the power to have it stripped from you too. You remember that before you try to threaten me."

Matt looked at William with a disgusted smirk. "Good evening, Gentlemen."

Chapter 2

Annie Lenning waited in the Willow Falls Bank for Walt Delaney to finish helping Carl Snow and his wife with some banking business of some kind. She stood close to Truet Davis as he looked around curiously at the small bank. They stood politely five feet back from the counter to give the other customers some privacy.

"It's a small bank," Truet stated.

"It's a small town," Annie replied simply. They had come into town late on a Friday afternoon with Adam Bannister before the bank closed for the weekend. Adam had gone up the street to talk to his brother Steven at the Blacksmith shop.

The door opened, and three men walked in behind them. Truet glanced back and saw a man about five foot nine with neck length brown hair with a stocky build. He looked quite unfriendly with hard-cold green eyes on a hardened face and a brown goatee. Truet nodded and the man nodded quietly in return. Truet turned back to face the banker and couple in front of him.

"Miss Annie, how are you doing today?" the man behind them asked.

She looked back and answered with a slight bit of hesitance in her voice. "I'm doing okay, you?"

He nodded. "Not bad. Don't worry; I need to get some money out of my savings," he said with a humored smile. "I hear you are going into the horse trade?"

"I am. We're preparing now, but in the spring, we should be up and running."

"Is the Big Z getting out of the cattle trade?" he inquired.

"No. Adam is taking that part of the ranch over. I will be breeding and selling horses."

The man narrowed his eyes with interest and nodded approvingly. "Very good. I have not seen you in ages, and I've wanted to wish you my condolences for your husband. I played cards with Kyle a few times, and he wasn't a bad man."

"Thank you."

One of the men who came in with him stood behind Annie. He was a bit taller, younger, and heavier than the first, but looked similar with a rounder face. He said, "I'd say she looks like she could ride. She looks good from here anyway." He smiled as he looked Annie up and down.

Truet turned his head and looked at the young man warningly. He had failed to stop a man named AJ Thacker from talking to his wife, Jenny Mae, in a sexual manner like that and he wasn't about to let that start up again unchallenged. The chubby young man wore a gun belt, but his coat covered it.

The young man widened his eyes and glared at Truet. "What farm boy? You want to say something?" he challenged.

Truet smirked slowly and faced forward again.

"What are you smirking at , plowboy?"

The man who had spoken with Annie said, "Knock it off, Vince."

Vince scoffed. "Plowboy gave me a dirty look. If he wants to back it up, we can go outside."

The first man's tone grew harder as he glared at his younger brother, "I said, knock it off! Or we'll go outside."

Truet looked back over his shoulder to look at the young man who appeared to be in his mid to late twenties. "I don't mean to cause any trouble with you. But I won't allow you to talk about her like that."

"Oh, you won't?" Vince asked, growing more threatening.

Truet shook his head as he looked back at the young man evenly. "No, I won't."

Mister and Misses Snow finished their business and left with a friendly hello to Annie before leaving quickly. They appeared nervous and barely glanced at the three men behind Annie and Truet as they walked out the door. Annie grabbed Truet's arm and guided him towards the counter, "Hello, Mister Delaney, I need to put these cashier's checks in my account. One is for Uncle Charlie's account as well."

Walt Delaney looked at Truet. "Truet, how are

you today?" he asked.

"Good."

"How long are you in town for?"

"I'm heading back on Sunday morning."

The man who had talked with Annie asked, "Truet? Are you Truet Davis?"

Truet turned to face him and finally saw the third man who had entered. His eyes stayed on the third man who had neck length straight black hair, a beard, and a left cock-eyed eye. He recognized him from a recent wanted poster in the Marshal's Office. It was Bo Crowe. He was startled to see him standing so close to him. His gun belt was covered by his coat as well. Truet forced his eyes to look at the man who had spoken to him. "I am." His senses grew wary as his gun was covered by his buttoned-up coat making it harder to grab if he needed to.

The man with green eyes nodded. "I've heard of you. You're the new deputy marshal. I'm Morton Sperry. That's my kid brother Vince and my cousin Bo." He raised his hands innocently and explained, "I don't want any trouble, Deputy. We just came in to get some money out of my account."

Truet nodded but was alarmed to be facing three outlaws of such a notorious reputation in the Willow Falls Bank. "Nice to meet you."

"I heard about you. You gunned down Farrian Maddox."

"He didn't leave me any choice," Truet said simply.

"And AJ Thacker. I didn't like him much," Morton said. He stared at Truet as if studying him. "Never mind, my brother. He's still young and dumb."

"No harm done." His eyes shifted back to Bo Crowe, whose dark eyes remained on Truet like a predator's stalking prey. He held Bo's gaze with an upwards turn on the corners of his lips.

Morton said, "I figured we'd meet someday, but I wasn't figuring it would be in the bank with Miss Annie. Are you two courting now?"

Truet nodded. "We are."

Morton nodded with a slight smile. "Well, that's a good family. My two older brothers fought with Adam and Lee in the Snake War. My brother Dwight came home in a box, but my brother Alan said the Bannister brothers saved his and Dwight's life more than once. I can't say we've always walked on the right side of the law and we made friends with men who didn't either, but it was always a rule, and everyone who rode with us knew you don't mess with or touch the Big Z Ranch or any member of that family. I've made it clear that I'll hunt anyone down that does, myself. And if I don't, Alan will, when he gets out of prison. We've never allowed anyone to mess with Annie's family. It's the least we could do after what Adam and Lee did for our family."

Annie looked back at Morton with a playful scowl. "Uncle Charlie might have something to do with that, too, right?"

Morton smiled sadly and nodded slowly. "That too. I do apologize for my little brother's lack of respect, Miss Annie."

"Thank you."

The door opened, and Adam Bannister stepped into the bank. He nodded at Morton with a curious expression. Mister and Misses Snow had mentioned to him that the Sperry's were picking a fight with Truet.

"I was just talking about you, Adam," Morton said.

"Good stuff, I hope."

"Always. I was just telling Truet how you and Lee saved Alan's life in the cavalry. One of the times was the Coffee Creek Battle, wasn't it?"

Adam nodded. "Lee saved a lot of us there; my hands were full. I saved your brothers a few times and I'm sure they both saved us, too. We all tried to watch out for each other. Dwight was killed after I was discharged for my wounds, which I was sorry to hear. He was a good friend of mine."

Morton nodded sadly. He turned to Truet. "I remember Matt when we were kids. He may not remember me, but we played together sometimes when his parents brought them over to my Uncle's dairy. When you see Matt, tell him we don't want any trouble, okay?"

Truet nodded. "I will."

"Matt Bannister?" Bo asked spitefully.

Morton nodded. "Yeah, Truet's a U.S. Deputy Marshal. Matt's his boss."

Bo looked at Truet with hostility in his empty dark eyes. "He just killed a bunch of my friends down in Prairieville. You tell him Morton might want to be his buddy, but I don't."

"I'll let him know."

Vince Sperry looked at Adam carefully. "You saved my brothers? You don't look all that tough to me. I bet my brothers could whip you. Huh?" he asked Morton. "I bet I could too."

Morton slapped Vince across the side of his head quickly with a scowl on his face. "Shut your mouth! Do you not know when to be respectful? You're lucky I don't let Adam take you outside and show you how respect is earned the old-fashioned way! He could paint the bank's walls red with your blood without even working up a sweat on a hot day. You better just keep your mouth shut!" He looked irritably at Adam. "I apologize for him."

Adam chuckled lightly. "Oh, I was going to ask him if he'd like to come out and show me a few things. Morton, you have a good day."

Annie hooked her arm around Truet's. "Let's go. Morton, you take care."

"You too, Miss Annie." He looked at Truet. "I hope we don't cross bad paths, Truet."

"Likewise."

Bo Crowe added as Truet and Annie left the bank, "I think we'll cross paths soon enough."

Truet paused at the door and looked at Bo. "Have a good day."

Chapter 3

Mattie Sperry sat in her wooden rocking chair, holding her year-old granddaughter on her lap with a wool blanket wrapped around them both. Even with a fire in the cookstove and a large fire in the fireplace, the uninsulated clapboard house was drafty and hard to keep warm in the winter. The older Mattie got, the colder the winter's seemed to get. The house had been added onto over the years. Every summer, it seemed like her boys were building another room onto the house to make a little more space to their growing home of children and grandchildren. Unfortunately, none of her boys had acquired her own father's carpentry skills. Their house was not attractive, warm or cozy, but it was what it was, just big enough and good enough to live in. She remained silent as she listened to her son Vince argue with Morton. It seemed the boys had run into the new deputy marshal Truet Davis in the Willow Falls Bank. Vince had been humiliated by his older brother when he tried to start a fight with Adam Bannister and Morton didn't appreciate it.

"Why are you afraid of him?" Vince asked irritably. "He's a big guy, but he wasn't carrying a gun. You acted like he was more dangerous than you and everyone knows that ain't true."

Morton glared at his younger brother with his hard green eyes. "Get it through your head, Dwight and Alan fought with Adam in a war. That is something you and I will never understand because we weren't there; those men, everyone one of them, are a brotherhood that is sacred to Alan. I'll tell you right now Alan would've beaten you senseless if he was at the bank today for you just being disrespectful to Annie. Not one family member of any of those soldiers has ever been robbed or mistreated by us and it will stay that way. Out of respect for Dwight and Alan, we don't cross those family lines. And I will tell you one more thing, Alan isn't afraid of anyone, but he told me that he would never want to fight Adam or Lee Bannister because he'd lose. You're no match for Adam. You know Steven Bannister is the blacksmith over there, right?"

"Of course, Steven's a good guy," Vince said with a shrug. "He's funny."

"Good. I don't want you thinking you can rob him or pick a fight and get away with it, because I'd beat you as you've never been beaten before. From now on, watch yourself over there in Willow Falls. You don't want to cross any lines with anyone named Bannister, Fasana, or Ziegler. I assure you that's the last family I ever want to fight with. Hell, Vince, Matt Bannister, and William Fasana just took out the entire sheriff's office down in Prairieville by themselves and you think you're going to insult their sister and pick a fight with Adam? If you had shot Adam, let's say, I promise you half of our family would be dead before the shooting was over. I've heard the stories from Alan and I'm telling you right now, that's a battle you don't want. From here on out, if I tell you to be quiet, shut your mouth!" He looked at his mother. "By the way Truet was looking at Bo, he must know Bo's wanted. I'm willing to bet Matt Bannister and Truet will be coming here for Bo soon."

Bo Crowe sat near the fireplace and nodded. "I believe so. If anyone has seen the wanted poster, it's going to be the marshal's office. He's the only one who's got the spine to come after me." He looked at his Aunt Mattie. "I don't want to bring any trouble to the family, so I'll be leaving in the morning."

Mattie frowned. Her dark gray hair fell lazily onto her shoulders. Her square face was weathered by a life of hardship and wrinkled into a permanent deep frown. Her hazel colored eyes showed a lack of softness. She spoke pointedly, "Where are you going to go? It's freezing outside and the snow's too high to cross the mountain, I'm sure."

Bo sneered slightly. "I have friends."

Mattie looked at Bo over the tip of her nose. "I have an idea. You won't like it, but it will help us all out a lot. I believe Mort's right; the marshal will come looking for you if he has the guts to show up here. Some say he does and if he does, then let's welcome him in. Think about this idea, Bo. If I turn you in, I can collect the reward, and that's a lot of money we could use to get through the winter with."

Bo shook his head with a scowl forming on his face. "I'm not turning myself in, Aunt Mattie! I'm not going to prison or be hung so you can have some money. Are you kidding me?"

"You're not going to prison. Just listen to me. We need money to survive and you are worth five hundred dollars. You can pretend to hide in the cellar or one of the hiding boxes around here. I'll verify I can get the money first and if I can, then I'll tell the marshal where you are. You give yourself up willingly and let him take you to jail…"

Bo laughed. "That's not sounding good to me, Aunt Mattie."

"Shut up and listen!" She snapped. "*Then*, these boys of mine will meet up with your brothers, if necessary and put the fear of god into your accusers. They'll fear for their lives and drop the charges against you. You'll be released without ever having to go to trial and will walk out of jail a free man. Plus, you'll earn some of your reward money as well."

Bo grimaced and then thought about it for a minute. "What if he doesn't give you the money?"

Mattie took a deep breath. "If the marshal does not agree to give me the reward money, then I won't help him find you. And he will not find you, Bo. We have two cellars: But I'm talking about hiding you in the hiding box under the chicken coop. He can search the property all day long, but he'd never find you there unless I tell him you're there. My boys will tell the marshal you're not here and try to hide you, but I'll make a deal with him in private, so he believes it. I'll tell him we're starving and my boys are going straight. You don't live to be sixty-five years old and not learn a little about how people think. If we just smile and hand you over, the Marshal's going to know he's being duped. But if my boys are unfriendly and I put them in their place, why then the marshal might just pay me for being honest and turning your thieving butt over to him. We are out of money, Bo. This opportunity can help us get through this winter without any bloodshed being risked. As you can see, I have many mouths to feed and I don't want my family to go hungry."

Bo looked at the Sperry family and the younger children that played around the house. "Aunt Mattie, how long do you figure I'd have to sit in jail?"

Her eyebrows raised. "Just long enough for us to wire your brothers and if they don't want to confront your accusers and witnesses, then my boys will find a way around the snow and get over to Prairieville and do it with your brothers. I don't believe anyone will want to go to court after these boys get a hold of them. Two weeks maybe, if that. It depends on how fast your brothers get to work."

"Two weeks in jail. And what do I get out of it other than watching you all eat my bounty away?

Especially Vince."

"I'll save you fifty dollars."

"Fifty?" Bo cried out. "There's a five-hundred-dollar bounty on my head and all I get is fifty?"

"And your freedom, yes. I need the money, Bo. I have plans that I need the extra money for."

"What kind of plans, Ma?" Vince asked.

"Never you mind, just plans of mine." She looked at Bo. "I need your help, Bo. Consider this my way of robbing the marshal and you'll be free to go gamble and carouse without worrying about being arrested. You won't have to run anymore. That's worth more than going to prison. What do you say?"

Bo wasn't pleased. "I suppose two weeks in jail beats years in prison. But I better be set free, or I'll come back here when I get out of prison and raise some hell!"

Mattie's face lit up with a rare smile. "Wonderful. Just remember, do not draw your weapon at all and give up! It won't do any of us any good if your killed or one of my boys are, or the marshal for that matter." She looked at her sons. "No guns when the marshal gets here. Now, when can we expect him?"

Morton spoke, "Truet said he was going back on Sunday, so Monday would be my guess."

"Let's talk about what's going to happen, so we all know," Mattie said. She had been wondering how she was going to come up with the money to pay for an extraordinary birthday present for Morton in June.

Chapter 4

Wes Wasson rode into Branson in the darkness of a Saturday evening. He rode through the streets until he stopped in front of a modest house and tethered his horse at the porch corner post, removed his hat, and pulled down the wool scarf that covered his face. He knocked on the door and waited with a grin.

When the door opened, he recognized one of his blonde-haired nephews. But he couldn't tell which one it was. Both boys looked like they had water-soaked cotton-growing out of their heads. The tall and thin young man looked but didn't recognize him. Wes covered his lips with his finger and whispered, "I'm your Uncle Wes. Where are your parents?"

The young man motioned towards the right of the stairs where the family room was. The house was silent except for the crackling of the woodstove heating the home. Wes stepped into the house and walked into the family room where he found his older sister, Florence and her husband Frank, sitting in a pair of wooden rocking chairs with pillow covered seats. Frank was reading a book and Florence was knitting a scarf. He spoke loudly, "I came all the way up here from California just to find you two old folks sitting around?" Wes laughed at the expressions of their faces when they recognized him.

Florence set her knitting needles down and stood up with a stunned and emotional expression growing on her face. "Wesley! Oh, my goodness," she said as she wrapped her arms around him, feeling the warm tears filling her eyes. "Wesley, it's so good to see you!"

Frank stood up with a smile. "How long has it been?" he asked as he hugged Wes as well.

"Oh, heck, fifteen years at least," Wes replied. "How are you, old man? It looks like you've put on some weight. That's not good for an old cavalryman," he teased while lightly slapping Frank's growing belly.

"That what's happens when you become a civilian and take up an easier life. And Florence keeps making some pretty tasty cookies and pies."

Wes turned to his nephew. "And this must be Bruce?"

The young man shook his head with a disappointed fading smile. "No, I'm Paul. Bruce is down at the saloon with his friends."

"Paul! My word, you were just yay high and barely picking your nose without eating it the last time I saw you. I come back, and you're a grown man tall as a tree almost, with a scratch of a beard even. How are you, boy?" he asked and hugged his nephew.

Paul stood six foot four and thin. He had straight white hair that lay flat against his head to his mid-ear, or so. He had a scruff of a youthful blonde beard and mustache on his thin, but handsome oval face. His blue eyes were sincere and sensitive, like his mother's. Paul worked at the sawmill and still lived at home with his parents and his older brother, Bruce. "I'm good. I'm taller than you now," he said awkwardly with a teasing smile.

"Why you little snot licker," Wes said and grabbed his nephew by the waist and drove him into the davenport playfully as Paul laughed. "I can still whip you; you cotton topped wench! Say, how about you and I walk my horse down to the stables and then let's go find your brother and see what this town has to offer for a good time, huh?" he asked as he stood up. He looked at his sister and brother in law. "Yeah, I came to see you two, but you're too old for me now. I'm still too young to sit idly in a house. Besides, I need a drink after such a long ride."

Florence frowned. "Wesley, you just got here, and I haven't seen you in years. Sit down and talk to me for a while. What have you been doing with yourself?"

He sat down heavily and slapped his nephews' leg with a hard slap. He grinned as he heard his nephew cry out. He looked at his sister. "Oh geez, you don't want to hear it. Trust me on that."

Frank frowned. "Are you in trouble? Matt

25

Bannister's the marshal in town here in case you are."

Wes laughed. "No, I'm not in trouble!"

"Well, what have you been up to since we saw you last?" Frank asked.

Wes frowned and hesitated. "Oh, not much, really. I made a living and had fun doing it." He smirked at Frank and added, "You know, Lieutenant?"

Frank squinted his eyes questionably. "No, I don't. And don't call me Lieutenant. I gave all that up twenty years ago."

"Well, nineteen years ago, you did. Sis, I have been supporting myself legally for all this time doing various things from waring with the Calvary on the plains to tending a hardware store in Sacramento to gold mining, gambling, some farming and a little hunting too." He slowly grinned. "I'm doing well and just came to visit with you all for a while if that's okay? I hoped to make it here by Christmas, but I'm late. What else have I been up to? I never married and I probably never will because I enjoy having a good time. Speaking of, I need a drink." He looked at Paul, "Hey, Cotton Top, let's go get my stuff off my horse and then take my old lady to the livery stable. We'll go find your brother and see what we can stir up."

Florence appeared concerned. "Wes, don't cause any trouble down there with my boys. They're good boys."

Wes laughed. "So am I! I'm not going to corrupt your boys. I may not have been around, but I love the boys too. They'll be fine. I mean, what kind of trouble could we really get in? I know what you're going to say," he paused to stand up. "I'm not young and rowdy anymore, Sis."

"Well, I'm glad to hear that."

He grinned. "Now, I'm forty-seven and rowdier than ever!" He laughed.

***

Wes Wasson was five feet and ten inches tall, with a stout body build with his broad shoulders. He had straight brown hair that was cut short and had a square face with broad cheekbones. His eyes were small and far apart, with lines at the corners from his laughter over the years. He had a concave nose and wore a goatee most of the time, but his face was covered with a weeks' worth of whiskers. No one recognized him when he walked into Ugly John's Saloon and walked up behind a table where a group of men played a game of cards. The snow-white hair of his nephew Bruce Ellison was unmistakable. He approached Bruce from behind under the glares of two of Bruce's friends who sat with their backs to the wall observing him carefully. Wes smiled and put a finger to his mouth to keep the two serious-looking men quiet. He grabbed a handful of Bruce's hair and pushed his head forward down to the table and spoke loudly in Bruce's ears. "You're under arrest. Don't move, or my deputy will shoot!"

Bruce grimaced in pain and shouted, "For what?"

"Murder. Bruce Ellison, we've been searching for you since you left Sacramento, but I finally caught you! You're going to hang!" he said with a grin as he held Bruce's head down.

"What are you talking about? I haven't been there since I was a kid!" Bruce spoke desperately.

Wes laughed and let go of his hair. "I know."

Bruce stood up quickly and turned to face his attacker, furious about someone interrupting the game and ruining his best hand of the night by exposing it to the table when they grabbed his hair. "Uncle Wes?" he asked in disbelief.

Wes laughed as he looked at his oldest nephew. "You've grown from a piss ant to a fire ant, Bruce. Good for you."

Bruce chuckled as he hugged his uncle. "What are you doing in town?"

"Visiting for a while. Me and your fence post of a brother came on down to liven this place up. So, what do you have going on around here, just cards?" He asked, looking at the men that sat around the table.

"Yeah. Grab a chair and pull it over. Paul, come on over," he called his little brother over to join then. "Uncle Wes, these are my friends, this is Bobby Alper, Richie Thorn, Charlie Walker, and that big guy is Jack Sperry." He lowered his voice, "Don't say it too loud, but Jack and Charlie are part of the Sperry-Helms Gang."

"Gents. I'm Wes Wasson, nice to meet you all. Let me join your game. The first round of drinks is on me."

Charlie Walker was older than the others; he appeared to be in his early thirties with shoulder-length brown hair and a thick beard covering his face. He was a small man, but his cold brown eyes didn't look to be afraid of anything. He looked at Wes evenly as Wes shook hands with the rest of them. Slowly, Charlie shook Wes's hand. "Good thing you showed some fooling around when you walked up behind Bruce, or you would've gotten yourself shot if not beaten half to death."

Wes widened his eyes. "I figured! You boys don't look like a friendly bunch to go messing with." He turned to Bruce. "So, where are you working at Bruce? Tell me about yourself."

Bruce Ellison was shorter than his brother at five foot eleven. He was stocky and had plenty of lean muscle definition from working in the mine. His white hair was the same cotton white as his brother's and just as flat and lifeless, except it was a little longer and covered his ears. Bruce was clean-shaven except for a blonde mustache. His blue eyes glossed over with the effects of alcohol. "I work at the silver mine with Bobby and Ritchie. And that's about all I do. What have you been doing for all these years, Uncle Wes?" He turned to his friends and added, "Uncle Wes was a soldier with my Pa way back when."

"Yeah, I was," Wes offered. "I joined up at eighteen and was in the Cavalry for fifteen years or so. We did a lot of Indian killing your Pa and I. Frank, Bruce's Pa was my sergeant. He's ten years older than I am. He was married to your Ma when I joined up. We had some good times for sure. It was tough living, but it was exciting."

"What have you been doing since then?" Bruce asked again.

"I did what I knew how to do. I sold scalps to the California Government," he laughed, knowing it would start a conversation.

"What?" Jack Sperry asked, surprised.

Wes explained, "California was offering good money for Indian's scalps, so I hunted them down and took their scalps. As I said, it was good money and that's what I made a career doing for some fifteen years in the cavalry."

"Did you kill them?" Paul Ellison asked, sounding disturbed.

Charlie Walker chuckled. "No, he traded a blanket for them."

"Of course," Wes answered. "California didn't want their hair for wigs. They wanted them dead. It was good money. I did that for a few years and when they got harder to find, I went where the Indians were and joined the Kansas Fifth Volunteers for a couple of years and then retired from the cavalry and moved back to Sacramento and started working doing whatever I could."

"You killed people?" Paul asked with disgust.

"Not people...savages."

"They're people, Uncle Wes."

"Technically, maybe. But if you saw what the Indians did to soldiers or even settlers, you wouldn't be calling them people. It's not human what they would do to the bodies of the dead. Ask your Pa; he's seen his share of the most disturbing crap you could imagine. I scalped the Indians I killed, but I did not mutilate their bodies and cut out their hearts …" He paused for a moment as a small smirk came to his lips. He continued, "I never gouged out their eyes and deformed them in miserable ways anyway. I saw it repeatedly on the Kansas prairie and places around there. When you find your friends lying on the ground unrecognizable and chopped to pieces, sometimes it can leave a lasting impression. We were there to stop that from happening to civilized people who just wanted to raise a family on a homestead." He paused. "I can tell you right now you don't want to know what happened to some of the white women and children they'd take or left behind. And for heaven's sake, don't tell your Ma, I told you that much. She's got a sensitive soul and a soft stomach too." He laughed.

Ritchie Thorn leaned forward over the table towards Wes. "How many Indians have you killed?"

Wes raised his eyebrows and exhaled in thought. "Hard to say."

"Twenty, thirty?" Ritchie asked.

"No, heck no. Hell, I probably killed more than that at Bear River."

"A hundred?"

Wes shook his head, questionably. "I couldn't tell you. But a lot."

Charlie Walker narrowed his eyes. "You were at the massacre of Bear River?"

Wes smiled. "It wasn't a massacre; we didn't get them all!"

Bruce Ellison stared at his uncle with his mouth open while his friends laughed. "My Pa never talks about it, but I knew he was there. He quit the Cavalry soon after that, right?"

Wes nodded as he took a drink. "He did as soon as his enlistment was up. Your Pa was fine with fighting man against man, warrior against warrior, but you can't fight a better cavalryman than you are. I don't like Indians, but I have to admit I've never seen better horsemen than our opponents in the Midwest. On the field of battle, we would take a position and shoot, but those Indians were like yellowjackets buzzing everywhere and you couldn't win, because they'd strike you hard and leave, and if you chased after them, you'd be ambushed. They are very tricky and quite gifted at stalking and hunting us like a pack of wolves. Your father was fine with fighting like that. He thought it was honorable for both sides of the field. Attacking villages and killing everyone in sight, including women and children, he couldn't stomach. The fight at Bear River was tough, but we won. It was a job, and we did it. And I'd do it again and again because campaigns like that won the west. If we were still trying to win the west fighting those heathens on the battlefield, we would still be fighting them fifty years from now. They were very tough, and I miss those days. I miss the challenge."

Charlie Walker looked at Jack Sperry with a grin. "So I know that it was a California group of soldiers that attacked at Bear River. So how could you be there and in the mid-west too?"

Wes chuckled. "I just explained that a minute ago. When I left the California Volunteers, I hunted scalps, and when that job died out, I went to Kansas to fight over there."

Charlie Walker looked at Jack Sperry with a smile. "We should sign him up with the gang."

Jack nodded as he listened to Wes.

Ritchie Thorn offered, "I heard once that Chusi's family was killed at Bear River. He's an old Indian that lives around here. He's the town drunk."

Wes looked at Ritchie with interest. "Shoshone?"

Ritchie nodded. "Yeah, when he attacked us in the street, he said he was a Shoshone warrior. Remember that?" he asked Bruce and Bobby.

Bobby nodded. "Yeah, I do. He kicked me in the lower forty-eight."

Wes looked at Bruce seriously. "He attacked you?"

Bruce nodded slowly. "Yeah, he came running across the street and jumped up and drove his knee into my chest. But we got even; I stomped on his chest," he added quickly, not to lose any creditability.

Wes raised his eyebrows. "Well, I'll have to meet him. I can't let him get away with that."

Ritchie pointed towards the door. "No problem. Bobby, run down and see if Chusi's in the Thirsty Toad and if not check the other saloons. And then come back and let us know."

Wes scoffed. "Let's all go find him. Come on, you guys, let's go have some fun."

Charlie Walker smiled. "Bruce, I like your uncle already."

Paul Ellison was hesitant. "Uncle Wes, Chusi is a

harmless old man. You guys should just leave him be."

"Yeah," Bruce agreed slowly. "He isn't hurting anyone."

"Bull!" Wes exclaimed loudly. "He kneed you in the heart, right? That hurts and potentially could have killed you. Let me tell you something, Bruce, it's great to be a nice man, but a true man never lets someone get away with a strike without retaliating two folds harder! It's time to be a man, instead of a cotton topped giggling boy. We're going to find this man and see if he recognizes me or not." He chuckled. "Dang, I might be the one that killed his family. And I want him to know that."

Paul Ellison's eyes widened as he took a deep breath. "I'm going home. I don't want to be any part of that. I like Chusi and I won't watch you humiliate him."

Wes laughed. "Talk about a cotton topped, soft spined boy! Paul, I'm not going to humiliate him. Come on, let's have some fun. I'm your favorite Uncle Wes, and you haven't seen me in a long time. Trust me; you'll laugh your cotton-tailed butt off."

Chapter 5

Chusi Yellowbear stood at the bar inside of the Thirsty Toad Saloon. He had sold his hides to the tannery in Natoma and had close to twenty dollars in his pocket. He had bought the dry goods he would need for the month and needed nothing more. He was self-sufficient between his garden, trapping, gill netting for fish, dried berries and fruits, wild roots, and hunting. He also did some begging on the street when he needed some money for a drink. He stood alone and sipped his glass with a sorrowful expression on his face. He had shoulder-length black hair that was heavy with gray. His aging face was weathered and his dark eyes appeared tired and older than he was. A permanent frown had taken over his once lively smile. He wore black and red checkered pants and a heavy brown sweater made of wool that had a few small tears on the front of it. On his feet were a pair of deerskin moccasins that he had made himself. His deerskin coat was rolled up beside his feet.

John Riggs, the owner and operator of the saloon, walked down the bar to Chusi and asked, "Hey Chusi, are you doing alright? I told you, you'd like that scotch better than that cheap whiskey you always buy. Am I right?" John had bought the Thirsty Toad a few months before and was trying to compete with the other saloons by bringing in a higher quality of drinks, a piano player playing music and hiring ladies to keep the men coming in. There were plenty of places to drink and gamble on Rose Street, but the main three saloons were Ugly John's Saloon a few blocks down the road, The Comstock Loaded Barrel Saloon, and The Thirsty Toad. All three competed to bring in the men.

Chusi nodded once. "It's good."

If there was anything John could say about Chusi, it was he didn't say anything that didn't need to be said. He was the first old Indian John had the opportunity to meet and hoped to get to know him well enough for Chusi to tell him about the early days and ways of living before the nation was settled. But getting the old man to talk about his past at all was difficult at best. The rumor was he had lost his entire family. John didn't know if that was true or not, but by the sorrow in Chusi's eyes, it wouldn't be hard to believe. It would be a devastating thing for anyone, whether they were Indian or not. Some saloons would not permit Chusi inside, but John welcomed him. He supplied John with fresh venison, homemade jerky and fresh fish for his dinner table whenever he asked for it. John smiled. "I told you Scotch is better. Do you ever eat frog legs?" he asked curiously.

Chusi nodded. "Yes."

"I was thinking about maybe having a frog leg dinner one night this summer, what do you think? Do you think a lot of folks would want frog legs?"

He smiled faintly. "It would take many frogs."

"I know. I was thinking if you could start catching them a week in advance and keep the frogs in a pit or something, we might have enough. I'd pay you for it, of course."

He nodded. "If you want."

The door opened, and Ritchie Thorn, Bobby Alper, Bruce Ellison, and his younger brother, Paul, all came inside along with Charlie Walker and Jack Sperry. Another man came in with them that John did not know.

"Great," John said under his breath. He spoke to the men as they walked down the bar towards Chusi, "I don't want any trouble fellas, or you won't be allowed back in here."

"Trouble?" Ritchie asked loudly. "John, relax, there isn't going to be any trouble." The men circled the old Indian. "Hi Chusi," Ritchie said with a hard slap to his back. 'How are you tonight?"

Chusi stared straight ahead at a picture of a nude woman on the wall. "Good," he said with no emotion. Fear was something he no longer felt, but he was uncomfortable being surrounded by men of low character such as those who looked for trouble now. He already knew three of them carried guns and three did not. The way the men were circled would have made it easy for him to pull his knife and spin with an extended right arm and slice all of their throats, except for the tall Ellison boy, he liked him. Chusi took a drink without showing any concern.

Ritchie continued, "We'd like to introduce you to our friend, Wes. Wes thinks he might know you."

"Hello, Old Timer," Wes said with a small smirk on his lips. Chusi merely glanced at him and turned back to stare at the wall.

John spoke from behind the bar, "You boys leave him alone. I mean it."

Jack Sperry waved a hand at John. "Yeah, we heard ya."

Paul Ellison had enough. "I'll see you all later," he began to walk away.

Wes frowned. "Where are you going, Cotton Top?"

"Home," he answered as he left the saloon.

Chusi took advantage of the moment to move over to a small table in the corner to get away from the men. He sat with his back to the wall facing the bar. He didn't mind sitting alone or being harassed sometimes; it was just a part of life as he knew it, and there was no changing that. He watched the men drink and laugh among themselves over comments he couldn't hear. He heard his name spoken a few times, but he ignored it and enjoyed the warmth of his scotch. Chusi thought of where the best place was to catch as many frogs as John would want to have might be. The mountain ponds and wetlands held many bullfrogs that would be easy to catch with a hook and red yarn.

Chusi's eyes lifted when he noticed the man named Wes come towards his table, holding his drink. The man had the look of trouble on his face as he neared. Wes pulled out a chair and sat down across from him.

"You don't remember me?" the man asked with smiling eyes.

Chusi shook his head uninterested. "No."

"Well, it's been a long time. Are you Shoshone?"

His eyes met Wes's. "I am."

Wes's smirk faded to a slight sneer as his eyes slowly hardened and stared into Chusi's.

"Why?" Chusi asked, feeling uneasy. His knife yearned to be used, yet he had no idea why. He noticed the other men were all stepping nearer with grins of anticipation.

John asked from the bar, "What's going on over there?"

Ritchie answered, "Nothing, John. They're old friends."

Wes's lips turned upwards, just a touch as he looked down and then back up at Chusi. "I heard you were at Bear River in January of 1863. Is that so?"

Chusi eyes narrowed slightly as he slowly nodded once. His breathing grew more profound.

"I'll be damned; me too," Wes said with a growing wicked grin. "I heard you lost your family there, is that true?"

Chusi's eyes hardened as he nodded once with a slow forming sneer.

Wes grinned. "Well, I'm probably one of the

men that killed them. I killed a lot of you savages there. It's one of the things I'm most proud of in my life. Tell me, do I look familiar? I gunned down every one of you I could. Maybe even your wife and children. You escaped by running into the river like a coward, didn't you? Yeah," he laughed softly. "You did. Well, while you were running away like a scared jackrabbit, I was having a ball blasting away your tribe." He shrugged nonchalantly. "I'll guess I have taken more scalps just from your family than you ever have, old man." He waited with his hand resting near his reversed gun handle on his left hip for Chusi's response. He was expecting Chusi to leap over the table.

Chusi sat quietly and stared at Wes with his dark eyes. His reaction was quite disappointing for those watching.

"Did you hear me, old man? I said I'm the one that attacked your camp that morning. It was brutally cold out, remember? Heck, you know, you dove in the river, didn't you?" He chuckled lightly. "Ya scurried away like a rat while we butchered your family down one after another. I've seen it a thousand times. I hunted people like you in California for a living and on the Kansas prairie too. I still have a pretty woman's scalp from your tribe. It might even be your wife's long black beautiful hair that used to smell like woodsmoke years ago."

Again, there was no response. Chusi just stared at him without as so as a twitch to his lips.

Wes blinked and squinted in frustration. "Did

you not hear me? Do I need to speak up? Hey, old man." He spoke louder as he leaned slightly over the table. "Did you hear me? It was me! I did it."

Chusi turned his head towards his left slowly and then looked back at Wes. He could grab his knife and slice the man's throat in a second, but he calmly took a drink instead.

"Don't ignore me, you dirty savage!" Wes shouted as he slapped the table with a loud slam of his hand. His beady eyes burned into Chusi. "Do I need to go get your wife's scalp? Do you want it back?"

"Hey!" John Riggs yelled, coming towards them. "Alright, all of you out! I told you to leave him alone."

Charlie Walker put his hand on his revolver and looked at John. "Back off! This might be your place, but this doesn't concern you."

"If it's in my place, it does concern me!"

Charlie raised his eyebrows questionably. "Not today, John. Your choice," he said as he removed the leather loop of his revolver's hammer. His cold eyes never left John.

John put his hands upwards to surrender to the situation. "Finish your conversation and get out of here, please." Charlie Walker wasn't a man to be tested or to argue with and everyone knew it. He was a member of the Sperry-Helms Gang and if that didn't speak loud enough, then nothing would until the sound of his gun being fired did.

"Are you deaf?" Wes shouted angrily.

Chusi looked back at Wes with nothing expressed in his eyes. "You didn't do it."

Wes frowned. "Yes, I did! Are you calling me a liar? I killed thirty, forty maybe fifty of your friends and probably your wife and kids too." He lowered his voice with a sneer, "And I enjoyed it more than you know!"

Chusi shrugged and finished his glass of scotch. "The man that killed my family had hair like his." He pointed at Bruce Ellison's cotton white hair. "I watched him." He stood up and looked at Wes, who mirrored him. "I will be going."

Wes began to laugh. "Oh, my word! There was only one man in our entire regiment with hair like that." He laughed. "Sergeant Ellison!"

"My Pa?" Bruce asked, surprised.

"He was the only one with hair that white!"

Ritchie pushed Chusi up against the wall. "Where do you think you're going? We still owe you a beating for that one night in front of the hotel. Remember that?" He hit Chusi in the stomach with a solid right fist. He held Chusi in place with his left hand and hit Chusi in the face and did it again.

"He kicked me in the lower forty-eight. Step aside, Ritchie," Bobby Alper said and kicked him in the testicles as hard as he could. "Payback!" Bobby yelled as Chusi fell to the floor in anguish. Bobby helped Richie stand him back up. He looked at Bruce. "Your turn."

Bruce was still trying to process it was his father that killed Chusi's family.

Wes put his arm around his nephew. "Give him your best shot. Hell, even if you broke his jaw, it wouldn't hurt him more than your Pa did. Put him out of his heathen misery, bud."

Bruce stepped forward and lifted Chusi's head with his left hand. "You shouldn't have interfered that night. Remember, you drove that knee into my chest? That hurt. So, will this." He followed his words with a right fist to Chusi's face while Ritchie and Bobby held his arms. Bruce began beating him with hard rights and lefts to his body and his face.

"Let me in there!" Charlie Walker said with a grin. "Chusi, I haven't got a problem with you at all, but I like to hit people."

"Don't touch him!" U.S. Deputy Marshal Jed Clark shouted as he entered the saloon and walked quickly towards them. "Let him go!" he ordered.

Charlie sighed. "Mind your business, Jed!"

Jed said nothing more but drove a hard right cross into Charlie's face and knocked him down to the floor. Jed pulled his revolver quickly and pointed it at Charlie and pulled the hammer back. He looked at Jack Sperry, who was glaring at him. "One move and your friend's dead. Now, let him go." He glared at Ritchie and Bobby. They did as they were told and Chusi sat slowly in a chair and laid his head on the table. He was bleeding.

Jack Sperry said, "Jed, I didn't know you could be so demanding. If you arrest my friends, you know we'll just talk to the sheriff and they'll be out."

Jed smirked slightly. "I don't work for the sheriff anymore, Jack. If I took him to jail, he'd stay there and there's nothing you and your gang could do about it. Or do you think you and your brothers are going to scare Matt like you do the sheriff?"

Jack Sperry was the biggest of his brothers at six feet even and close to two hundred pounds. He had dark brown hair that barely covered his ears and was usually unbrushed and had a slight curl at the ends. He had a round face with thick eyebrows and the Sperry green eyes. He had a full-faced short dark brown beard and mustache. He shrugged his shoulders. "He's just a man."

Jed nodded. "Yeah, a man that would make you wet your pants if he wanted to!"

Jack laughed. "I doubt that."

Charlie looked up at Jed and hollered. "You're going to pay for that!"

"Am I? Well, you let me know the cost, huh? You two get out of here. You four stay here." Jed waited until Charlie and Jack had left the building before he turned to Chusi. "Chusi, do you want me to arrest these men for what they did to you?"

Chusi looked up at Wes and then at Bruce. "No." There was a wild look in his eyes for the first time. "I'm going now," he said and grabbed his coat and left the saloon.

Jed looked at Wes Wasson. "You must be Uncle Wes?"

Wes was surprised. "Yeah, how'd you know?"

"Your nephew Paul came to my house and told me what you were doing to Chusi."

"Why that sniveling rat-tailed dog. I never figured him for a whipped pup." He laughed lightly. "Oh, well. It'll take some more time than I thought to turn him into a man, I guess."

Jed was filled with disgust. "Tormenting an old

man is far from being a man. Get out of my sight and don't go around Chusi again. None of you."

Wes smiled. "Ah, being a former soldier, I can tell you I fought to make this country free. That means I can go around anyone I please, and there is nothing you can do about it. It's a free country, Deputy. Thanks to men like me."

Jed chuckled sarcastically. "Maybe, but so far, I think appreciation is owed to much better men than you."

Chapter 6

Matt took a bite of his salmon fillet and raised his eyebrows, impressed. "That's really good. Do you want to try a bite?" he asked Christine. They were eating lunch together in the Monarch Restaurant.

Christine nodded and took a bite off his fork. "That is good. Would you like some of mine?" She had ordered chicken and dumplings soup.

"No, thanks." He took a drink of his water. "That's not going to be too hard for you to eat, is it?"

She frowned slightly. "I don't think so. Doctor Ryland said I could start eating solid food again, but not steak or any kind of nuts yet. Chicken is okay." Christine had been shot in the abdomen and was finally recovering well enough to walk around. She could not dance yet and would have to rest for another month or so before doing anything physical to allow her abdominal muscles to heal from the surgery Doctor Ryland had performed. To Matt, it was a miracle that she was alive and eating lunch with him. To say he thanked the Lord for that miracle of saving her life was far too low of praise. He thanked the Lord daily for the privilege of having Christine with him still.

"Well, you take it easy. I'll take you back home when we finish here. I know it's tough, but you need to stay down and rest."

She sighed. "I'm tired of not doing anything. I can't lift anything heavy or be on my feet for too long; the only thing I can do is read. I'm not a writer or I'd write a book, but I'm so bored. You know when I do start dancing again, I'll be so out of shape that I'll be covered in sweat. No one will ever want to dance with me again. I'll be disgusting."

Matt grinned. "Um..." he shrugged. "I think you'll be fine. If you get too sweaty, I'll still dance with you."

"You might have to because I'm not feeling too pretty now days, you know. I have a big scar across my stomach now. It's just not pretty."

His smile faded as he watched her sincerely. "Christine, you're bored and not feeling like yourself quite yet. But that will change when you get back on the dance floor."

She set her spoon down. "Helen and Sam moved their wedding to Valentine's Day. She doesn't want to dance anymore since Edith was killed. And it's not the same anymore without Edith. The fun is gone without her." She paused. "I don't know if I want to keep dancing, Matt. I can't imagine going down there and dancing and not seeing Edith there or pretty soon, Helen either. They've always been there for me. You just don't know how important someone is to you until they're gone. Every time I walk by her room, I want to knock once and go in, but she isn't there anymore, Connie is. I miss her, Matt." Moisture filled her eyes.

Matt frowned sympathetically. "I know you do." He reached over and took hold of her hand softly. "I have an idea. I know we've been undecided on a wedding date. So why don't you find a calendar and pick a date for our wedding? You can start planning the wedding however you want it and find a dress you like. It would help keep your mind occupied while you are recovering. And when we get married, we'll kick Truet out on the street and we'll have our own home. Then, Sweetheart, you will never have to dance again, except with me."

She looked at Matt sadly. "I don't want to pick a date without you helping. Would you prefer a Spring or Summer wedding?"

Matt narrowed his eyes in thought. "Late Spring?"

"Do you want to have it in the church?"

"I think if we're making a covenant before God to be married, then yes. And I don't know how you'd feel about it, but I'd like to get married in the Willow Falls Church with Reverend Ash doing the ceremony. But I'm not set on that. We could have our wedding in our church here too."

She frowned. "All my friends are here. I've never been to Willow Falls. Maybe we could go there sometime and talk to the Reverend about it before deciding on that? Because all our friends here would have to go there. And it's a pretty long ride, isn't it?"

"Sixteen miles."

She nodded with a skeptical expression. "How about we compromise and have Reverend Ash come here to perform the wedding if that's important to you?"

"We could. I thought it would be easier for Aunt Mary and Uncle Charlie."

"Yeah, but it wouldn't be easier for your Uncle Luther or your other relatives that live here. Another thing to think about is where everyone would stay the night at? I doubt there is a large hotel there from what I've heard about Willow Falls."

Matt chuckled lightly. "There's not much there."

She tilted her head. "Then let's get married here in our church. This is our home, after all."

"All right. We have settled that much. Now when?"

She smiled. "We'll have to look at a calendar."

Matt's eyes narrowed when he noticed Truet Davis coming into the restaurant and pulled up a chair to their table uninvited. "Sorry to interrupt, Christine. You're looking fantastic by the way."

She smiled. "Thank you."

"Matt, I was introduced to Morton Sperry and his brother Vince at the Willow Falls Bank yesterday."

"And?" Matt asked, waiting to hear more.

Truet shrugged. "Morton was very nice. I didn't know his older brothers were in the same cavalry unit as your brothers. They have a lot of respect for your family. Vince Sperry is an idiot, but Morton seemed very sincere about that anyway. That's not what I came in here to tell you, though. Bo Crowe, from that wanted poster in the office, was with them. He wanted me to tell you that he doesn't mind having some trouble with you. In other words, you don't scare him."

Matt took a drink of his water. "I'm happy to hear it, I suppose. Alright, we'll ride over there in the morning. I'm curious to see why the Natoma Sheriff didn't let me know Bo was there. Surely, he must have seen him too."

"I wanted to tell you that real quick since I just got back in town. I'll see you two later," Truet said and left the restaurant. He no sooner walked out the door when he came back inside. "Matt, you better come look at this." His tone was quite serious.

Matt got up and followed Truet outside of the hotel. Across the street, Chusi Yellowbear was yelling at no one in particular and swinging his knife around dangerously. Luckily there was no one around him as he stumbled a few steps one way, then a few steps the other and screaming in his native tongue.

Matt walked across the street slowly with Truet. "Chusi. Hey, Chusi," Matt spoke as he got closer to him.

Chusi was quite drunk; it was plain to see as he turned to face Matt. Tears streamed down Chusi's face as he pointed the knife at Matt angrily and yelled furiously in his native tongue. Chusi stepped off the boardwalk and almost fell as he stepped towards Matt with his blade pointing outwards.

"Chusi, put the knife down, my friend." Matt could see Chusi looked to have been beaten up by his swollen and blackened eye.

Chusi stood in the street and lifted his head up in the air and screamed wildly and then looked at Matt with a fury in his eyes that was alarming. Matt knew Chusi meant to harm him. He stumbled quickly towards Matt, with his knife being drawn downward to plunge it in an upward manner into Matt.

Matt shook his head. "Chusi, don't do this!" he warned as he backed up a few steps away from Truet. The danger of stepping backward on the rough frozen ground was risky, but he wanted to get Chusi's back turned towards Truet. He pulled the leather thong from the trigger of his revolver to have it readily available if needed. Matt backed away from Truet, and Chusi kept stumbling towards him with a dangerous sneer and low guttural words he couldn't quite comprehend. Chusi turned his back to Truet as he followed after Matt, Truet took advantage of the moment and slammed the butt of his revolver over Chusi's head, knocking him unconscious.

Matt stared at Truet, speechless. He have never seen Chusi act like that or have that crazed look in his eyes before. Matt spoke in disbelief, "I think he would have killed me if he could've."

Truet turned Chusi onto his back. "He's been beaten up."

Matt nodded. "It's not the first time that's happened, but I've never known him to act like that.

Can you take him to jail and lock him up? I think we'll leave him in there for a couple of days to cool off." He picked Chusi's deer horn handle knife off the ground. "Let's see if we can borrow someone's horse and I'll help throw him over a saddle. I have to walk Christine back to the dance hall and then I'll meet up with you later."

Truet replied, "Go finish your lunch with Christine. I can handle this just fine."

Matt exhaled bewildered by Chusi's wild eyes expression. "I wonder what got into him?"

"Matt, Christine's waiting. Go finish your lunch. I'll throw him in a cell and we'll find out later."

Chapter 7

Frank Ellison had gone to bed before the boys had come home the night before. His son, Bruce, had tried living with his friends Ritchie Thorn and Bobby Alper out at the Slater's Mile for a while but had recently moved back home. His complaint was living with his friends in a small cabin was just too crowded and filthy for his liking. It was better to walk the three miles to work than to live in a pig pen and still walk a mile. Frank figured Florence's cooking might have something to do with it too but having him home was nice. However, Bruce's tendency to go drink and carouse with his friends wasn't appreciated by his God-fearing parents. Frank knew the reputation of the Thorn brothers and knew Ritchie was no good for anyone. Bruce had become friends with Richie at the silver mine, and now they were carousing in town together all the time. Hearing that Bruce was with Jack Sperry and the likes of Charlie Walker the night before was a concern of its own. If there was anything Frank knew about, it was the likelihood of becoming what you hang around. Outlaws and ruffians were not a good collection of friends to have, and it concerned Frank and Florence, a lot. Paul was a good-hearted boy with good friends, but Bruce, for whatever the reason, was choosing to pass his time with elements that would only bring him trouble.

Frank had fallen in love with Florence Wasson many years before and married her. He was a corporal in the cavalry at the time in the 2nd California Volunteers. He had talked Florence's little brother, Wesley, into joining as well. Frank was promoted over the next two years to Sergeant and was a natural-born leader who loved being in the cavalry. However, when they were led into the Idaho Territory and marched through a bitterly cold January day to end the hostilities of the Shoshone tribe, it changed him forever. Frank respected the Indians for their tactics and skill. They were great warriors and anyone back east saying a soldier with a rifle was worth fifty Indians, was a fool. They had no idea just exactly how tactical, courageous, and skilled the tribes could be. They could also be brutal and natural predators as lethal as a pack of wolves at a Sunday school picnic, even against the trained cavalry. When the battle of Bear River was over, Frank lost a part of himself there amongst the hundreds of bodies of warriors, old men, women, and God forgive him, children. For a man who loved his wife and his children, to murder a full tribe to the last as the objective, was inconceivable. The Indians did not attack them; the 2nd California Volunteers attacked the tribe. The warriors fought bravely to protect their homes and families, but they were overwhelmed by manpower, weapons, and ammunition. Frank would have liked to have not been there or held back altogether, but he was a sergeant in the military with orders to follow. His men were watching him, and so were the officers over him. He did his share of killing indiscriminately, and it haunted him for years. He wasn't the same after Bear River, and he lost his devotion and wanted out of the service. He was promoted to Lieutenant despite his lack of enthusiasm, and when it came time to re-enlist, he left the cavalry. He wanted to go home and be with his wife and children and never kill anyone again.

Wes, on the other hand, took a dark turn somewhere on that morning at Bear River. They had been hoping to join the fight against the Confederacy, but they were sent to Bear River instead. They were unleashed like wild animals on a tribe that wanted peace. When the killing began, Wes was one of the first to fire a shot, and one of the last to stop shooting. Wes wanted to kill Indians, and it didn't matter if it was a man or an innocent woman or a baby in her arms, he was animalistic that morning.. Frank had been around long enough to know men could do horrible things, but when it was over, he was shocked by the depravity of his men, especially Wes, who had done the unimaginable.

Frank was glad to leave it all behind him and knew how blessed he was not to be born an Indian.

He knew people were people no matter the race and there was not one father in that encampment on Bear River and elsewhere, that didn't love his wife and children as much as Frank loved his own. That thought was one that never left him as he raised his children. It haunted Frank and someday when he faced the Almighty God of Heaven, he prayed the Lord would forgive him for the blood he was responsible for. The only thing he was proud of was that he had never become callous to killing. There were no memories that he wanted to talk about or missions or battles that he desired to brag of. He preferred never to mention he was in the cavalry at all, let alone being a lieutenant or being part of a bloody massacre. Wes, on the other hand, loved to talk about it and had no remorse.

Frank was not exceedingly happy to see Wes step into his house the night before, nor pleased that Wes invited Paul to the saloon to meet Bruce and his roughneck friends. It had given Frank a bad taste in his mouth at the time and now he was finding out why. Paul told him at work what Wes wanted to do to Chusi. Frank never knew too much about the old Indian man that he'd see around town, but when he heard Chusi was at Bear River, his heart dropped. Frank had been filled with a sense of anxiety ever since hearing it at noon. He had hoped Deputy Marshal Jed Clark had gotten to the saloon before Wes could bring up such painful memories to the poor old man. He had not.

Wes laughed. "Frank, I love you, man, but it happened, okay? We have nothing to be ashamed of. You, me, and the rest our regiment did what we were commanded to do. We did our service and that's all. And yeah, I am proud of that. We saved an untold number of American lives."

Bruce had just gotten home from work when Frank asked them about the night before. "Pa, it's not a big deal."

"Not a big deal?" Frank questioned bitterly. "Son, you weren't there! I promise you somewhere in that encampment there was a family just like ours and a father like myself, watched his sons fighting to save their family and being killed before his very eyes. I promise you; children watched their mothers and fathers dying right before being killed themselves. And you think that's no big deal? Do you think it's no big deal to shoot a three-year-old with a .45 caliber shell? Over and over again?" he raised his voice angrily as tears filled his eyes. "What about shooting a beautiful young woman running for her life down, even before she has a chance to live it? Do you think pointing your weapon at a man who is just trying to protect his family from you, is no big deal? They were people just like you and me; a different culture is all that separated them from us. And then we find out later that they weren't looking for a fight and hoped a peace treaty could be made. It was stupid kids probably about your age that caused the trouble with the settlers and the tribe had to pay! That's like you and your worthless friends, causing some trouble and Matt Bannister coming in here without saying a word and killing us all! That's exactly what happened!

Yeah, it was a big deal. And that poor old man out there somewhere we see walking around drowning himself in alcohol, probably lost all he loved in that massacre. Now I understand why he drinks! To my shame, I was a part of that. Now you know, and I never wanted you all to know that. That's a part of my past I don't want to think about." He turned to look at Wes. "And you had no right to tell them! You know how I feel about the extermination of that camp."

"Frank, look, I'm sorry if I crossed any lines here, but the truth is you're a hero. Why not be proud of it?" Wes asked.

"Because there's nothing to be proud of, Wes!" Frank shouted. "What did you say to that old Indian? Did you tell him you were there?"

Wes grinned. "Well, yeah, he knows now. He didn't remember me, though."

Bruce laughed. "He sat down with him and asked Chusi if he remembered him. And then he told Chusi he could have his wife's scalp if he wanted a piece of her back."

Frank shouted as he ran his hand through his hair. "Why? Why do you thrive on causing other people pain? What is wrong with you?" His eyes burned into his brother-in-law.

"Now you sound like the Sergeant I knew." Wes looked at Bruce. "He used to yell at me all the time."

Frank's heart pounded, and his face reddened with fury. "Wes, I don't want you around my boys or my home anymore. It's been one day in Branson, and you're already causing trouble. That old Indian did nothing to you. How could you do that to him? Honestly, why? No!" he shouted, raising his hands. "I don't even want to hear it. Just get your things and get out of here! You're trouble. You've always been trouble and you'll always be trouble!"

"Frank…" Florence said, surprised to see her husband so upset. "He's my brother."

"Yeah, I know! And it hasn't been twenty-four hours and he's already caused trouble! I don't want to talk about that day, and it's all he wants to talk about. Wes, I want you out, right now!"

"Pa…" Bruce said.

"Shut up, Bruce!" Frank warned.

Wes exhaled. "Sorry for causing any problems. I'll behave."

"No, you won't. I don't want you here."

"Fine. I'll go get a hotel or something." He stood up. "But you know, Sergeant, I may have asked Chusi if he remembered me killing his family. And do you know what he said?"

"No, and I don't care!"

"Well," Wes said as he grabbed his coat and put it on over his gun belt. "He said I didn't do it. The man who killed his family had hair like him." He pointed at Bruce. "The only person who had hair like that was you." He shrugged. "Since I probably will not be back, I thought I'd let you know that. I'll be around for a few days, Sis."

"Get out!" Frank shouted with a shaking bottom lip. His eyes fought to hold the water that filled them.

"He did say that, Pa," Bruce added. "Uncle Wes,

I'll clean up and we'll go to the dance hall tonight."

"Hey, that sounds great. Don't tell your cotton mouth, brother. He'll get the marshal to come tell us to leave the women alone." He laughed as he walked out the door.

Frank left the house suddenly slamming the back door behind him and walked quickly to the privy and sat down. He wept bitterly.

Chapter 8

Matt stepped into the Marshal's Office about nine at night and said hello to his deputy, Phillip Forrester, who was watching over their prisoner, Chusi Yellowbear. "You don't have to stay here all night, you know. You can go home if you want. I'll lock it up when I leave," Matt said.

Phillip yawned with a slight grimace. The scar on his cheek from a recent wound still hurt some when he yawned and stretched the skin. "I think I will. Chusi ate his dinner and wants out. I told him he'd have to wait until you said he could be released."

"I'm not releasing him tonight. Maybe tomorrow night, we'll see how he behaves. Get out of here, Phillip."

Matt went into the jail and closed the steel door behind him. He took a seat on a bench along the wall facing the jail cells. Chusi was lying on a bottom bunk tracing something out with his finger on the bunk above him. He had glanced at Matt and went back to what he was doing. "Do you want to talk about it?" Matt asked.

"What?"

"Whatever's bothering you."

"No."

"Can you tell me why you were swinging a knife around on the street? What were you yelling today?"

"No."

"This isn't getting us very far, is it?"

"No."

Matt sighed. "Chusi, we're friends. I know something has to be wrong because you never act like that. Not even when you get beat up by a gang of thugs."

"Just drunk. It was the scotch, maybe."

"I doubt that. Maybe you just don't want to tell me and maybe you'll stay in there until you do. But, I, for one, have better things to do than sit in here and talk to myself." He stood up to leave.

Chusi spoke in his native tongue with a sharp tone. He sat up on the bed and glared at Matt with a hostile expression. "Let me out of here!" he shouted.

Matt looked at him curiously and replied, "I can't do that yet."

"Why? I was drunk; now, I'm not!"

Matt sat back down. "You had a wild and crazy look in your eyes today. You might've killed someone if they hadn't gotten out of your way. You were coming at me."

"No!"

"You acted like you wanted to kill me. If Truet weren't behind you, I would've shot you. So, if you think you are here just to rest, I'm afraid not. You are under arrest. Now tell me what made you so outraged? Who beat you last night?"

Chusi sneered and lay back down. "Let me go home."

"I can't do that. Should I go home, or are we going to talk? I'll let you know now that tomorrow I'll be gone all day, so now is your only chance until tomorrow night at least. But I probably won't feel like talking then, so maybe the next day. I'm fine with that too."

"The food is good."

"Very well," Matt said, standing up. "Let me ask you, is there anything I can do to help you?"

"Yes, let me go home!" His widened dark eyes revealed the hostility burning within him.

"I can't do that. You might get drunk and end up stabbing somebody accidentally. And I would hate to see you hang over something like that."

Chusi smirked bitterly. "It may not be an accident."

Matt frowned. "That's what the jury will think either way. You have a bucket, use it. Phillip will not let you out of jail tomorrow for any reason until I get back. Last chance, are you sure you don't want to explain to me why you acted like you wanted to kill me?"

"No."

"So be it. Goodnight, Chusi."

The door closed, and Chusi scrolled his wife's name with his finger on the bottom boards supporting the mattress above him. Under her invisible name, he wrote the names of the three children that made up his family. Omusa, his beautiful bride, was his joy in life with her playful spirit and elegant laugh. Chusi had loved her like the sun loves the earth on a warm spring day. They had three children; their firstborn was a beautiful daughter named Sitsi. Chusi still remembered the first time he held her in his arms and looked into her eyes. She was perfect. She was the pride of his soul. Then two years later, Omusa gave birth to their first-born son, who they named Chogun. He was a more crying baby, but a warrior he was to be. Omusa gave birth to another son named Lootah, who was a very loving child. Omusa was twenty-eight years old and six months pregnant on that cold morning when the soldiers came.

He and his family were with the tribe for the winter camp along Bear River. In the morning, they could see the steam rising from two hundred soldiers coming towards them in the freezing weather. A small group of men had caused some trouble among the white settlers, but despite their foolish actions, hopes were high that a treaty could be signed that morning with the white soldiers. The Shoshone were warned of rumors of the soldiers' hostile intentions and a few had left, others were warned by dreams and left, but most were confident a treaty could be signed and any bloodshed would be avoided. Most believed their peaceful winter camp filled with families and laughter would be unharmed. As the soldiers got closer, some warriors took defensive positions as a precaution just in case the rumors were true. While the Chief, Bear Hunter, hoped it would be a peaceful meeting, the mothers nervously gathered their children near them, knowing there was no promise of a friendly meeting. The soldiers attacked without warning or cause. There was no chance of talking of peace or an opportunity to surrender. Once the first gunshot was fired, the screaming began, and neither the guns nor the screaming stopped until there was no one left to scream. Chusi and the other warriors fought with everything they had to save the lives of the tribe, including the lives of their wives, sons, and daughters. If ever there was a motivation to fight, it ran strong through the Shoshone warriors' blood that day. For over two hours, they fought the soldiers with every weapon they had. The guns they did have were soon out of ammunition and their bows, spears, and knives were no match for the arms of two hundred soldiers. Every Shoshone was killed on sight; the women and their children were shown no mercy and murdered like they were lice. If there was ever a moment of pure evil, it was being an Indian on that morning when a pair of soldiers gunned down a young mother carrying her beautiful baby boy.

Chusi watched the soldiers shoot his little sister in the back while she ran away and then execute his infant nephew like a threatening wolf pup. Chusi watched in horror as a soldier with white hair, aimed his revolver, and shot his beloved wife while she was trying to save their three children. Omusa was frantic and leading their children with the baby in her womb towards the river to escape the horror in the icy water. All of them were gunned down like rodents before Chusi's very eyes. Sitsi was ten years old, Chogun was eight and little Lootah had just turned five. The soldier stood in place and shot one after the other from a short distance. Lootah was standing among the fallen bodies screaming in terror, was the last.

Chusi had screamed and tried to leave his position to help them, but he was under the fire of three soldiers. He shot his last arrow at the man who had killed his family and missed by barely an inch. The soldier turned towards him and aimed his revolver, but when he pulled the trigger, he was out of bullets. The sound of constant gunfire was everywhere as bullets hit all around him. Warriors fell one after the other as the bluecoats began to swarm viciously like hornets at an exposed nest. The screams of pain, cries of fear and yells of fierce anger died down one by one.

Chusi had fought brutally and killed a few soldiers, but when he saw his family being killed along with hundreds of others, he knew he could stand his ground and die with them or abandon the fight to help those who did survive. Chusi ran to the river and dove in as a soldier shot at him. He faked being hit, rolled in the water like a dying beaver and resurfaced face down as the current took him downstream. Thought to be dead, the other soldiers let him drift down the river.

Now twenty-one years had passed, and he had never been able to let it go. He could not stay and see the broken spirits of those who knew he failed to protect his family or dared to die trying as other warriors had. He had nowhere to go and he had no life to live with the guilt and sorrow he had come to know. For twenty-one years, he had regretted not being able to kill the soldier with white hair. He shot one arrow and it missed. He would not miss the man again. There was blood owed and only blood could satisfy the thirst he had for revenge. He would fulfill the debt of his family's blood that was spilled that morning, and there would be no offer of mercy or warning, just as the soldiers had done. He traced the names of his family on the board over his head again. He screamed and hit the board above him with his fist. His heart pounded, and the strength of a warrior's blood flowed through his veins. It felt good to be alive again.

Chapter 9

Willow Falls was not on the main road that traveled from east to west. To get to Willow Falls, one had turn right where a sign pointed towards town on the main road. The main road did, however, go right through the town of Natoma. As they passed the road to Willow Falls, Truet asked Matt if he wanted to invite the Willow Falls Sheriff, Tom Smith and his deputy Johnny Barso, to join them in the quest to arrest Bo Crowe from the Sperry family home. Matt had declined and the four men rode past Willow Falls and continued towards Natoma.

"We might run into trouble," Truet had warned.

"We might. But I don't want the Sperry's thinking we're cowardly enough to need extra men to face them. Once they start thinking they got you intimidated, then they'll become bolder, and you either have to face them or become like Sheriff Wright. I'd rather face them boldly the first time we meet."

Nine miles down the road, they entered the small town of Natoma. It was an attractive town built at the base of the mountains along Heather Creek. As they entered town they passed a schoolhouse on the left, an acre or two of grass, then the Avery Saloon was on the left corner, as the main road took a wide right turn and followed along the creek as it led out of town. Matt stopped his horse in the middle of Natoma and looked around. To his right was a little white church, a general store, and the stage stop at the Gregory Hotel and Restaurant. Around the corner on the right was the livery stable and straight across the road from the livery stable was the Natoma Glove factory not far from the Natoma Tannery and Leatherworks. A street went up a hill to the left where most of the houses were. Matt turned his horse left and rode past the Avery Saloon and the post office and tethered his horse in front of the Sheriff's Office and went inside with his three deputies. The four men had been riding for hours in the snow and cold and it felt good to enter the warmth of the Natoma Sheriff's Office.

The old man reading a book behind his desk looked upward, surprised to see someone enter his office before noon. He frowned, not recognizing any of them. "Can I help you?" he asked as he stood up uneasily. He was not wearing a gun belt. "I'm the Sheriff, Zeke Jones."

Matt introduced himself and then his deputies. When they had all shook hands, Matt added, " Not so long ago, a wanted poster for Bo Crowe was sent to every law office around here, and I wired you a message to let me know if you saw him. You must know he's related to the Sperry-Helms Gang."

Sheriff Jones shook his head nervously. "No, I wouldn't know. Those boys don't talk to me," Zeke said. He was in his sixties with gray eyes that seemed much too lifeless. He had short gray hair on the sides and bald on top of his head with multiple age spots. He wore a short gray mustache on his clean-shaven face. The office was filled with cigarette smoke.

Matt gazed at him and knew it was pointless to argue. The man feared the outlaws and sat behind his desk day in and day out, pretending to be a lawman for no other reason than a paycheck and something to do. "Truet saw him with Morton Sperry two days ago in the Willow Falls Bank. We're going to bring him and need you to show us where they live."

"Oh, they're just up the road half a mile or so. The last house on the road, you cannot possibly miss it. It's a two-story house painted black years ago, with rooms added onto it in every direction it looks like. This road dead-ends at their house. It just doesn't get any simpler than that." He shrugged uneasily. "You know, you can't go wrong."

Matt grabbed the man's gun belt off a coat rack and handed it to him. "That's fine, but you still need to come with us. We might need your gun hand if things go wrong."

Anxiety filled the old man's eyes. "Marshal, I'm not feeling so good today, so if you don't mind…"

Matt raised his voice, "I do mind! Now put your

gun belt on, grab your rifle and let's go! " He turned to his deputies, "Jed, you and Nate go down to the livery stable and tell them you need the sheriff's horse."

"Sure, Boss," Jed said and left the office.

Matt looked back at the frightened old man harshly. "You wear a badge on your chest. It's time you use it. You're coming with us whether you feel like it or not. So, grab your weapons and your coat and get ready to go!"

Fear was all that showed in the old gray eyes of the sheriff. "Marshal, if I go, it's going to break the peace here. I'm alone here. Maybe you don't know, but the last Sheriff was assassinated fishing along the creek by one of them after Allan Sperry was arrested. . I don't want that to happen to me."

"I wasn't here then , but I am now. If you're in trouble or need help, walk next door to the post office and wire me. I'll be here in a few hours. And if you know who assassinated the sheriff, we can arrest him today too."

"No, I don't know. I took the job after he was killed."

Matt grimaced a bit. "And you never investigated it, did you?" he asked, already knowing the answer.

Zeke paused before answering. "I had nothing to go on. They're all family around here, no one talks."

Shortly, Matt saw his deputies arrive with a horse already saddled and ready to go. "Let's go."

"Marshal, please…" Zeke's bottom lip quivered.

"Get on your horse and let's go!" he shouted.

They rode up the hill, passing houses until there

was nothing but forest on both sides of the road, the road then dropped down a hill and rounded a curve where they stopped about a hundred yards short of the two-story black house. A small pasture fenced off on the right side of the house went down to the creek and up to the barn on the backside of the property. A Conestoga wagon with a canvas top was on the left side of the house on an access road to the barn. The property appeared overall to be cluttered, overgrown and poor. The snow on the road revealed many horse and human tracks going back and forth to town. A dog barked as they watched the blue smoke coming from two chimneys. The house had a wide-open front porch that was covered but was nothing more than boards laid level on the ground under a lean-to with four support posts holding the porch roof up. It had four empty chairs sitting under it.

Truet shook his head. "There's no sneaking up on them here, that's for sure."

Matt looked at the property in thought. He did not like the way the house was set up or the congestion of the woods so near to the house and having only one view of the homestead. There was no easy access to the backside of the property to see what was behind the house.

"I don't like this," Jed said simply. He pulled his rifle out of its scabbard.

Matt nodded in agreement. "Well, let's ride in. Watch the windows and the corners of the house. Truet, you got the shotgun. Spread out as we ride up there and no one shoots first unless it's necessary."

Nate frowned. "I have the shotgun."

Matt shook his head. "Not this time. If anything happens, I need experience first and foremost in a matter of seconds. Give it to Truet."

Nate handed the Parker Shotgun to Truet and a handful of shells.

"Here," Truet verified there was a bullet in the chamber and then handed Nate his Winchester. "It's loaded."

Matt took a deep breath and nodded. "Let's try to keep this as peaceful as we can. And Sheriff Jones, if this goes to hell, you better be shooting, because if one of my men is hurt and I find you hiding behind a bush, I'll shove that badge down your throat faster than you can believe. Are we clear?"

He nodded his head nervously.

"Let's ride in nice and calm."

Chapter 10

Mattie Sperry and her daughter-in-law, Bernice, had made a substantial breakfast to feed the house full of people. Seventeen people were living in the house, including her nine grandchildren ranging from a baby to fifteen years old. Six of Mattie's grown children lived at home and only one was married. Morton was single, Jannie was single and had her four kids, Henry and his wife Bernice had two children, Vince and Jack were both single and her youngest daughter Daisy was single and had her three little ones. The constant fighting and crying between the kids could drive sane women nuts, but it was so consistent that it had become a part of her life.

To support such a tribe of Sperry's, it took labor and the boys all had ways to make money, if it wasn't cutting wood and selling it, it was working at their uncle's dairy or the tannery. Bernice worked at the glove factory and so had Mattie for a few years. The boys and their gang did some illegal things here and there to make ends meet, along with some blackmailing and extortion as well. They did what needed to be done to support and feed the family.

Mattie looked at her nephew, Bo, sitting in a chair looking grumpy from being woken up by the kids' screaming earlier that morning. He had spent much of the evening at the saloon with her adult children drinking and Bo wasn't feeling his best. Mattie's sister had married a half breed Indian and had five boys and one daughter and all of them had the beautiful native long black hair. They were a good looking bunch of kids and the five boys had their father's physical strength and brutality too. The Crowe family were a wild bunch, but they had good hearts and were respectful towards the family. Mattie's brother was Gerry Helms, who owned a dairy on the other side of town. He helped Mattie out when she needed it or one of her nephews on the Helm's side did. The Helms, Sperry's and Crowe's were all cousins and were close as far as family goes. Some people said they were no good, but the fact was no one dared to speak like that to any of them. There was a certain respect that their family had and it was merely the knowledge that you don't mess with any of them. No one in town got in their way and that was their due respect.

Duke, the family dog and Chow, Bernice's little dog, both began barking. It wasn't the barking of a coyote near the chicken coop; it was the bark of an approaching stranger. "Bernice, who's coming?" Mattie asked curtly. Her eyes shifted to Bo alertly. "Get your moccasins on, just in case."

Bernice, an attractive redhead, peeked out the covered window and saw five men on horseback about a hundred yards away at the curve of the road watching the house. "It must be them. There's five of them and they have rifles," she said fearfully. She turned around and clapped her hands to herd the kids. "Come on, all of you, into my room right now!" She began picking up the babies and herding the others.

Mattie stood up. "Daisy, get Mort and Jack and tell them to hurry up! Bo, grab some blankets and go get in that hole!"

He pulled on his moccasins as fast as he could. "I was really hoping they wouldn't show up," he said bitterly. "You know, I'm going to be riding back to Branson in the freezing cold, right?" he asked his Aunt.

She scowled. "You're being paid for it! I told you to dress warm. Now go."

"I don't know why I agreed to this," he complained.

Mattie shouted, "So you don't spend years in prison, you selfish fool! Now get your butt outside and get in that hole. Morton! Jack!"

Morton came out of his room, tiredly running his hand through his hair with a yawn. "Let's go," he said. He walked out the back door with his brother Henry and Bo. The chicken coop had already been slid over to expose the watertight box buried in the ground. They opened it and there was a padded floor, blankets, a small kerosene lamp if needed, a jug of water and a box of food stored in there. Bo climbed down into the wooden box and they replaced the wooden lid with holes drilled in it and slid the chicken coop back over it. They went back inside the house and waited for a knock on the front door.

With all the kids taken into a backroom, Mattie sat down in her chair and waited. Morton, Henry, his wife, Bernice, Jack and Vince all remained in the living room with their two oldest nephews. Mattie sighed, "It ain't even noon, they must want Bo bad to leave so early on a cold day."

Morton nodded. "I've always heard Matt was like a bloodhound. I knew he'd be coming today."

Matt and his deputies rode to the front porch with a larger dog nipping at the horse's feet. It seemed odd that no one in the house had come out to call off the dog or to meet them at the door. "Don't shoot the dog unless you have to," he said as he dismounted. The dog stayed three feet back, crouching forward barking and growling but didn't come any closer. Matt slid his rifle into its scabbard and pulled the leather thong off the hammer of his Colt Peacemaker. "Jed, go around the left side and watch the back. Nate, go to the right. Truet since you already know them, you and the Sheriff come with me. No shooting unless you must. But watch yourselves," Matt said and waited until Jed and Nate had carefully gone around the house. He stepped onto the long front open porch and knocked on the door as he and Truet both stood off to the side.

"Who is it?" came a man's voice from behind the

door.

"I'm the U.S. Marshal, Matt Bannister. I'm looking for Bo Crowe. It would be easiest for him just to let me take him in." Matt had Sheriff Jones stand behind Truet for his safety.

"He's not here."

Matt nodded, expecting to hear those words. "Can we talk through an opened door?"

"Marshal, you're not going to come in shooting, are you? We're unarmed in here, and we have women and children in here too."

"I can't see that with the door closed. But no, we're not here to start any trouble, we came for Bo Crowe. He's a wanted man, and I hope he'll surrender peacefully," Matt explained.

The door opened slowly. A rough-looking man stood in his socks, holding a cup of coffee and looking at Matt. "I'm Morton Sperry, Marshal." He looked strangely at the Sheriff. "Zeke, what are you doing here?"

Zeke shook his head with a shrug.

"Truet," Morton acknowledged him.

Matt answered while eyeing him carefully. "My deputy saw you with Bo in Willow Falls a few days ago. Bo is wanted for crimes committed in Aurora County and we're here to get him."

Morton shook his head. "He's not here anymore. He left yesterday. I think he's going west."

"Do you mind if I look around?" Matt asked, with his eyes locked onto Morton's.

Morton shrugged his shoulders and stepped back. "You can look until you're satisfied." He waved for Matt to walk past him.

He hesitated. "I'd prefer you not being behind me."

Morton nodded wordlessly and stepped into the family room. Matt stepped into the darkened room full of men and two ladies. He immediately scanned the room to verify no one had any weapons. His eyes danced from face to face reading any signs of hostility or potential danger. Only two of the men showed any hostility at his presence, one he recognized as fifteen-year-old Tad Sperry, who he had caught urinating on his friend Chusi Yellowbear a couple of months before. The other man was heavier than the rest, perhaps taller and was ill-tempered, Matt could see that in the younger man's face.

Tad grimaced. "Uncle Mort, that's the man who pulled my hair and made me yell that I peed like a girl that morning in Branson! I told you it was the Marshal!"

Morton looked at him irritably. "Do you pee like a girl?"

"No!"

"Then shut up."

A couple of the men were laughing at their nephew quietly. Morton waved around the room. "Marshal, these my brothers, Jack, Vince and Henry. That's my little sister Daisy, you've met my nephew, Tad, and this is our mother. You all, this is the Marshal, Matt Bannister that we've all heard about and his deputy Truet. He's courting Annie Lenning, Matt's sister."

Matt was followed in by Truet, who carried a Parker Shotgun. He was followed in by Sheriff Jones. Matt paid careful attention to where the family members were sitting as Morton introduced them. Though they all seemed uneasy, the only one showing any hostility was Vince, who was sitting on the davenport, glaring at him. Matt ignored him and nodded to the youngest sibling named Daisy, who looked to be about twenty. Matt looked at Mattie kindly. "Ma'am, as you might've heard, I don't want any trouble, but I am looking for Bo. Do you know where he is?"

She looked at him with an unfriendly expression. "I never met your mother, but I knew your father many years ago. He was friends with my husband."

Matt frowned. "My father knew a lot of people around here. Is your husband here?"

She sneered. "No, he ran off years ago. He wasn't worth a pot of beans."

"I'm sorry to hear that. Misses Sperry, as I said, I am looking for Bo. I'd appreciate it if you could tell me where he might be. I won't say your son's a liar, but the mountain passes are probably snowed in. I have my doubts Bo left this valley."

Morton exhaled irritably. "He's not here, but as I said, you can look for yourself. I imagine your men are looking outside as we speak, right?"

"They are," Matt acknowledged.

Morton chuckled. "Come on; I'll show you around. Relax Marshal, like I was telling your sister the other day, I have nothing but respect and gratitude for your family. You're safe here."

"I appreciate that," Matt said without letting his guard down. "Truet, stay in here, and make sure no one leaves."

Mattie stood up. "Morton, I'll show him around. You stay here with the boys."

"No, Ma, I can show him around."

"No, I said I'll do it and we don't need you making it more uncomfortable. Now go sit down!" she snapped.

Morton shook his head with a grin as he stepped near her rocking chair to sit down under the teasing of his brother Henry.

Mattie said to Matt as she stepped past her cookstove towards a hallway, "These boys can be tough as nails, but they still listen to their Mama. It doesn't matter how big they get; I'll still smack them upside the head any time I feel like it." She turned and glared at Matt with stern eyes. "Now, why would you make my grandson, Tad, say something so embarrassing as he pees like a girl?"

Matt was taken off guard by her sudden change of direction and her cold eyes. He answered, "I caught him and some other boys urinating on a friend of mine who had passed out in an alley."

Mattie shook her head slightly. "The boys got a mean streak, I'll admit, but he's a good boy. Come, this room belongs to my daughter, Jannie, and her kids." She opened the door, and Jannie Sperry was still lying in bed. "Jannie, wake up! This is the Marshal, Matt Bannister."

"Miss," Matt uncomfortably. The room smelled of stale smoke and alcohol. Jannie Sperry was just waking up and was not attractive at all. She was in her thirties with long brown hair and a face that looked to be as worn out and weathered by alcohol and men as anyone Matt had ever seen. She pulled the blanket back, revealing a bare leg. "Are you cold, Marshal? I could warm you up."

"I'm okay, thank you," Matt replied.

"Get out of bed and do something around here," Mattie spoke shortly as she closed the door. She led Matt into an empty room and turned to face him. "Marshal, how much is the reward for my nephew?"

"Five hundred dollars."

"Would it be possible I could get that reward if I turned him into you? I'll tell you what Marshal, my family is near starving and we need the money, or I'd never consider betraying one of my own. If you promise me, I'd get the reward money right away and not keep it from me; I'll tell you where he is. If not, you'll never find him." Her face was set in stone, but her eyes revealed her anxiousness for her deal to be agreed upon.

Matt took a deep breath. "Misses Sperry, I try to be as fair and honest as I can. If you turn him in, yes, you will get the reward. You would have to come to Branson to collect it, but yes, it would be yours. I don't cheat people out of what's rightfully theirs."

"Would he be tried in Branson?"

Matt shook his head. "No, I'd hold him until the mountain passes are clear and take him back to Prairieville. It's not a Jessup County warrant."

"My sons are going to be very angry with me."

"Where can I find him?" Matt asked.

"Will you write me a promissory note, promising me the money?"

"If you want me to, sure. But like I said, I try to do what's right. You got my word that I'll not keep it from you. What's due to you is yours."

"I don't trust anyone. Let me get a paper and a pen. You write that note, and then I'll tell you."

When she came back into the room, Matt wrote a promissory note for the reward and signed it. When he did so, she took it into Jannie's room to have her read it to her. She stepped into the hallway while Jannie cursed her mother for betraying her cousin. Mattie pointed towards the back of the house. "We have a hiding box under the chicken coop. He's in there. I need my money, Marshal."

Matt nodded. "Come to my office tomorrow and I'll make sure you get it."

***

Morton and the other Sperry boys were most displeased with their mother for telling Matt where their cousin was hiding. To quiet them, Mattie had yelled and ordered them to slide the chicken coop over while Matt identified himself. Bo Crowe pushed the box's cover open and surrendered without incident. He glared at his aunt and said little as Matt took his weapon and shackled his hands in front of him. Matt told his deputy Jed Clark to go with Henry Sperry into the barn and get Bo's horse for the ride back to Branson. Matt and the others led Bo through the house to wait for his horse to be brought around front.

The Sperry family gathered on the front porch apologizing to Bo for their mother's treason. Mattie wept and repeated through her tears that her family was starving and shouting at her complaining boys to get a job if they did not like it.

Matt listened and watched, not particularly liking the feeling he had brewing in his stomach. Something just wasn't right, but he couldn't quite place it. His eyes watched the angry faces of Morton and his little brother Jack as he argued with his mother, and the emotionless face of Vince Sperry as he sat on a porch chair glaring at Matt. The giddiness of the young lady, Daisy, and the scowl on young Tad's face, yet Tad's eyes were lightened with excitement. There was something that did not feel right about it. It didn't feel sincere.

They could hear Henry and Jed talking as they stepped past the corner of the house, leading an attractive Arabian horse around the front and tethered it to the rail near where Matt stood with Bo.

"We got it, Boss," Jed said. He walked back behind the horses to get on his mount. Jed circled behind his horse and stopped in fright and tried to draw his revolver, but only had enough time to try warning his friends. Charlie Walker stood at the corner of the house with a double-barreled shotgun pointed at Jed. Charlie pulled the trigger drilling a hole into Jed's chest, driving him backward as his horse reared in fright.

Matt stood on the porch with Bo Crowe beside him, keeping his eyes on the family when he heard the shot. He looked to his left and saw Charlie Walker step around the corner, turning the shotgun towards Nate, who was on his horse trying to control it from rearing. Matt drew his revolver quickly and shooting from his hip, he pulled the trigger and feathered the hammer as quickly as it landed on the firing pin, to fire again and again. Three quick shots had found their mark hitting Charlie in the left abdomen, the upper abdomen just below the sternum and one in the right lung. Charlie fell to his back, pulling the trigger of the shotgun firing harmlessly into the forest behind him.

Bo Crowe tried to nudge Matt to make him miss, but the shots were already fired. Matt slammed the butt of his revolver over Bo's head with a bitter curse and pushed him to the ground as Matt went quickly to his fallen deputy.

"Watch them!" he shouted to Truet while pointing at the Sperry family.

Truet turned his shotgun to the family and told them not to move. Nate, getting his horse under control, stared in shock at the bloody body of his friend, Jed Clark. Matt kneeled at Jed's side, feeling for a pulse in his neck. Jed was already dead. Matt closed Jed's wide-opened eyes.

"Charlie!" Jannie Sperry screamed and ran towards Charlie.

"Jannie, get back here!" Henry yelled under cover of Truet's shotgun.

Jannie fell over Charlie's body sobbing bitterly.

Matt stood up aware that Charlie wore his revolver on his hip.

"You killed him! You killed Charlie. He never did anything to you, you bastard!" she screamed and tried to reach for Charlie's gun.

Matt grabbed her by the arm and stood her up and pointed her towards Jed's body. He yelled, "That's what he did! You're damn right I shot him!" He spun Jannie towards her family and walked her by the arm and guided her forcibly into a chair. He glared at Henry Sperry. "Did you know he was back there?" he demanded to know.

Henry shook his head. "No. He stays in the barn. He has a room, but no." Henry's answer seemed quite sincere. "I mean, I knew he came back with Jack yesterday, but no!" He was stunned.

Morton raised his hands innocently and shook his head. "None of us knew, Marshal. He was out all night with Jannie. I thought he'd sleep all day like usual."

Matt glared wildly at the members of the family one by one, looking for any trace of someone hinting to a setup. All of them, including Vince, seemed to be genuinely surprised and shocked by the whole thing. Matt looked at Truet, "You and Nate put Jed on his horse and take him and Bo into town. I'll be along in a bit. I want to talk to the family for a moment." Matt reloaded his revolver silently with a sneer on his face as the two deputies did so. He forbid any Sperry to enter the house and stewed in his thoughts as he frequently glanced up at the family members until his deputies were well out of hearing distance.

Matt let his hardened eyes roam over every one of them. They settled on Morton. He holstered his revolver finally. "If I find out this was a planned ambush, I'll be coming back for your heads! We came peacefully, and my deputy is dead. If Charlie Walker acted alone, we're good. If not, I won't come peacefully again...ever. I try to be a fair man, but that blood on your property belongs to my deputy and I'm not doing very well with that. If this was an ambush, please," he stretched his arms out to his sides. "Go get your guns and let's continue it right now."

Morton shook his head with his mouth open just a bit. "I swear, it wasn't an ambush. I had no idea that would happen. I'm sorry..." He shrugged innocently, not knowing what else to say.

Mattie looked frightened. "Marshal, we had no idea, honest. My boys don't want any trouble with you and as their mother, trust me, I don't either. I don't want to lose any of my boys. Charlie slept in the barn. I don't..." she broke down weeping.

Matt took a deep breath and exhaled. "Henry, will you go saddle Charlie's horse for me? I'm taking him back with me, so everyone can see what happens if you shoot one of my deputies." He looked at Jannie, who was sitting in the chair weeping. "Ma'am, I apologize for mishandling you. It wasn't right."

She cursed him and then covered her face and sobbed.

Before long, Henry came back with Charlie's horse, and Morton walked over to his friends' body and kicked it angrily. "You stupid son of a..." He looked at Matt. "I'm sorry about Jed. I never wanted anything like this to happen; whether you believe me or not, I'm telling you the truth."

Matt looked at him severely. "You lied to me at the door, why should I believe you now? I don't know how many times I have to repeat myself, I'm a fair man, but I don't like being lied to!"

Morton looked to be sincerely sorry. He shrugged helplessly and looked like he wanted to speak, but held back, "I'm sorry. Let me help you get Charlie on his horse and we'll tie him down. Honestly, Marshal, I was hoping we'd get along like we did when we were kids. Do you remember us playing together and my uncle's dairy?"

Matt shook his head. "No." He looked at Mattie, who was being held by Daisy. "As I said, come by the office and I'll make sure you're paid." He stepped into the saddle and backed his horse up for a reasonable distance before turning his horse and riding it up the road and around the bend leading Charlie's horse behind him.

Chapter 11

The ride back to Branson was long, cold, and quiet. Matt, like the others, didn't feel like talking. As they neared Branson, Matt told Truet to take Bo Crowe to the jail and told Nate to deliver the two bodies to the Funeral Parlor. Nate was to say to Solomon Fasana that Matt would pay for Jed's funeral costs, but Jed's wife would come down and make the arrangements that she wanted to make. As for Charlie Walker, Matt gave clear instructions; he wanted Charlie put straight into a pine box and brought to the Marshal's Office and propped upright for everyone to see what happens when a U.S. Deputy Marshal is killed. Truet tried to talk Matt out of doing that, but Matt was determined to have Charlie placed there with the note to make the message loud and clear. Matt was going to ride ahead of them into Branson to notify Jed's wife and children of his death before the gossip reached them before he did.

Two hours later, Matt came back to the office

and found a small crowd gathered around the front of his office, quietly gazing at the bloody body of Charlie Walker that was setting in front of his window. Solomon had propped the pine coffin up with boards nailed into the boardwalk. Matt walked past the crowd, not saying a word as he entered the office. Truet, Nate and Phillip were all quietly discussing the loss of their friend.

Matt removed his hat and looked at his deputies. He was going to speak, but nothing came out. He had spent the last hour and a half with Jed's wife and children having to explain to them what had happened. It was one of the worst experiences he had ever had the great displeasure of doing. He took a deep breath. "I don't ever want to have to do that again. There was nothing Jed could have done and unfortunately, it happened. I don't have to say it, but that is the risk of being a lawman. It could have happened to any of us. You three need to consider if you want to continue to be in this profession after seeing what can happen today. If you choose to stay here, just know I'll do my best to protect you, but bad things can happen." He shrugged.

A man came into the office with a curious smile. "So, you killed Charlie Walker, huh? About time someone stands up to the Sperry-Helms Gang…"

"Get out!" Matt shouted with enraged eyes and pointed at the door. "Get out now, before I smack that smile off your face!"

The man left with a frightened expression.

Truet frowned. "Matt, are you all right?"

"Nate, go home. Truet, you might as well go

home too. Phillip, take an hour off and bring our guests some dinner at eight o'clock. I want to be alone for a while."

"Yes, Boss," Nate said quietly.

When Nate and Phillip left the office, Truet sat on the edge of one of the desks and said, "It wasn't your fault, Matt."

Matt's breathing grew slightly harder, and his eyes glossed over somewhat. "It *is* my fault! We should've searched the whole damn place before letting my guard down. I won't make that mistake again. I knew something was not right; I could feel it. Anyway, go home. I'm going to lock the office up to be alone for a while."

Truet stood up. "Are you keeping Chusi or letting him out? He keeps asking."

"Chusi can stay another night and think about answering me when I speak to him. Did Bo say anything?"

"Not a single word."

"He will eventually."

"It wasn't your fault Matt."

Matt shook his head slowly, sadly. "Jed has a twelve-year-old boy and three more younger than that. He was their only means of income, Truet. Not only are they dealing with the shock of him not coming home again, but Wanda, his wife, is scared to death how she's going to feed her family. I don't know how I'm going to do it, but I'm going to keep paying his wages to support them. I won't leave them empty-handed." His eyes filled with thick tears. "I'm not kidding; I don't ever want to do this again. If you ever plan on marrying Annie, I want you to go work on the ranch. I don't want to tell my sister and my nephew and nieces that you were killed because you're working for me. That's non-negotiable."

Truet smiled sadly. "If I married Annie, I'd have no choice but to work on the horse ranch anyway."

"Go on home."

"Are you going to be all right?"

"I'll be fine."

When Truet left, Matt locked his office's front door and went to his desk and sat down. He no sooner sat down when he heard someone knocking on the front door. He stepped out of his private office and saw the reporter for the Branson Gazette Newspaper knocking on the door. The reporter wanted to talk to him about what had happened, no doubt and earn his pay off Jed's death. Matt waved him away and went to the steel door for the jail cells and opened it and disappeared inside.

"Chusi, do you want to talk to me today?" he asked.

Chusi Yellowbear sat on the edge of the bottom bunk bed and stood up expectedly. "Time for me to go?" he asked.

"Not until you tell me why you were swinging a knife around. You aggressively came at me, Chusi. I've seen you drunk many times and you've never had that enraged look in your eyes. Why were you so angry?"

Chusi looked at Matt emotionlessly. "Bad whiskey."

Matt shook his head. "No, there's more. You're still fuming over something. I can see it right there on your brow. I'm your friend, so tell me what it is so I can maybe help. Are you mad about those idiots beating on you?"

"I want to go home."

Matt sighed. "I can't have a madman walking around town, swinging his knife around at invisible enemies. When you want to talk, you let me know."

Chusi stepped angrily towards the bars. "Let me out of here!" he screamed.

Matt looked at him, calmly. "No."

Chusi glared at him and quietly stepped back and sat down on his bunk. Matt stepped over in front of the cell holding Bo Crowe. "How do you like my jail, Mister Crowe? I imagine you'll be here for a while, so I hope you don't mind it."

Bo was lying on the bottom bunk facing the door. He sat up on the edge of the bed. "I don't mind it. I'm sorry about your deputy, Marshal."

"Thank you."

"I'm sorry, I didn't shoot him myself," Bo added simply with a slight smirk.

Matt stared at him. "I suppose he'd still be dead, but it would be you decorating my office instead of Charlie if you had."

"My brothers would've equaled the score. You cannot win, Marshal. You may have wiped out the Dielschneider family, but they're not Crowes. I'll go back to Prairieville and go to court, but I promise nothing will come of it. So yeah, I'll sit in here and be your guest until the snow melts."

"Did you know Charlie Walker was there?" Matt asked.

"Of course. Charlie sleeps in the barn."

"My presence wasn't a surprise, was it? No one seemed surprised to see me."

Bo shook his head slowly. "We figured you'd be coming when we saw your deputy in the bank. So, I hid. If it weren't for my aunt and her greed, I'd still be there tonight," he said bitterly.

"I imagine if you expected me, there was time to plan an assassination. That is why no one mentioned Charlie, right? Charlie takes out two of my men with the shotgun, who else had a weapon?"

Bo furrowed his brow. "There was no assassination planned. Charlie did that on his own. No one mentioned Charlie because he sleeps most of the day. Jack and Charlie had just gotten back from Branson yesterday. Last night we all went out drinking and Jannie and Charlie were out until really late. She woke me up when she came stumbling into the house." He shrugged. "There was no assassination planned. I was just going to hide until you left. No one likes being in jail, Marshal," he explained.

"And Morton and the rest of the Sperry-Helms Gang?"

"What about them? You were not coming for them and they knew it. They're not going to start a fight over nothing."

"With their chosen profession, a fight is kind of inevitable, isn't it?"

Bo chuckled lightly. "Marshal, that's up to you.

They won't come looking for a fight, but they won't run away if you start one. You already lost one deputy. You'll only lose more if you ever do."

Matt looked at Bo and then nodded thoughtfully. "You're about half right. Have a good night."

Chapter 12

Frank Ellison heard the news of Jed's death and that the body of Charlie Walker was in front of the Marshal's Office. Jed was a friend of his and he wanted to see the body of the man who killed him. Frank walked to the Marshal's Office and stared with others at the bloody corpse under the evening's lantern light. It filled him with a sense of anxiety, knowing Charlie was a friend of his son Bruce's. Frank worried that one of these days, Bruce might be persuaded to join the outlaw gang or fall into the trap of having the wrong friends at the wrong time and end up in a box such as the one that held Charlie.

He saw Matt Bannister unlock his office door and step outside and lock the door behind him. Matt ignored the bystanders asking him questions and began to walk away. Frank stepped quickly to his side. "Marshal, can I talk to you real quick?"

"No. I don't want to talk about Jed or Charlie," he answered firmly.

"No. It's not about them. It's about the Indian, Chusi; I need to tell you something. I would go to the sheriff, but I'm afraid it would fall on deaf ears."

Matt turned to listen to him. "What about Chusi?" He could read the anxiety on the older man's face.

"I'd rather not say on the street, can we go inside?" he asked.

Matt nodded and led the way back to the office and let Frank inside before locking the door behind him. They went into Matt's private office and sat at the desk. Matt asked, "So what's wrong with Chusi?"

"My name's Frank Ellison. I haven't met you yet." He shook Matt's hand.

"Ellison? Any relation to Bruce?"

Frank nodded shamefully. "He's my son."

"Okay. What do you have to say?"

Frank hesitated. "Marshal Bannister, have you ever heard of the 2nd Cavalry California Volunteers?"

Matt shook his head slowly.

"The Bear River Massacre?"

Matt nodded while observing Frank's nervous fidgeting. "I have."

"I was a sergeant with the California Volunteers and we were ordered to...eliminate the Shoshone that morning. It was what we were ordered to do, you will understand. We did. We killed indiscriminately, men, women and children." He shook his head emotionally. "It was horrible and I've never forgiven myself for my part in it." He wiped his eyes.

Matt closed his eyes, already knowing Chusi had lost his family there.

Frank continued, "There were some who enjoyed what we did. One of those was my brother-in-law, Wes Wasson. I got out of the Cavalry as soon as I could afterward, but he stayed on. Wes showed up here a couple of days ago and took my boys to the saloon. Chusi was there and somehow, Wes found out Chusi lost his family there apparently. I didn't know that." He paused to take a breath before continuing, "Wes went to Chusi and bragged about killing Chusi's family, and Chusi pointed at my boy Bruce and said the man who killed his family had hair like Bruce's." Tears slipped out of Frank's eyes. "Marshal, the only man who had that color of blonde hair in our whole regiment, was me. I killed Chusi's family and now, thanks to Wes's mouth, Chusi knows. I'm furious at Wes and kicked him out of my house, but I'm afraid Chusi's going to seek revenge against me."

Matt sighed. "Oh, crap." He thought in silence for a moment. "I arrested Chusi yesterday morning for walking around yelling at no one and swinging his knife around. He even came at me and I'm supposedly his friend."

Frank was concerned. "I don't know what to do. If I were him, I'd want vengeance, wouldn't you?"

Matt nodded. "I would. Mister Ellison, I have Chusi locked up in the back. He's not talking to me but wants out of jail. I was wondering what was making him so angry. I knew it wasn't just being beaten up by your son and his idiot friends; now I know. As for your concerns, I don't know what to tell you. I can't keep him locked up forever."

"Do you think he'll come after me?" Frank asked.

Matt nodded. "Wouldn't you?"

Frank shifted uneasily in his seat. "Yeah."

"Did you scalp them?" Matt asked pointedly.

He grimaced. "Heaven's no! But Wes did."

Matt scoffed, followed by a heavy sigh. "Chusi was a proud warrior, and you all declared war on him and his people. What happened that morning destroyed him and the fire inside that made him a man. He lost a large portion of his people, his relatives and friends, he lost his family and he couldn't save them. Can you imagine what that does to a man? I will tell you this; he isn't the same man that he was last week, you know a broken-down drunk with nothing to inspire him. Chusi is different now. I think your brother-in-law woke up a sleeping giant, and there's not much I can do about it. People think bows and arrows, knives and tomahawks are nothing compared to guns, but I can tell you from my own experience because I am part Nez Perce, those weapons are both efficient and deadly."

"I know that!" Frank shouted.

"What I'm saying is if we don't head this off, he'll be a walking assassin and no one will hear him until it's too late." Matt shook his head in frustration. "People pick on him and they push him around thinking he's a weak and helpless coward, but the fact is he was a broken man. What people like your son don't realize is they're messing with a sleeping lion that could tear them apart, even at his old age. All Chusi needed was a purpose for living and in the Indian culture, vengeance has more power than you know. That explains a lot." He shook his head in disgust and looked at Frank pointedly. "Mister Ellison, I was just fifteen when I hunted down and killed all five of the men of the Dobson Gang. I gave them no quarter and I had no mercy. It was a personal vendetta for killing my friend." Matt furrowed his brow as the thought occurred to him. "The same thing happened today though, didn't it? Charlie Walker killed my deputy and he's out front with a note pinned to his chest, stating this is what happens when you kill one of my deputies. Yeah, I'd say blood vengeance runs strong in our native blood."

"What should I do?"

Matt shook his head slowly. "I suggest you come back to the jail cells with me and try to explain it to him. Let him know how sorry you are. Ask for his forgiveness and…pray he has it in him to forgive you. And then, I'd start carrying a gun."

"That doesn't sound very helpful, Marshal."

Matt shrugged his shoulders. "What do you want me to do about it? I cannot keep him forever, so you might as well try being reasonable with him and see how that goes. If he wants to come after you, he will. So why not try talking to him when it's safe to do so?"

***

Chusi stood up like the hair on a cat's back when approached by a dog when he saw Matt lead Frank Ellison into the jail cell. Chusi's eyes widened with recognition and then sharpened like daggers into the soul of Frank.

"Chusi, this is Frank. He would like to talk to you," Matt said uneasily.

Frank was nervous. "Um, I don't know how to say this..."

Chusi spoke, "I know who you are. You murdered my family. I saw you!" His chest heaved with deep breaths, "I prayed we'd meet again. Now we have. You can leave now."

Bo Crowe's hands grabbed the bars of his cell door to peek out and see who was talking to Chusi. An interested grin was growing on his face.

Frank nodded shamefully. "I'm afraid I did. I know there's nothing I can say to make you forgive me, but I am so sorry. We were given orders that day, and it wasn't my choice. I didn't want to; we had no choice." His eyes filled with tears of regret and shame.

Chusi slowly grabbed the bars as he glared at him. "You shot my wife and children. Babies. You," he shouted, "killed them!"

Frank nodded. "I did," he said, barely audibly. "It's the biggest regret of my life. It really is. I had no idea it was your family."

Chusi was enraged. "All of them were my people, my family! You had me in your gun sight too, but your gun would not shoot. I escaped your death!"

Frank shook his head. "I don't know..."

"Do you know who my wife was? Do you know which children you murdered were mine? Tell me!" A dangerous scowl formed on his face.

Frank shook his head as his emotions took over. He fought from sobbing. "No..."

Bo Crowe laughed softly. "Oh, Man! Your future plans are gone."

"Shut up, Bo!" Matt exclaimed.

Chusi glared at Frank with a ferocity that left no doubt that he would cut Frank's throat if he could. He yelled, "Answer me!"

Frank wept. He looked up at Chusi. "I don't know."

Chusi's lips snarled. He spoke calmly with a threatening tone, "You killed so many. My bride was pregnant and you put a bullet in her back as she ran with my children towards the river. You shot my three little ones and I barely missed you with an arrow. You aimed your pistol at me, but there were no more bullets. Do you remember now?" he shouted.

Frank thought back painfully. He nodded, "Yes," he said meekly.

Chusi pointed at him through the bars. "I saw you!"

Bo chuckled quietly. "Wow, you murdered his family? I'm glad I'm not you, Pal!"

Matt stepped over to Bo's cell door and pointed at him. "One more word and I'll shackle and gag you for the night! Do you understand me?"

Bo laughed. "I'm not say anything."

"Will you forgive me. Please." Frank pleaded

with desperation in his eyes.

Chusi's eyes glared into Frank. "You left my bride's and our children's blood on the ground while you took their hair. My heart has bled tears for years, and you stand here and plead like a woman? My people were not even given a chance to do that! I have nothing more to say to you." He walked over to his bunk and sat down and glared at Frank. His face had become as emotionless as stone.

***

"It wasn't my fault! Honestly, please. Don't you understand it was orders. I was just following orders," Frank pleaded.

A small smirk turned Chusi's lips upwards. . "I will do as you did."

Frank stared at him questionably for a second and then understood what the ferocity in his eyes meant. Frank's eyes widened in horror. There was no question of what Chusi meant. "Please...I have a family."

Chusi jumped off the bed and ran to the bars reaching for Frank. He yelled, "So did I! It didn't matter to you; it does not matter to me!"

Matt grabbed Frank's arm, "Let's go!"

Frank pulled his arm out of Matt's grasp and pointed at Chusi as a rift of rage went through him. He yelled, "You leave my family alone! If you go near them, I will kill you! Do you hear me? My sons and my wife have nothing to do with this. This is between you and me! Do you hear me?" he screamed. "You and me!"

Chusi stared at Frank with his lips curled upwards slightly. "I'll be out of jail soon."

Matt grabbed Frank and forced him out of the jail and closed the door to the sound of Bo laughing.

Frank took several deep breaths as he calmed down and looked at Matt through water stained eyes. "He's coming after my family, isn't he?"

"Sounds like it."

"What am I supposed to do?" Frank shouted. "It was twenty-one years ago. What am I supposed to do now? Can you hold him here?"

Matt nodded. "I can for a day or two, but not indefinitely. I will try to talk to him over the next few days and see if I can reason with him. In the meantime, stay in touch and I'll let you know if I get anywhere. It's best to let Chusi calm down and see how he feels in a few days."

"And if he doesn't calm down and comes after my family?" Frank asked urgently.

Matt looked at him pointedly. "Then I suggest you put your cavalry hat back on and protect your family. There's only so much I can do until he does something."

He stared at Matt for a moment. "That's where this is heading, isn't it?"

Matt tilted his head with a slight shrug. "It might. I'll do what I can to reason with him, but you have to tell your son and his friends to leave him alone. That crap is not going to help."

When Frank left, Matt closed the door and exhaled. He didn't feel like going to see Christine or talking to anyone about his heavy heart nor bothering to get something to eat; he just wanted to go home and get on his knees with the comfort of his Bible and spend some time with the Lord and pray.

Chapter 13

Wes Wasson was in his small hotel room lying on the bed when there was a knock on his door. He sat up with some excitement growing in his eyes. Wes found Branson was relatively dull when everyone was working. He visited his sister for a few hours, but he was ready to meet up with his nephew Bruce and his friends for another night of drinking and making some memories together. He was surprised to see his brother-in-law, Frank, at his door. Frank didn't wait to be invited in; he stepped past Wes and sat in a chair.

Wes closed the door and looked at his old Sergeant. "I'm surprised to see you here. I take it you're not done berating me yet, huh?" He grabbed a bottle he had on a table, pulled the cork, and took a drink.

Frank held out his hand for the bottle. He took a long drink when it was handed to him. "No, I'm not." His eyes shot a hard glance. "Wes, you've always had a big mouth, you do know that, right?

Remember at camp that time when you got Big Dale Tompkins angry enough to wanna snap your neck? It took three of us to pull him off you."

Wes grinned. "Yeah, he was mad."

Frank shook his head. "Dale was the easiest going man I've ever known. There were bets if he was a real human or not because he never got angry, frustrated, or bothered by anything. But he wanted to kill you!"

Wes laughed lightly. "I know. I won the fifty-dollar jackpot on who could irritate him first. I overdid it, I think." He laughed.

"My point was your mouth can cause a lot of trouble. I went to see that Indian today. I apologized for what I did, for what we did…"

Wes grimaced. "Why? We did what we had to do. There's nothing to be sorry about."

"Yeah, there is," Frank said sadly. "We didn't give them a chance; we just attacked. His wife and children were no threat to us."

Wes scoffed. "And when you find a mouse nest in your house with babies, do you cuddle them up close and raise them or do you stomp on them? Look, we're never going to agree on this, I'm proud of it, you're not, okay? I get it. We are not the same, and that's normal, so why are you here? To tell me I talk too much again?" He chuckled. "I've always known that."

Frank looked at him, somberly. "Wes, that Indian, was arrested by the Marshal for going crazy in the street yesterday morning. I went to see Charlie Walker's body in front of the Marshal's

Office and told him what we did, and he took me back to see Chusi…"

"Wait… Charlie Walker, isn't that Bruce's friend?"

Frank nodded. "The same. The Marshal killed him in a gunfight."

"Matt Bannister, right?"

"Yes. So, I was talking to Chusi and…"

"Why did they get into a gunfight? Charlie seemed like a good guy to me."

"He killed Matt's deputy!" Frank replied sharply. "Let me finish!"

"Fine. But I want to meet Matt before I leave town. I've read a lot of stories about him, you know. I met a guy one time who watched Matt kill one of his own friends in a saloon back in Wyoming. Can you imagine having to kill your friend?" he laughed. "It kind of reminds me of Big Dale, because we were friends until that day. He never liked me much after that." he laughed.

"Chusi is going to come after my family," Frank said simply with no humor on his face at all.

"What?"

"You heard me. Chusi is going to come after my family when he gets out of jail."

Wes chuckled. "No, he's not. He's going straight back to the saloon to have a drink after being without one for a few days. If you are worried about him, fine, I'll dispatch him for you when he leaves to stumble back to an alley. There are enough dregs of society around here that no one will know who did it. Is that what's bothering you?"

"You act like it's no big deal."

Wes shrugged. "It's not. You forget I have been hunting Indians for a long time. Your family will be fine."

Frank took another drink of the whiskey bottle. "Matt said something that bothers me. He said the man's changed. He said it's like Chusi has a reason to live now and that's killing me. He said, Chusi is an awakened Lion, a predator, and now all of a sudden, I feel like prey."

"Prey?" Wes asked with disgust. "Frank, you were a soldier! You've gotten soft over the years. Are you sewing quilts nowadays too, Sergeant? We did what we were told to do. That's all there is to it. Get over it and if Chusi has a problem with it, we'll finish the job. And I won't think a thing about it. How long is he in jail for?"

"A few days. Matt will let me know when he's out."

"And what did Matt say about it?"

Frank smirked. "He said I need to put on my revolver and protect my family."

Wes nodded. "Well, it sounds like what you need to do then. Frank, you need to take my sister's bustle off your waist and put your gun belt back on. You've gotten too soft, Old Man."

Frank chuckled for the first time.

"Seriously, it'll be fine."

Chapter 14

Christine Knapp dressed warmly and walked with Bella's husband Dave, who carried a small wicker basket across town. Her wounds from being shot by Martin Ballenger had healed, but her abdominal muscles were still weak and on the mend. Luckily for her, Dave was helpful enough to agree to carry the basket and walk to the Marshal's Office with her. She had been for the most part in bed for about four weeks now. In truth, she was excited for Spring to arrive and melt the ice and snow. She could walk on the boardwalks easily enough because city ordinances required each business to sweep the snow off any boardwalks in front of their establishments. Crossing the streets with the uneven ground with many ruts covered by the frozen snow and ice was hard for her to do alone. She feared slipping and losing her balance on the ice and falling because her abdominal muscles were still quite tender. She could not go for a walk without someone being with her and it was frustrating not to be able to leave when she wanted to. But most of all, she was grateful to be alive. She knew Chusi Yellowbear had been arrested and wanted to make him a bread pudding as a gift. He had saved her life once and she felt it was the least she could do for him now that he was in jail. She had heard the upsetting news of Jed Clark being killed and knew Matt was hurting. He sent word to her last night that he was going home to sleep rather than visiting with her. She wanted to see Matt when she got his message, but she had no one to walk with her across town. She was anxious to see him and make sure he was doing okay.

Dave and Christine turned onto Main Street and saw the pine box holding Charlie Walker's body on the boardwalk; they passed by it slowly. Christine read the note pinned to his blood-stained chest in disgust. She entered the office with a repulsed expression on her face. "Good morning, gentlemen. Is Matt here?"

Phillip smiled with one cheek lifting higher than the other. The scar on his left side of his face had pulled the skin a bit tighter but had healed well. "Good morning, Christine. Matt went to the courthouse a few minutes ago. He'll be back pretty soon."

"I have a bowl of pudding for Chusi. Is he still here?"

Truet Davis stood up from his desk. "He is here, come on back, Christine. How are you feeling today?"

She grimaced as she came through the three-

111

foot partition gate. Dave stayed outside, gazing at Charlie and talking about him with another man who stared at the corpse as well. "I'm a little sore but doing okay. Truet, why does Matt have that man out front? Isn't that kind of morbid?"

Truet nodded as he opened the steel door to the jail cells. "It is. I advised him not to, but he insisted. He was upset after Jed was shot. We all were, but he thinks it was his fault. Anyway, I don't want the prisoners hearing that Matt was upset, so let's not talk about it in here. Matt will be back pretty soon. Chusi is right in here."

Inside the jail, Chusi's head lifted off his pillow when he saw Christine enter the jail with a basket. He stood up. It was the first time Chusi had seen her since she had been shot. He smiled at her kindly. "The Angel is alive and well. It's good to see you."

"Chusi, how are you?" she asked. Her voice brought Bo Crowe to his cell door to grab the bars and peek around the granite wall separating his and Chusi's cell to try to see who was talking.

Chusi nodded. "And you? How are you? You look like an Angel, as always."

She laughed lightly. "You're always so nice. When you get out of there, how about you have dinner with Matt and me? I have never been able to thank you for saving my life properly."

A noticeably sad expression came over his face. "The people would not like to see you with me."

She furrowed her brow. "Chusi, I couldn't care less about what the people think. If I'm having lunch with my friend, what they think matters not at all to me. I don't even care if they stop eating and stare or gossip for a month. Do you know why?"

He shook his head with an appreciative look in his eyes.

"Because I like you. And friends have dinner together sometimes. In fact, I brought you a present. I don't know if you like bread pudding, but I sure hope so, because I brought you a bowl of it." She opened the basket and pulled out a plain white bowl filled with bread pudding. She put a spoon in it to eat with. And then handed it to him through a slot in the door. "I hope you like it."

"Did you make it?" he asked as he took the bowl.

"I did. If you like it, I'll make some more."

He took a bite curiously. His eyes widened with delight and nodded his approval. He sat on his bed and finished the bowl of pudding quickly.

Truet stood in front of Bo Crowe's cell quietly just to keep his eyes on her with the two prisoners in there.

Bo Crowe said, "I like bread putting. Would you bring me some too?"

Truet didn't give her the chance to answer. "She's not here to talk to you, Bo. Go sit down and be quiet."

Bo looked at Truet displeased. "Don't treat me like a child, Deputy. I asked nicely. If the pretty lady wants to bring me some pudding, that's up to her, not you."

Truet raised his eyebrows. "It is up to me. You will have nothing to do with her at all."

Christine smiled awkwardly. "Truet, it's okay. I

can bring him a bowl of pudding. It's no big deal, really."

Truet's eyes darted to her sharply. There was a hardness in his eyes she had never seen before. "No, it's not okay. He's a rapist. So, talk to Chusi, but ignore everything this man says."

"Oh." She turned back to Chusi. "Is Matt treating you well in here?"

He nodded. "Very good."

"No," Bo replied. "This is like a fourteenth-century dungeon." He spoke to Truet, "I don't appreciate you saying I'm a rapist either, Truet. I never raped anyone. That girl's lying. I don't need to do that to anyone," he said with an arrogant smirk.

"I'll believe the girl over you," Truet said pointedly. "I've met your kind before and that's exactly who you remind me of, a man named AJ Thacker. Now, go sit down and shut up."

Bo chuckled lightly.

Christine smiled at Chusi awkwardly. "Is Matt going to let you go pretty soon?"

His lips pursed together. "Soon."

"Then, you'll join us for dinner, right?"

"Maybe."

Bo peeked through the bars trying to see her. "I'd go to dinner with you, pretty lady. It sounds like Matt's your man, but I could change that..."

Truet grabbed Bo's shirt extending his arm to push him back and then jerked him forward against the bars forcefully. "Shut your mouth!" he shouted with his eyes glaring into Bo's.

Bo raised his head with a scowl on his lips.

"When I get out of here, I'll teach you some respect."

"On that day, I'll walk you outside and give you a chance. But it might be a while because you'll be going to prison after you leave here."

Bo chuckled. "No, I'll walk out of here a free man. Deputy, I might even pay a visit to your pretty lady in Willow Falls when I leave here..."

Truet threw his right fist vertically between the bars and hit Bo in the face; he fell back and landed on the floor. He was stunned and wiped a bit of blood from his nose. Truet pointed at him angrily. "I won't put up with threats!"

"Truet, what's going on?" Matt asked loudly as he walked into the jail. He winked at Christine and ran his hand across her shoulders as he stepped in front of Bo's cell.

"He threatened Annie! He started talking to Christine like AJ Thacker used to talk to Jenny Mae. I hit him when he threatened Annie!" Truet was angry.

Matt nodded. "Go on out of here," he said and looked at Bo as he stood up. His nose bled, but luckily not severely. He watched Truet step out of the jail cell.

Bo sat down on his bed and said, "Your boy can hit, but I wasn't expecting it. Wait until I am. He won't be so lucky."

Matt spoke sternly, "No more. That's all I'm going to say to you, no more! Are we clear?" Matt asked, but his eyes burned into Bo with a deadly seriousness that didn't need to say anything more.

Bo looked at him and looked away, unable to

match Matt's hardened gaze. "Yeah, we're clear."

"Good." He nodded and stepped forward to hug Christine.

"How are you?" she asked with her usual sincerity.

He nodded. "I'm okay. Let's go out in the office and talk."

She collected her bowl and spoon from Chusi and Matt closed the steel door behind them as they left.

Truet looked at Matt. "Sorry, Matt. He reminds me of AJ. There's no way I'll listen to him threaten Annie. So, I nailed him."

"You don't need to be sorry about that. Bo knows if he tried anything like that, it's a death sentence. His family knows that too."

Truet sighed heavily. "I'm not going to be nice to him."

"Be fair with him, that's all you need to do. Go cool off somewhere. I'll be in my office talking with Christine."

Truet shook his head as he stared out the front window. "No, you're not. And I'm not leaving either." He nodded outside.

Matt looked out the window and saw the Sperry family staring at their friend in the pine box. "Dang. Christine, I'm going to have to talk to you later. I need to speak with these folks and I don't want you here when I do. But I'll see you tonight, okay?"

Her brow furrowed with concern. "Matt, is everything okay?"

He smirked slightly. "I don't know how they're going to like seeing their friend propped up out there. Let me walk you to the door."

Chapter 15

Matt opened the door and guided Christine through the group of Sperry's and the other men who glared at him after seeing Charlie in a pine box. "Dave, Thanks for walking her up here. I'll see you later tonight."

Morton Sperry spoke bitterly, "You brought Charlie back here just to post him up with your note pinned to his chest like he's some kind of a trophy? You couldn't resist writing he was a member of the Sperry-Helms Gang either, could you? He's our friend, you son of a..."

Matt cut him off, sternly, "He shouldn't have shot my deputy if he didn't want to be a decoration then. Unless there is a lie somewhere in that note, I don't want to hear about it."

"You have some nerve, Marshal. I won't forget it," Morton replied with a scowl.

"Good. Then it won't happen again," Matt responded simply. "Well, come inside, I have something for your mother."

"Do you have the money?" Mattie asked quickly. She was dressed warmly in a wool sweater over her gray flannel dress and wool socks above her boots. Her heavy coat was buttoned and she wore a lamb's skin hat with flaps that covered her ears.

Matt replied shortly, "I told you I would. Come inside." He entered the office and had Truet hold the partition gate open as the large family walked through it. Matt handed an envelope to Mattie. "I have an agreement with the bank to get the reward money faster than usual to those who come forward to help me. This is a bank cashier's check for five hundred dollars. You can cash it at the bank or put it in your bank account if you have one. You'll have no problems either way."

"Thank you, Marshal," she said as she opened the envelope and looked at the check. She grabbed her son Jack to read it to her, verifying that it was good.

A tough-looking man with short brown hair and a goatee glared at Matt with hostility. "We're taking our friend back home with us. And if I were you, I would start taking some lessons from Sheriff Wright."

Matt had been too busy to notice the man had slipped the loop off the trigger of his short-barreled .45 revolver. "If I were you, I'd slowly secure your weapon." Matt's hand moved to remove the leather thong from his trigger. "Now."

The others grew quiet and put their attention on the two men as an uncomfortable tension filled the office. The man smirked just slightly and narrowed his eyes. "Are you going to put me in a pine box out front too?"

Matt raised his eyebrows. "That's up to you."

Mattie slapped the man's arm. "Jesse, stop being such an ornery cuss and do as he says. We didn't come here for trouble, and we don't need you to start any. Do it now!"

He sneered and nodded. He did so without another word.

"Thank you," Matt said. "You must be Jesse Helms?"

He nodded. "Yeah, and you don't scare me."

"I didn't intend to," he answered and put his attention back to Mattie. "Would you like to visit with Bo?"

"We would, Marshal."

"There will be no weapons of any kind allowed in the jail cell; I will verify that before you go in. You can lay your weapons on the table over there, which includes any knives, pocket revolvers, or anything else that can be used as a weapon. If I find one item, none of you will be allowed back there. Are there any questions?"

"What if I refuse?" Vince Sperry asked with his chest puffed outwards.

"You can wait outside."

"And who is going to make me?" Vince asked with a quick look at his cousin, Jesse.

"I will," Matt replied plainly. "Let's be plain and simple; none of you will walk over me like you do, Sheriff Wright. He's weak, I'm not and neither are my men. If you want to play rough, that's the only game I know, so you're welcome to it." He looked at Vince. "In case you don't understand that, in other words, you'll remove your weapons, or you will wait outside." He looked at Jesse Helms, "You don't scare me any either."

Morton was pressing his lips together irritably. He answered for Vince and Jesse, "We understand, Marshal. Let's do as he says, boys, for Ma."

Matt opened the steel door and allowed them in to see Bo after they were searched. He left the steel door open but did not follow them inside.

***

Mattie looked at Bo and the bit of dried blood on his nose. "What happened to you?"

Bo shook his head as he shook hands with his relatives. "Nothing really. The deputy Truet hit me for talking about his woman."

Morton glanced at the office with aggravation. "You'll be out of here soon enough."

Mattie whispered as she showed him the cashier's check. "We got the money. We're going to trade it for paper money and when we have that, we'll send a wire to your brothers. I think you'll be out in a few days if they do their job right."

Bo smirked. "They will. And then I'm going to teach that deputy some respect."

Mattie shook her head. "No, you're not. You're coming back to our place and leaving that deputy alone. They already have Charlie out front; we don't need you out there too."

"Aunt Mattie, nothing's going to happen to me," he replied with a scoff. "I might even help my new friend Chusi out with a little act of vengeance when we're done in here."

Jack Sperry laughed. "No, you're not. My friends are the ones that beat him up. I'm staying in town tonight to have some more fun with them."

"Really?" Bo asked. "I was looking forward to it. I'm part Indian, you know and I wanted to get my hands on that old soldier too."

"Oh, you're talking about that!" Jack exclaimed. "That's Bruce's Pa and Uncle Wes. His Pa is the one that killed Chusi's family. Isn't that right, Chusi?" he asked loudly with a laugh. He continued to Bo, "Bruce's Uncle Wes is the one that scalped them."

"What?" Morton asked with interest.

Jack moved over in front of Chusi's cell. "Chusi here, he can explain it best. He was there. What happened to your family? How come you didn't save them, you ran?"

Chusi narrowed his eyes coldly at Jack and laid down on his bed silently.

"Come on, tell them what happened to your family," Jack repeated louder.

Matt stepped into the jail cell. "Leave Chusi alone, or I'll escort you out of here."

Jack grinned. "I was just asking him a question. Chusi, tell my brothers what happened to your family."

Matt shouted, "Out! All of you get out of here. You are not going to stand in here and question him about something he has tried to forget for all these years! Let's go."

Morton led the way as he guided his mother out of the jail cell. The others followed. Jack slapped the bars of Chusi's cell. "Wes is looking for you when you get out. He said the job wasn't completed back then."

"That's enough!" Matt shouted.

"You!" Chusi spoke loudly as he laid on his mattress with his hands behind his head on the thin pillow.

Jack looked back at him.

Chusi spoke, "I will find him."

Jack grinned. "I hope I can watch it when you do."

Chusi nodded once and then stared back up at the top bunk emotionlessly.

"Get out of my office," Matt said as Jack walked past him.

Jesse Helms paused in front of Matt. "My cousin's nose is bleeding."

Matt met his gaze evenly. "Yes, it is."

Jesse glared at him for a second and then walked towards the table to get his weapons. As they were leaving, Jesse paused at the door and looked back at Matt. "We're taking Charlie."

Matt shrugged uncaringly. "Please do."

When they had left, Truet looked at Matt. "I don't think they like you anymore."

Matt smirked as he watched them load the pine box into their covered wagon. "Well, it was bound to happen. But if nothing else, now they know we won't put up with them and that's an important bit of information for them to know."

Chapter 16

Matt rode his horse to the Ellison's house and tethered her to a hitching post. It was past dinnertime and dark out when he knocked on the door and waited until Frank opened the door. "Marshal," he said, surprised to see him. "Come inside, please."

"Evening," Matt said, stepping inside. "Frank, I was hoping to find you and your son and brother-in-law at home."

"You're in luck; it's dinner time. Are you hungry?"

"No. I don't want to interrupt, but if I could talk to your family, that would be great."

"Of course. Hang your coat up and come sit down."

Matt removed his heavy buffalo coat and laid it on the floor after trying to hang it on an unstable coat rack.

Frank called his family from the dinner table into the family room to have a seat. He introduced Matt to his wife, Florence, their youngest son, Paul and Wes Wasson. Matt already knew Bruce Ellison.

"Is Bruce in trouble?" Florence asked, anxious to know why the famous marshal was in her family room.

"No," Matt answered with a shake of his head.

"Then why are you here, Marshal?" She wasn't rude but more worried.

Frank asked her to sit down in her chair as he brought a kitchen table chair for Matt and set it where he could talk to them all. The two boys and their uncle Wes sat on the davenport. "Thank you," Matt said, sitting down.

Frank said to Florence, "He's here to talk about that old Indian."

Wes Wasson looked at Matt curiously. "You know, I've read stories about you and you're not what I was expecting. I thought you would be older and be more beat up and dangerous looking. I wasn't expecting you to look a bit like an Indian yourself. Lose the beard and add a summer in the sun, you'd look Indian."

Matt raised his eyebrows. "I am. My grandmother was Nez Perce."

Wes chuckled. "I never read that."

"I wouldn't believe too much of what you read about me anyway. I've never talked with a writer. So, where they are getting their information, I have no idea. As far as I'm concerned, they're all a bunch of liars for selfish gain off my name. I'd shoot them all if I could."

Bruce Ellison stared at Matt with disgust. "Like you shot Charlie?"

"No," Matt answered irritated by the statement, "I'd only shoot them once, I shot Charlie three times and I'd do it again if he stood just a little longer. I know he was a friend of yours, but he killed Jed for no reason and would've killed Nate, Truet or myself next if I had not shot him. It's unfortunate because Charlie had no cause to do that; we were not after him. And now two men are dead because of one man's stupid decision."

Matt looked at Frank and then at Florence, who sat curiously listening to them talk. "Misses Ellison, I am here because I'll be letting Chusi Yellowbear out of jail tomorrow and because of some foolish choices made by your brother and your son, your family might be in danger."

Wes scoffed and then laughed sarcastically. "That's more dramatic than a Shakespearean play, Marshal!" He mimicked Matt's voice, "'I'm just here to tell you you're in danger because of your brother and son.'" He laughed. "Marshal, there's five of us here, and he's an old broken-down old man. I think we'll be fine."

Bruce grinned. "Chusi can't do anything, Marshal."

"Can't or won't, Bruce?" Matt asked, "It seems to me, not so long ago, he was whipping you, Ritchie Thorn and Bobby Alper, all at the same time when you three tried robbing a lady in front of the Monarch Hotel," Matt said reminding him of when the three friends tried to rob Felisha Conway. "He wasn't even mad at you then."

Florence's eyes narrowed in on her oldest son.

"You tried to rob a woman, Bruce?"

"No, Ma, I didn't. It was just some fooling around." He answered with his cheeks turning red.

Matt answered quickly, "And that fooling around hurt a bit, didn't it?"

Bruce was angered by Matt, bringing it up in front of his parents. "We were beating him pretty good until William showed up."

Matt smiled. "Right." He looked at Frank and his wife. "Last week, Chusi was a broken man and would've allowed teenagers to harass him without fighting back because he had nothing else to lose. The only reason he fought Bruce and his pals that night was because I had asked him to watch over that lady for me. Anyway, I arrested Chusi the other morning for going a bit crazy on the street. Like I told your husband, Chusi is a friend of mine and he was still coming at me with a knife. If my deputy had not knocked him out with a revolver, I would've had to shoot him. I wondered what had happened to him because he wouldn't talk to me and then I found out what these two said to him. I'll tell you right now, Chusi is not the same man he was. There is a new spirit in his eyes and a new breath of life in his lungs. There's a blood vengeance burning in him and that puts everyone in this room in danger, even you, Misses Ellison."

"Me? Why me? I don't even know him!" she exclaimed with a perplexed grimace.

Matt narrowed his eyes pointedly. "You have to understand that the Indian culture isn't like your own. The soldiers, like your husband and brother, who entered that winter camp, did not know any of the people they killed. They just killed and Chusi, I'm sure fought like a wild dog to save his people. He watched your husband shoot his wife, who was pregnant and his three other children. They had names and had a life, which was Chusi's life."

Wes interrupted him, "Come on, Marshal. We know what we did. They were orders! We couldn't sit down and have coffee with the heathens!" he chuckled.

Matt looked at him harshly. "The only heathens there that day were you, soldiers! I've seen the cruelty on both sides in Wyoming and up through the great plains. I've met the Cheyenne and other tribes and I've heard their stories of what the soldiers did to them. I've seen bodies on both sides just as desecrated as each other. And don't forget my own tribe was forcefully removed and at war with the cavalry just a few years ago. I can tell you right now, some of the greatest people with the greatest hearts I've ever met were Indians. And Chusi is one of them; he has a great heart and he's a very good man. But you just spat the most painful experience of his life right back into his face. Honor to an Indian isn't like the obedience of a U.S. Soldier. It's personal and the only way to correct a wrongful death is by blood. Frank killed Chusi's entire family and that's bad enough, but you," he spoke to Wes, "scalped them and bragged about it to him! Are you kidding me?" Matt shouted and then paused to regain his composure.

Wes grinned. "Yeah."

Matt continued, "You just resurrected a Shoshone warrior and he'll be coming for your blood. You took four or five people from him, and he'll be coming to take one for one, wife for wife and child for a child. He'll go after Frank for the killing and you for scalping his family."

"Let him come…" Wes invited.

"No, listen to me!" Matt raised his voice. "Your actions put this whole family in danger. Frank's been walking around this town for years and Chusi never recognized who he was until now. That's the difference you made! Now Chusi's a new man with a purpose and it's destroying this man and his family! Understand it's not just a purpose in our language, it's a blood lust, it's a matter of getting his honor back and that's stronger than any type of vengeance you may understand. He'll gladly die for that purpose, by the way. I can't hold him in jail to protect you; I can't hold him in jail to protect him. I have to let him loose and see what happens because there's nothing I can do until he does something. I'm not here to be dramatic; I'm here to warn you and to tell you to leave him alone if you see him on the street."

Frank grimaced and said, "Marshal, if he's coming after my family, I'm not going stand by and wait. I'll take the offensive and end the threat early."

Matt responded, "If you take the offensive and kill him, you'll be arrested for murder. Self-defense is one thing, cold-blooded murder because you scared is another. Listen to me; he will come after you if I can't persuade him not to. I'm going to talk to him tomorrow with my fiancé. He listens to her for some reason. I pray he listens and realizes there's more to live for than seeking vengeance for something that happened so many years ago. It's not going to bring his family back. My hope is he is willing to forgive the wrongs and leave you all be." He looked at Wes and Bruce. "But you have to leave him alone. I promise if I'm able to reason with him and you blow it," he shook his head. "Any blood will be on your hands."

Florence spoke, "Bruce promise the Marshal you'll stay far away from that man. You too, Wes. We don't need any trouble and I don't want an Indian sneaking into my house."

Bruce nodded with a slight smirk. "Me neither, Ma."

Wes sighed. "Try talking to him, Marshal. Just let me know how it goes because I'd hate to shoot an innocent man. You do realize he probably killed some of our fellow soldiers, maybe even my friend that died there."

Matt's eyes remained on Wes.

"What?" Wes asked with a sarcastic grin. "Oh, I promise to be good. I don't want anything bad happening to my family."

Matt replied irritably, "I'm wondering if I'll be wasting my time talking to him while you're here. I have a feeling you're looking forward to starting a fight with him. I'll warn you right now; don't, or you might be in for quite a bloody and painful fight." Matt stood up. "Do not underestimate that old man. You folks have a nice evening."

Chapter 17

It was a sunny day, and the warmth of the sun slowly began to melt the snow and ice. Matt stood beside Christine and his deputies at the graveside service of Jedidiah Clark. It had been an excellent funeral service for a good man. Matt's heart was broken for Jed's family and as he watched them grieve, it troubled him even more that he hadn't been able to save his friend. There was nothing he could have done, but because it had happened, he was irritated at himself for having overlooked every possibility. Guilt plagued him like a hovering dark shadow reminding him that he should have searched every outbuilding and barn on the property before letting his guard down. He believed the Sperry's had no knowledge of what Charlie Walker was going to do and if there was anyone to blame aside from Charlie, it was himself. Matt had already decided to keep paying Jed's wife his monthly wages; it was the least Matt could do to help them and to honor his friend. He paid for the funeral costs and was having a memorial marker made for Jed that honored his sacrifice for years to come with a U.S. Deputy Marshal's badge engraved into the granite below his personal information.

When the funeral reception was over, Matt and Christine took a buggy back to the Marshal's Office to talk to Chusi. Matt entered the jail and scowled when he smelled the odor of Chusi's dog crapping on the jail cell floor again. He had sent Nate to Chusi's camp early that morning to bring the dog into town so it could be fed and kept warm. It had taken a while for Nate to find Chusi's home out in the woods, but eventually, he returned with the dog. Matt couldn't say he loved the dog, but Chusi did and that was what mattered.

"Chusi, I'll make you a deal, clean up your dog's mess and I'll let you out of here." Matt unlocked the cell door and the dog came forward, wagging her tail frantically and jumped up on him, wanting to be petted. Matt bent over and rubbed its ears and neck. "You're one ugly dog, do you know that? You are! Yes, you are! Just the ugliest and stinkiest dog ever!" he said in a friendly high-pitched voice as he pet the female Red Tick Hound. It had solid red spots around its ears and on its sides and a blotchy mixture of red and white everywhere else

Chusi smirked as he watched Matt. "She likes you."

Matt looked at Chusi with a grin. "It's a one-way relationship because I don't like her." He looked back at the dog. "No, I don't. Nope, your just too ugly to like," he said with the same high-pitched voice as he spoke to the dog.

Chusi spoke, "Thank you for having Nate bring her here."

Matt stood up straight. "You're welcome. When you finish cleaning that mess, let's sit down and talk for a bit."

***

"The Angel," Chusi said with a slight grin when he saw Christine sitting at a table near the woodstove in the main office with the same small basket she had the day before. The dog went to her and she carefully leaned over to pet it while Matt closed the steel door to the jail cells behind him. Truet Davis, Nate Robertson and Phillip Forrester sat at the table as well with cups of coffee in front of them.

Matt sat down at the table and motioned for Chusi to join them at the table.

Chusi sat down, feeling a bit uneasy when he saw Christine's sad smile and moist eyes as she looked at him. He sat between Nate and Phillip, facing Matt, Christine and Truet. There was a cup of coffee waiting for him.

"What's this?" he asked, motioning to the others at the table.

Matt leaned forward over his elbows on the table. "We want you to know we care about you here in this office. We all think of you as our friend, Chusi."

He nodded once. "Friends, yes." He picked up his cup of coffee and took a drink.

Matt continued, "I don't want to see you get hurt and I don't want to arrest you again, either. I'm curious to know what your plans are when it comes to Frank Ellison and Wes Wasson now that all that stuff has come out."

Chusi's eyes fell to the table's top. He made no reply.

Matt continued, "There are only two ways it can end if you go after them. Either you'll be killed or if you did kill them, I'd have to arrest you and you'd sit in that jail until the day you're executed. Either way, it would be the end of you and we don't want that. None of us sitting here with you want that to happen. So, we're asking you to promise that you'll let it go. I know they've said some horrible things…"

Chusi glared at Matt bitterly. "It's what they *did*, not what they said!"

"That was twenty-one years ago. You heard what Frank said, what he did haunts him to this day. What more than can he do than to apologize and ask for your forgiveness? He knows how wicked it was. Frank quit the Cavalry as soon as he could after that day. What more can he do to prove he's sorry for what he did?"

Chusi looked at the top of the table emotionlessly. "Die like a man. He's scared!"

Matt grimaced. "Of course, he's scared. He's afraid you're going to want to hurt him and his family." Matt paused as he noticed Chusi nodding his head. "Is that what you're planning to do?"

"Can I leave?" he asked, still looking down.

Matt knew all too well that his view of the

world was quite different than the way Chusi saw the world. There was a vast difference between the white man's customs and values and the customs and beliefs of the Shoshone man sitting before him. Most of Chusi's life was lived in the freedom of the frontier in a teepee with his family. He was a proud hunter, a warrior, a strong and courageous man who lived without a city or a town, but with the love and respect of the proud Shoshone people. Forgiveness over a cup of spilled milk was one thing, but there was no forgiveness for spilled blood, except for spilling the blood of the one who made the first cut. Chusi had only been living in the white man's world for twenty years of his life at most and the depth of his morality was ingrained in him from his youth. Matt was not having any luck trying to get him to understand the concept of forgiving the men. At the same time, Matt wondered if he would be so willing to forgive someone if his wife and children were killed. Indeed, Matt feared losing Christine when she had been shot and if he had caught Martin Ballenger before the crowd lynched him, Matt wondered if he would have shot Martin. Granted, he had shot and killed the Dobson Gang in his youth, but he had grown spiritually since then. There is no doubt he would want to shoot Martin Ballenger, but Matt believed he would have had enough self-control to arrest Martin if he had surrendered.

Truet spoke, "My wife, Jenny Mae, was pregnant when she was killed, Chusi. I know what that feels like to have your family taken from you violently by another man. I remember exactly what that rage felt like and I'm sure you feel like I did. But the comfort I have is knowing Jenny Mae is in Heaven and I'll see her again. I have to keep moving forward in my life and let the past go, or I'd be stuck in despair. Do you know what I mean? It won't do any good to end their lives and yours for something that's not going to bring your family back."

Chusi looked at Truet with a touch of hostility in his eyes. "You killed those men that killed your wife, yes?"

Truet nodded slowly. "Three of them. The fourth was hung."

Chusi was incensed. "Then, you got your vengeance! I have none. If those same men walked around town today and laughed in your face, would you still sit here and say these things? Or would they be just as dead as they are today?" His eyes burned with the same intensity that he had on the morning he was arrested.

Truet bit his bottom lip thoughtfully. "That's a tough question. What I can tell you is I was a soldier too and being in the Cavalry, you don't make the choices. You do what you are told to do or else. What those men did to your people was horrible, but the one responsible was the highest officer in charge, not the mere soldiers doing what they were told. Frank was a soldier, but not the one who made the decisions. He told you, himself, how sorry he is." He shrugged compassionately. "He asked you to forgive him because he knows it was wrong. And that's what Christians do. We ask the Lord to forgive our sins and we ask the people we have wronged to forgive us, too, just as we are supposed to forgive anyone who asks us to forgive them."

"Were you at my camp too?" Chusi asked bitterly.

"No. I was in the Calvary ten years later or so on the great plains. We fought the Cheyenne, Arapaho and Sioux mostly. But I know the skill and honor of the warriors on the battlefield. I know what you could do to those men and they would not see it coming. I know that and so does Matt. I know you have not gotten your justice, but revenge is only going to lead you to the grave no matter how it turns out. I understand your anger; trust me. I honestly do, more than anyone else sitting here because the men that murdered my wife did laugh in my face about it. And I killed them. The difference is; there was no justice, no law for me to go to. The fact is simply this, if you do as I did, you'll only be killing yourself."

Christine spoke softly, "Chusi, I'm going to be marrying Matt and I want to see you at our wedding. I want to see you playing with our children if the Lord blesses us with any. I want you to be a part of our family. I want to see you at our family dinners, and I want you to be a part of our children's lives. You lost your family and Matt's father is never here and I don't have a father, so I want you to join our family and be a Grandfather to our children."

He smiled slightly as warm moisture glistened in his eyes.

She continued, "I am a woman and it doesn't matter if your wife was Indian, black or white, we are still women and I can tell you if I were killed like I almost was not long ago, I'd want Matt to keep living and do it well. I'd want him to be happy with someone else, just like Jenny Mae would Truet, I'm sure. I'd want him to keep living a long, happy life without me. I'm sure your wife would want the same. Can I ask what her name was?"

Chusi closed his eyes slowly. "It doesn't matter."

Christine frowned sympathetically. "Chusi, what was her name?" she asked softly.

"Omusa."

"Omusa. That's a pretty name. Was she a beautiful young woman?"

He nodded sadly.

"And your children? What were their names?"

He sighed silently. No one had ever cared enough to ask the names of his family. He spoke softly, "I waited for Omusa for a long time to be my bride and I have loved her and only her. Our daughter, Titsi, was the oldest. She was as beautiful as her mother. Our first-born son, I named Chogun; he was a strong and stubborn, boy. Our second-born son, we named Lootah. He was a loving little boy. Omusa was big with our fourth child when she was shot and killed." The soft, warm smile had disappeared and the angry glare returned in his eyes. "The soldier, Frank, I remember his white hair, shot her in the back as she ran with our children towards the river. When she fell, Titsi tried to help her up, but her life was ended too. She was ten years old. Chogun was crying out for me to help him when he was shot too." Chusi's eyes grew thick with tears.

"Chogun was eight years old. And my baby, Lootah, was only five. He was crying for his mother when Frank stood over him and pulled the trigger like he was a rat!" He looked up at Christine with hard, reddened eyes that appeared to be a mile deep in a liquid that refused to fall. "How can I forget what I heard and saw?" He held up a hand showing five fingers. "Lootah was five! And now that man begs me for forgiveness?" He shook his head with a scowl. "No. He killed five of mine; I will kill five of his!"

Christine wiped the tears from her eyes. "What happened to you is horrible, Chusi. It makes me wonder why God allows such evil things to happen, but then I remember that God never wanted such horrendous things to happen. Sin and evil bring destruction and that was an evil thing. I want you to know, I see you for the man you are right now and I know you're a good man, even after all the wickedness you have seen. The woman you married must have been amazing to have won your heart and your willingness to wait so long for her. So I must ask, do you think she would want you to end your life to get vengeance for her and your children? If she was here for just five minutes, what would she say to you?"

He clenched his jaw emotionally. "She'd say... avenge my children!"

"Chusi..." Christine sighed.

Matt spoke pointedly, "I can't let you kill Frank or touch his family for what he did. He would have gone to the military jail or been shot himself if he had refused to do what he was commanded to do. It changed his life too. And those memories still haunt him today."

"I remember it differently."

"That was then; this is now!" Matt shouted with a harsh tone to his voice. He immediately took a deep breath and paused with his eyes on Chusi. "You're going to do whatever you're going to do and I'm not going to hound you about it. You know the consequences. However, Christine just told you we would like for you to be a part of our family and play with our children and teach them the Indian ways. There are good times ahead if you can control yourself and not harm an innocent family. Be a better man than them, so you can watch over my family like it was your own. You're only sitting here because you matter to us, Chusi. Let the blood they owe you go."

He nodded but said nothing. "Can I go?" he asked sadly.

Matt nodded. "You may."

"Chusi," Christine added softly, "I made you a big bowl of bread pudding. Bring the bowl and basket back without hurting anyone and I'll make you some more," Christine said as she slid the basket across the table to him.

"Thank you." He looked at Matt. "Can I have my knife? I must go check my traps."

Matt went into his private office and handed Chusi his knife in a deer hide sheath. "Think about what I said, Chusi. I buried one friend today. I don't want to lose another."

Chapter 18

Chusi walked his red dog out of town and through the forest to his teepee near where Spider Creek emptied into the Modoc River. He made a fire in the teepee's firepit and went out to pull in his trout line that had been soaking for three days. There were two trout on his line and he cooked those over the fire for his dinner. He had some of the bread pudding as well. His traps would have to wait until the next day when there was more light as it was a three-mile hike to his traps.

Chusi sat beside his fire, staring at the flames with heavy tears once again in his eyes. They, too, refused to fall but clouded thickly in his eyes. He had gone back a few days after the massacre and found the bodies of those killed frozen on the ground. Many of the women had been stripped and ravaged and had their heads split open by an axe afterward. Children were not spared from any of the cruelty. He found Omusa where she had fallen, the baby in her womb had been cut out and tossed beside her.

All of his family members had been scalped and their hair taken as trophies. He had never seen anything more brutal and inhumane in his years of life. It was the whites who called his people heathens and animals but seeing the ghastly sights the soldiers left behind. It was incomprehensible to believe that the soldiers were human beings. He refused to leave the bodies of his family on the ground to be coyote and crow food, but there were far too many bodies to bury them all. He labored to dig graves and put his beloved family in the frozen ground without ceremony. His songs and his tears and cries over them, were the only lamenting for them.

His teepee had been burned like all the others, but inside wrapped in a surviving buffalo blanket were the beaded moccasins and beaded deerskin dress that Omusa wore on their wedding day and occasionally in better weather. The brightly beaded child moccasins for their children were also there. He took what he could and left with more sorrow than a man should ever know. Chusi left a broken man, a shadow of who he once was. He came west and roamed like a lost spirit until he settled in Branson and had become a burden to the town. Whiskey helped take the pain away and he remembered many nights screaming into the forest to release the agony of what he'd been through and vowing to avenge their blood if he ever had a chance to. Life is a funny thing; the soldier responsible was living in the same town as him.

Chusi exhaled as he stared into the flames of his

fire. He untied the buckskin strings around a folded deerskin and pulled out Omusa's beaded moccasins and held them. She wore them when they married and on every celebration. She wore them when they went into the white men's town; she wore them when she shined the brightest. A tear slipped out of his eyes and ran down his cheek, followed by another. He was thirty-eight then, strong, proud and his skin smooth. Now he was fifty-nine and his face had weathered and aged far more than the twenty-one years since he had last seen her.

Christine had asked him what Omusa would say to him if she could come back for just five minutes. He smiled slightly because he knew she would say, "*You're old!*" before she said anything else. What would she say to him if she had limited time to say anything? She would be saddened to know her family treated him so poorly. She would know he could not save her or their children any more than he had tried to. She would understand why he left an overwhelming losing battle to help the others who got away. She would know him and his heart was brave and wise. She would trust his decisions, but would she understand his life now? The whiskey? No. The loneliness? No. The begging on the street for more whiskey? No. Would she be proud of him if she was alive today? The answer was no. He didn't have a horse; he didn't have a band of family or friends. He had a dog and memories. All that had become of him was a drunk beggar who most white folks pushed around and made fun of. It used to sicken her to see her people begging for whiskey and food twenty-one years ago. He had become what Omusa despised.

The question Christine asked wasn't if she would be proud of him; it was if Omusa would want him to forgive the soldiers for what they had done? He was convinced that she would ask for a container of their blood for each child they murdered.

He laid down and pulled a blanket over him and closed his burning eyes. It had become a simple fact of life; sometimes, when he would've liked to talk to someone, it was then that he realized how alone in the big world full of people, he was.

***

Omusa Yellowbear stood in the middle of the creek, appearing more beautiful than Chusi had ever seen her. Her long black hair was shining in the sun, and her sparkling eyes were on him as he walked into the creek to meet her. He stopped short of her as there was an invisiable barrier of space between them that neither of them could cross. He could see Titsi, Chogun and little Lootah playing on the creek bank behind Omusa with a baby boy. His children were laughing, and joy was all that shined in their eyes. They smiled at him and went back to playing. Omusa held two large white flowers in her hands. She set them in the flowing creek, but they floated directly over to him. Chusi picked up the flowers and held them in his hands. He knew the one in his right-hand represented Frank Ellison and the one in his left-hand represented Wes Wasson. He looked up into Omusa's eyes and knew it was his choice to either crush the beautiful flowers and watch the petals float downstream or to let the flowers float away in one piece. Omusa did not say a word in one way or another, but there was such a peaceful reflection in her face that Chusi knew his rage would not please her. He set the flowers in the gentle current and watched them float over the rocks until they were out of sight.

He looked at Omusa yearning to hold her. She smiled at him gently and spoke in her soft voice, "A pebble thrown in the stream will remain forever, but the ripples will fade away and be remembered no more."

Chusi jerked his head up awake and ran out of his teepee and down to the creek. He looked longingly and could see where she had stood in his vision. He could see where his children had played a few moments before. His heart ached like it was falling miles within his chest. He dropped to his knees on the creek's snow-covered bank and began to weep. The vision, while he slept, had been so real. He could see her; he could hear her voice as it had always been. The sound of his children playing together was such a beautiful sound to him and now the only sound was the creek flowing and the birds chirping their morning songs to start the day. For a moment, he was so happy and upon waking, the heartache of missing them was all the closer than it had been the days before.

Her words still echoed in his ears. He took a pebble from the ground and tossed it in the stream.

He watched the slight ripples in the current and before he knew it, they were gone, and no one would have ever known something was thrown in the creek. The pebble was still there, but the effects it caused were gone. He tossed in another stone and watched the result. He tossed another and then remembered the barrier that kept them apart in his vision. His head raised as he began to understand. He picked up a pebble and looked at it; their love was as strong as a pebble but thrown into the creek, it is gone from the land of the living, separated by the barrier of water. The ripples are immediate and came in waves, like the sorrow and heartache that he had felt when she was taken away. The pain was supposed to fade the further the ripples went from the moment the pebble made an impact with the water. The ripples cease, but the pebble remains. Yes, the hurt can fade with time, but the love will always remain as strong, but separated by the space between life and death.

Chusi nodded. "Omusa, my love. I understand." The flowers were letting go. Letting go of his hatred, his guilt and his past. He nodded. "I will try."

Chapter 19

Matt frowned when he heard a knock on his front door. He had just woken up and was stoking the fire to put some heat in the house. He looked at the clock on the wall and sighed. It was too early for a social call. "Who is it?" he asked, going to the door.

"Chusi."

"Chusi?" Matt asked himself with a scowl as he opened the door. "Good morning, Chusi, what can I do for you?" he asked as he yawned. "Come in."

Chusi looked at Matt with a small smile, which wasn't normal for him.

Matt narrowed his eyes, wondering if Chusi was okay. "What?"

"I had a vision," he stated and remained quiet.

Matt shrugged questionably. "Were you marrying a red-headed beauty from Prairieville named Danetta, by chance?" He chuckled when Chusi grimaced a bit confused. "I guess not. Do you want some coffee?"

"Yes. No, not about the redhead. Yes, for coffee."

Matt nodded with a grin. "I figured. Have a seat, tell me why you're here so early. Is something wrong?"

"No. I had a vision, and I need you to do me a favor."

"What kind of a favor?" he asked as he handed a cup of coffee to Chusi.

"I need to go see the white-haired man, Frank that...you know."

"When?"

"Now."

Matt glanced at him, thoughtfully. "Now?"

Chusi nodded. "Yes. Can you take me, please?"

"Why?"

"To tell him we're, even."

"You're even? What makes you even?" Matt asked with a sense of alarm. "Yesterday, you were intent on harming him and now you're even?"

He nodded. "Yes. I had a vision."

"What was your vision?"

After Chusi told him about his vision and what he believed it meant, Matt agreed to take him over to the Ellison's house, but they needed to hurry because Frank would be leaving for work before too long.

They had hurried across town and knocked on the Ellison's door.

Paul Ellison opened the door. The twenty-one-year-old son of Frank and Florence. He was surprised to see Matt with Chusi. "Hi..."

"Good morning. Is your Pa home?" Matt asked.

"Yeah. We're about ready to go to work but come

147

in. Uncle Wes is sleeping still, but that's alright." He closed the door behind them and led the way into the family room where Wes Wasson was sleeping on the davenport. The lights were low, so not to disturb him. "Pa, Ma, the Marshal's here with Chusi."

"Chusi," Matt stated, "wanted to come to speak with you."

Frank and his wife were both stunned to see Chusi standing in their family room. Chusi was wrapped in a blanket and wore a hat over his head. His long, tangled hair fell over his shoulders. He stood straight and looked at them with his stern dark eyes.

Frank spoke with concern, "What's this? Are you showing him where we live so he can come here on his own, Matt?"

Matt shook his head and looked down at Wes when he opened his eyes, startled, to see Chusi standing in the family room, he sat up quickly, spouting out a sudden curse.

"Chusi, say what you came here to say," Matt said with a smirk at Wes.

Chusi stared at Frank with no emotion on his face. "You and me, are even."

Frank grimaced, not understanding. "What's that mean?"

Matt spoke, "It means you have nothing to worry about. He forgives you."

Frank shook his head slightly as a layer of water came over his eyes. His voice became emotional. "How? What I did was...unforgivable."

Chusi looked at him. "We're even."

Frank nodded. "Thank you." He bit his bottom lip fighting the years of shame that clouded his eyes. His wife put her arm around his shoulders comfortingly.

"Chusi," she said softly. "Thank you. You have no idea how much that day has affected him. He has nightmares about it still."

Chusi nodded once. "Me too. You, Miss, may not know how bad it was, but I went back and the soldiers had cut the baby out of my wife and many, many worse things too. For that, I should thank him," he nodded at Frank. "For killing my family quick, so they suffered no further shame. But I will be haunted by it no more." A slight smile moved the corners of his lips.

Florence covered her mouth with a gasp and began crying.

Matt had caught Frank's eyes shift over to Wes accusingly as Chusi spoke about his wife. It had become evident that one of the monsters that desecrated the bodies was Wes. Matt looked at Wes and wanted to immediately slap the slight smug smirk of humor off his face.

"We can go now," Chusi said to Matt.

"Alright, Chusi, let's go. You folks have a great day."

"Matt," Frank said from across the room, stopping Matt at the door. "Thank you."

Matt waited for Chusi to step outside then he closed the door with Chusi outside. He stepped back into the family room to face Frank. "I didn't have anything to do with it. He came to my place, wanting to come over here after having a vision as he calls it. If I were you, I'd be thanking Jesus. He had intended to take all of your lives last night. You have no idea how blessed you are."

"Oh, my Lord!" Florence gasped and sat down in a dining room chair.

Frank's lips quivered. "I will thank the Lord."

Wes groaned on the davenport. "Did he have a vision of me scalping his dead head if he showed up around here?"

Matt looked at Wes indignantly. "No. His wife and children came to visit him and asked for him to give you all grace. I would say that is a much greater vision. Now, I'll make this between you and me; I'm warning you right now, leave him be. Not one word, not one fight. If I hear differently, it's going to come down to you and me."

Wes looked up at Matt and scoffed lightly, shaking his head.

Frank spoke sharply, "You better believe Wes will leave him alone and so will my sons! If I hear of any of you harassing that poor man, I'll personally tear your heads off and kick it around in the streets!"

Matt nodded. "Have a good day, folks."

***

When Matt had left, Florence stood up and hugged her husband. "Is it true? Were terrible things done to those Indians?"

Frank sniffled and nodded. "I left the camp and

went upriver to be alone. I got on my knees and begged God to forgive me for what I had done. When I came back... Yes."

"Soldiers aren't supposed to do that kind of stuff," she gasped.

"They aren't, but they were."

"What were they doing?"

Frank broke the hug and looked at his wife. He shook his head. "I don't want to talk about it. I just wanted out of the Cavalry after that. If you want the details, talk to your brother, he was the one holding Chusi's baby when I walked into camp. I have to go to work."

"Wesley Wasson?" she asked, horrified.

Wes grinned. "Yeah and your husband has never liked me much since then, have you, Sergeant?"

Frank looked at him. "No. But I will tell you, leave Chusi alone. I don't want my family killed because of your lack of common sense and loudmouth."

Wes chuckled. "Oh, come on now. You were always afraid of the red man. Don't tell me you still are."

Frank shouted angrily, "No, I respected the Indians! Why do you think we attacked the villages, the women and children? It's because we couldn't beat them any other way! They were too smart, better mounted and better soldiers than we were. You were just too damn stupid to know that! You call yourself an Indian fighter. What we did was cold-blooded murder! What Chusi just did," he pointed at the door, "took far more courage, strength and character than either of us will ever know or ever have! He's suffered enough. And you better never say anything to him again!" Frank shouted. He looked at his son. "Paul, let's go. We're going to be late."

When they left, Florence sat in her padded chair and asked, "Wesley, how could you do that?"

He shrugged. "Sis..." he smiled. "You don't want to know about the things I've done. Let's leave it at that."

"I didn't ask that I asked, how could you?"

He shrugged. "Easy. And before I leave, I'll kill that one too. I just have to make sure it's self-defense so that the Marshal won't arrest me. Not that I'd be convicted for killing a rodent."

"You better make sure my family's not involved."

"Your family will be fine. I'd never put your family at risk of anything, Florence. You're all the family I have left."

Chapter 20

Phillip Forrester and Nate Robertson were in the Marshal's Office when the door opened, and a big man stepped inside. He was dressed in a cowhide coat and wore a floppy leather hat over his bushy dark hair and beard. He looked at the two deputies. "Where's Matt?"

"Matt's not here, Adam. He's having lunch with Christine, I think," Nate answered. He was taken back by the burning anger that showed in Adam Bannister's eyes.

The door opened again, and William Fasana and Steven Bannister stepped inside as well. Adam opened the three-foot partition gate separating the entry from the main office, inviting himself deeper into the office. The others followed him beyond the gate.

William spoke, "Boys, we're going to visit Bo Crowe. Do you want to open the main door, or shall I? I am a part-time deputy marshal when I'm needed, you know?"

Nate stood up. "Sure. No one's supposed to take their weapons back there, so if you'd leave them on the table?"

"Oh, I think we'll be fine," William said as Nate unlocked the steel door.

Nate could tell something wasn't right because Adam was usually quite friendly and so was Steven Bannister, but neither man looked friendly today. Both men appeared to be quite irritated, and the look in their eyes was making Nate uncomfortable. He didn't press his luck about leaving their weapons outside of the jail. William, as well, had a far more severe countenance about him than his usual playful self. William was the first to enter when Nate pulled the steel door open, followed by Steven and Adam.

William chuckled while he peered into the cell holding at Bo. "Well, would you look at that, a prisoner. And an ugly one too. Hey, I'm over here!" he laughed, noticing Bo's wandering eye.

Bo stood up and glared at William and Steven. He had never seen either of them before and was wondering who they were. "If you knew who I am, you'd shut up and walk away!" Bo said sharply.

William raised his eyebrows and extended his face mockingly by lowering his jaw with his lips pulled tightly closed. "Ohh...if I was scared, I would, maybe, but I'm not! Do you want to go for one of my guns?" he asked and moved his hip closer to the jail's bars to make his revolver accessible to Bo. William wore a reversed two-gun setup and had easy access to the gun on his left hip.

Bo grimaced. "Who are you?" He did not like the look in the two bigger men's eyes. William was getting on his nerves.

"Come on, take it," William challenged. "I dare you?"

The hammer thong was on the revolver exposed to Bo and removed from the one the long blonde-haired stranger's hand was near. Bo shook his head curious who the men were. "No. I'm not stupid."

Nate Robertson shook his head, growing more nervous. "William, don't do that. Matt's going to be angry about you doing that."

"Mind your own business, Nate," William said without taking his hardened blue eyes off Bo.

Steven ignored Nate as well. He spoke to Bo, "I'm Matt's brother Steven, this is my brother Adam and that's our cousin William Fasana."

Bo looked at Adam and then William. He had heard of them both for different reasons in the past. Hearing Adam's name, Bo now recognized him from the Willow Falls Bank the day he was there with Morton and Vince. He recalled Morton warning Vince never to start any trouble with Adam. He nodded slowly and spoke to Adam, "I've heard of you. So...what? Did you come here just to gawk at me? Do you want an autograph or something?" His sarcasm was quite evident in his voice.

Adam raised his eyebrows with interest and nodded. "Yeah, an autograph would be nice, but I just came in to shake your hand. I've never met a famous outlaw before." He put his hand through the bars to shake.

Bo smirked and shook his head slightly. "I'm not famous. And I don't want to shake your hand, either. My cousins might have high regard for you, but that doesn't mean I do."

Adam grinned. "Don't tell me you're scared to shake my hand? Any friend of the Sperry's is a friend of mine and I just came here to meet you. But it might ruin your reputation if I go out there and tell folks you were too scared to shake my hand. Especially when I add you were shaking like a cold hen . Worse, I'm just a simple rancher; I'm not even a gunfighter." He snickered joined by William and Steven.

"Fine," Bo said and took hold of Adam's hand and then felt the large, dominant hand of Adam grab his wrist joint and jerk him forward forcefully against the cell bars. Adam's eyes had grown cruel and he reached his left hand inside the bars and grabbed a handful of hair on the back of Bo's head. He rammed Bo's face between two bars and forcefully squeezed Bo's face between the four-inch space between the bars.

Bo grimaced in pain and cried out as pressure on his skull was building. He cried out loudly, but could not break free of the strength of Adam.

Nate Robertson stepped forward to stop Adam's brutality, but Steven Bannister pointed at him warningly. "Stand back, Nate! You don't want to be hurt and I don't need weapons to do it." He was stunned by the fierceness in Steven's eyes.

William added, "But I have weapons handy if

they are needed, Nate." There was no humor in either of the men.

Nate held up his hands as he stepped back. They were Matt's family and he could deal with them when he returned from lunch. "Fair enough," he said as he retreated.

"Does that hurt yet?" Adam asked as he strained to force Bo's head tighter into a vice-like grip between the bars.

"Yeah!" Bo screamed. "Stop! Please...let me go. You..."

"Hush! No need for bad language, right?" Adam asked and slapped the top of Bo's head with his right hand while his left hand continued to push Bo's head between the bars.

"I'm going to kill you!" Bo screamed.

"Whale tail!" Adam shouted out like he was playing one of his kids and slapped his big palm down on top of Bo's head, which stunned Bo momentarily..

William and Steven began laughing heartily.

"When I get out of here..."

"Whale tail!" Adam shouted again, and threw a hard downward jarring palm strike on top of Bo's head. "Only whale's spout out empty air . So stop that."

Bo began to whimper helplessly. He tried to pull his head out of the bars, but it was useless against Adam's strength.

"Now, that you're not spouting nonsense, look at me!" Adam sneered as he glared viciously at Bo from only a few inches away. "Truet told us you made a threat towards our sister, Annie. I'm telling you right now, you little piss-ant, if you even step on our land or go near her in any way, I'll find you and take you out to the mountains, slice your Achilles' tendons and use you for wolf bait! I'll sit back and watch and we'll see if you can scare the wolves away by spouting your idle threats! You better listen up good, because if you think *I'm* making an empty threat, try me! Do you understand me?" he asked with venom in his voice. He jerked Bo's head forward for effect.

"Yes!" Bo cried out painfully.

"I don't know, I don't think you do," Adam said doubtfully. He pulled Bo's head harder into the bars.

"Stop! Please, stop!" Bo began crying.

"Quit blubbering or I'll give you another whale tail!" Adam demanded. "Honestly, if you think this hurts, wait until I'm not playing! Make no mistake about it; I'm not anyone you want to tangle with." Adam added in a softer voice, "I'm a nice guy, but you got on my bad side when I heard what you said. So, I'm going to give you one last chance to convince me. Let me ask you a question, are you ever going near my sister?"

"No!" he exclaimed loudly. "I swear, I never will. I was just saying it to make Truet mad! I didn't mean it! I swear."

"Look at me!" Adam sneered. "That's funny because I do mean what I said. You'll be fertilizer on the forest floor if you don't believe me. This is your only warning." He pulled the top of Bo's head downward in between the bars to expose the top of his head while Bo cried out from the bars grinding on the sides of his head. With his head stuck in the bars, Adam let go of his hair and grinned at his brother and cousin. The grin turned into a chuckle. 'Watch this." Adam stepped his right foot back a little bit and drove a hard-right open palm into the top of Bo's head with the power coming from his hips. His arm went through the bars and Bo flew back and ended up on the floor against the far wall. He held his head and looked disoriented.

Adam pointed at him as he laughed. "This was a nice and friendly warning. Don't force me to get mean, because you won't like me."

Bo began weeping.

William grinned. "I thought you were tougher than that, Bo. Well, now you know what Adam will do. Me? I'll just shoot you if you ever threaten anyone in my family again." He looked at Adam with a broad grin. "That was like opening a bottle of champagne, wasn't it? Pop!" he laughed as they walked out of the jail.

***

Out in the office, Adam, William and Steven sat down at the table and had a cup of coffee waiting for Truet to bring Annie back from shopping and Matt to finish his lunch with Christine. William looked at Nate and Phillip. "Boys, there's no need to tell Matt about this, right?"

Nate scoffed. "Don't you think Matt will ask

about the scratches on the sides of Bo's head?"

Phillip was uncomfortable with answering. "I think Bo will tell him where those scratches came from."

"Do you think so?" William asked, faking concern.

Phillip answered, "Yeah. You could hear him screaming out on the street probably."

"Hmm. Well, maybe we should go back in and shove his head between the bars again until he promises not to tell Matt. I doubt Bo will ever shake Adam's hand again, so we'll need the keys."

"Ah…No," Nate said with a nervous grin.

William laughed. "I'm just kidding, fellas. Geez, you two need to lighten up a bit. You see, you boys can't be doing that stuff to your prisoners, but we can because we're related to Matt. That's how the law works; I'm sure it's written in the by-laws in some law book somewhere."

Before too long, Matt entered the office by himself. He looked awkwardly at his brothers and cousin and then grinned. "I didn't know we were having a family get together today?" he asked as he took off his coat to hang it and join his family.

"Yeah and you're late," William said irately.

Steven shook his head disappointedly. "We had this planned since Christmas, Matt."

Matt narrowed his eyes thoughtfully. "What? I don't remember anything."

Steven rolled his eyes. "Can you two believe this? Sit down, Matt, we need to talk to you."

"About what?" Matt asked as he took a seat at the

table with them.

"You didn't talk to us before you asked Christine to marry you."

"I didn't know I needed to."

"What?" Steven shouted quickly. "Listen, you don't want to talk to Lee or Albert because they're both henpecked. You need to talk to us because we rule our homes. We're afraid that Christine is going to change you into a… well, an Albert. You know a 'yes, dear' man, whenever she tells him to jump."

Matt grinned slowly. "Steven, I appreciate the concern, but that's what they say about you! And buddy, I've never seen anyone talk so big and then 'yes dear' away like a startled calf when Nora speaks." He laughed.

Steven grimaced and shook his head. "Nora does what I tell her. If I say 'I'd like some chili beans for dinner,' she does it!"

William laughed. "There's a difference between suggesting and demanding. I think she does that because she loves you or something. I don't know why, though, but she does."

"Yeah, you just keep talking tough, Steven. We all know when Nora's around, you're the sweetest little peach on the tree. And I'm glad of it," Matt said. "Seriously, though, why are you guys in town today? Are you staying the night?"

Adam raised his eyebrows and shrugged innocently. "Hmm…no reason."

Matt looked at him curiously. "What?"

William laughed as Adam shook his head, awkwardly with an innocent expression. "Well, a little birdie told us what your prisoner Bo Crowe said about Annie and…"

Matt's mouth opened, but nothing came out for a second as he stared at Adam. "You didn't hurt him, did you?"

"No! I didn't hurt him." He chuckled, "But… somehow, I'm not sure how he got his head stuck between the bars. I think he was trying to crawl through the bars to escape…maybe?" Adam shrugged questionably.

Matt closed his eyes. "And?"

William and Steven, both chuckled.

Adam smirked. "Ah…Do you remember when we were kids and you would catch mice and pop them on the head?"

Steven began laughing heartedly.

"I recall, yeah," Matt said without a smile. "Is he okay?"

Adam nodded. "Never better! Now he knows not to make threats towards our sister. I don't think you'll have to worry about him anymore. It turns out he's not so tough after all. Is he?" he asked William and Steven.

Steven shook his head, trying to hide his laughter.

William shook his head with a grin. "No, he's not so hard. Hell, he didn't bend the bars at all!"

Steven and Adam burst out laughing.

Matt stood up. "I'm going to see what you did. And he better not be marked up."

Adam grimaced. "Um, he scraped his face up a bit, only on the sides of his face, though. It seems my measurements were off by a fraction; the width of his face was a bit wider than the space between the bars. I mean, who knew?" Adam shrugged with his palms upwards in an exaggerated act of innocence.

"He's in my custody and I don't want him beat up while he's here. I already warned him about making threats about Annie or anyone else."

"We just backed you up a little, is all," Adam said. "All is well...now."

The front door opened and Wu-Pen Tseng stepped into the Marshal's Office with his two guards, Uang Young and Bing Jue. Wu-Pen had a smile and carried a box. "Marshal, good to see you."

"Wu-Pen, how are you?" Matt asked curiously as he stepped over to the partition to speak to him.

"Good. Good. I had this made for you. It is a Chinese dessert called Chongyang gao. It's a traditional Chinese dessert to remember and honor your friend, Jed. I was most sorry to hear what happened to him. Please, take the Chongyang gao and share it with your friends. I had much made. It is best when it's still warm." He handed the box over to Matt.

"Thank you, Wu-Pen. I appreciate it." He nodded to Bing Jue and Uang Young with a friendly smile.

"It's the least I could do." He paused and then said, "I made it very clear to my people that whoever was doing those horrible killings must stop now. Has there been another since then?"

Matt raised his eyebrows. "No. It's been pretty quiet and I hope it stays that way. But thank you for your help."

Wu-Pen nodded with a smile. "I do not know if

it was Chinese who did it, but I want it to stop too if it is. Very good, then. I'll leave you to your work. Good day, Marshal."

"Thank you for the dessert," Matt said as he watched them leave.

William furrowed his brow questionably. "Do you trust him enough to eat that...whatever it's called?"

Matt set the box on the table and lifted out a round ceramic plate with a round cake-like dessert on it. It was made of rice, it looked like, with dates, walnuts and something else placed on its top in a decorative display. It looked good. It was cut into triangles for easy serving. "I think so. Who wants to try it?"

Nate held up his hands defensively. "No, thanks."

Steven looked at Matt, inquisitively, "Why wouldn't you trust him?"

William answered, "Because there have been a couple of the wickedest murders you've ever heard of, and that man probably did them."

"Really?" Adam asked. "What he do?"

Matt told them quickly about what Leroy Haywood, Roger Lavigne and Oscar Belding had done to three Chinese men who worked for their uncle Luther out at the quarry pit. And then about Leroy being killed by black widow spiders and of Roger Lavigne's cabin being burnt down with him in it. He explained Oscar Belding was afraid he was next and Matt had warned Wu-Pen that he was a suspect.

Matt continued, "I suspect it was Wu-Pen and his

two guards, but I can't prove it. And I won't arrest a man unless I have proof, because being Chinese, he'd be strung up quick. And I don't want to make a mistake and have an innocent man hung. So until I can prove it was him, I can only suspect."

Adam smirked. "So, that's why he said that about talking to his people."

Matt nodded. "Yeah. And maybe he did. I can't rule out one of those Chinese men had a brother or a friend who works at the mine and knows those guys. Stranger things have happened, I'm sure. Who wants to try this...dessert? It looks like a cake of some kind."

Phillip Forrester asked, "Do you think it's wise to eat a cake from your murder, suspect?"

Matt chuckled. "Probably not, but I think he was sincere and it's just a nice gesture. I'm sure it's fine. He said it's best eaten warm, so let's try it."

William shook his head with a sour expression. "Unless he wants to get rid of you and your deputies so he can finish off Oscar in peace."

"William, stop it!" Matt said with a stern expression. "He isn't going to poison an entire office of people with everyone knowing who brought the cake."

"Give your prisoner a piece and let's find out," Adam suggested.

Steven stared at the dessert with a furrowed brow. "Cake isn't made of rice."

"Oh, you are all cowards," Matt said and picked a piece up and took a bite. It was warm, moist, sweet, and chewy. It tasted different but still good. He

165

nodded. "It's not bad."

William shook his head with a scowl. "I'm not touching it. He might've poisoned it."

Matt shook his head with a smile. "If he wanted to poison me, he would have had one of his people drop it off. Someone we would never see again. He's too smart and too careful to cover his tracks to be stupid enough to bring a poisoned cake here himself. It's fine. And it's pretty good, really. Come on, you cowards, try some."

Chapter 21

Steven Bannister sat on the edge of a padded chair in Lee Bannister's family room as he explained what Adam had done to Bo Crowe. "Bo was trying to pull his head out of the bars, but he couldn't do it. Adam looked at William and me with a big stupid grin, like a little boy about to steal a piece of candy and pow!" He shot his hand forward quickly. "He hits the top of Bo's head and he fired out of those bars like a cannonball and ended up against the far wall!" He laughed. "And then Bo started bawling like a baby." The room filled with laughter.

"No one told me you did that," Matt said with a smile. "Bo has some chaffing around his hairline and a headache, but no damage done unless it's brain damage."

Truet Davis sat on the davenport beside Annie. "I gave him a shot to the nose, but I wanted to do far more than that. He's a bleeder."

Albert shook his head. "If he's a rapist, I could make a big R branding iron, so you can start branding these heathen's foreheads, Matt."

"I would like to, but I think that's against the law, Albert. Make one anyway and I'll hang it in my jail as a deterrent. I could lock a man up and grab the branding iron and let him know I'm putting it in the woodstove for a while before the boys and I come back to brand him. It would give them a good scare anyway."

"Sure. I'd be glad to," Albert agreed.

"Yeah," Lee added, "It would be a joke until Adam comes to town and grabs William to go hogtie and brand all of your prisoner's asses, just for fun."

Adam smiled. "Only the bad ones."

William Fasana spoke, "I told Matt when we went to Prairieville it was the Crowe brother's territory and I didn't want him going alone. Little did we know we'd find the whole Sheriff's Office down there were criminals, but we're lucky the Crowe brother's stayed out of it or we probably wouldn't have made it home. I only met one or two of them, Adrian and Tyee Crowe. They are Bo's older brothers and I didn't like them. They are all a bunch of crazy homicidal killers. Their little gang is brutal."

Adam narrowed his eyes irritably at William. "How come you didn't say so earlier? Maybe like… when I was whale tailing their little brother?"

William laughed. "I wanted to see what you were going to do! Would it have made any difference?"

Adam shook his head. "No. I don't care about his brothers."

Matt offered, "Their cousins of the Sperry's and

the Helms. Which reminds me, Morton Sperry said you and Lee saved the lives of one of the Sperry's during the Snake War?"

Adam frowned. "Yeah, two of them were there. Dwight was actually a good friend of mine. His brother Alan was Lee's and William's friend."

William agreed, "Yeah, we were."

Adam continued, "In truth, we all saved each other on different occasions, especially in the Coffee Creek battle. That's when Lee saved Alan, me and others. William saved a lot of our lives, too, though. Lee and William saved more lives than I ever did. None of my friends came back from the war, including Dwight. All of Lee's did."

There was an uncomfortable silence that filled the room for a moment. Lee spoke softly, "No. I lost friends too. Alan Sperry survived, but he was never the same after Dwight was killed. He became an angry man and he stayed that way. When we came home, I went into the saloon business and kept investing and building, while Alan started a career in crime . He's in prison now. Our friendship faded a long time ago."

"I don't talk about the battles too often," William said, "After surviving the battle at Coffee Creek, nothing's scared me much after that. We went in as boys and came out as trained men ready to take on the world. I had a bad case of wanderlust and I left to sport the cards all over the west. I even went to the east coast and the Mississippi gambling halls, you hear so much about. The humidity down there was too much for this Oregon grown boy and the southwest was too darn hot." He paused and shook his head. "So, I came home eventually. And that's my story."

Annie stared at him, momentarily. "So, we went from the jail to the Snake War to gambling all within five minutes. William, no one cares about your wanderlust, we know!"

William smiled.

Adam said thoughtfully, "Dwight was a good friend and a great man, but he wasn't a great soldier. He wasn't made for it. We had a lot in common, him and I. We were both the oldest of big families, both of us were pretty sensitive guys. He was a good shot too, but he just didn't have the heart for soldiering. Alan did. He was a fighter and a good one, but Dwight just wanted to be married someday and be a teacher."

Matt asked, "Does anyone know if Alan is fast and efficient with his gun? I heard he was."

Lee nodded. "He was. When he gets out of prison, you need to know he is quick-handed and deadly. He's easily angered and reacts harshly. That helped him become one of the most feared outlaws, no doubt. Dwight was the nice one; Alan's the dangerous one. People talk about Morton Sperry, but as far I know, he's child's play compared to Alan."

"I'll keep that in mind."

"So, in short," Annie spoke to Matt, "if the Crowe brothers join up with the Sperry-Helms Gang and come after you to get even for Adam hurting your prisoner, you have nothing to be afraid of unless

Alan gets out of prison."

Matt smiled through a yawn. "I think they understand the war they would be starting."

Annie's expression became sincere. "When you get married, are you going to stay with the Marshal's Office, or are you going to find something safer to do for an income?"

Matt shook his head slightly. "I don't have anything else to do, Annie. Besides, the only law around here, is me. If I left the Marshal's Office, it wouldn't be long until I picked up my gun and put the badge back on to hunt someone down. I believe I'm where I need to be."

"So even if Christine asked you, you wouldn't quit?"

Matt shook his head slowly. "No. She knows what I do and how much I love doing it. It's all I know. I don't plan on giving up my badge for any reason or anyone. Christine understands the risks , but she refuses to let those risks scare her away from us having a life together. We both put our lives in the hands of the Lord and trust him to help us through a long life together. There's not a whole lot more than we can do, other than that." he shrugged. "There's no way I could be a storekeeper or something and watch a bank robber ride out of town and not be in the middle of the fight anyway, so why not get paid for it and tell the deputies what to do?" He nodded at his deputy Truet.

Lee spoke, "Let me ask you, Truet, if you and Annie ever get married, would you stay with Matt at the Marshal's Office or work at the ranch?"

Annie scoffed. "The ranch! The ranch comes with me and any devotion to me is devotion to the ranch and working it. And if he doesn't want to be a rancher and work hard to make it successful, then we will never be married. You don't have to ask Tru; I can already answer that for him. Like I've said before, Lee, I don't need a husband to support me, but I wouldn't mind one to help me."

Steven chuckled. "It sounds like she's setting the ground rules before you even ask her, Tru. Now you know, if shoveling crap doesn't sound as adventurous and exciting as being a lawman, you better move on. She's looking for a man that gets excited about shoveling crap."

Truet's cheeks reddened just a touch. "I went out to the ranch with Matt to help build Nathan and Sarah's house. Matt had left and when Annie saw me for the first time, I had a hammer in one hand, a board in the other and fresh cow manure on my boots and she knew I was the one for her, right then and there. To answer your question, Lee," he paused. "I wouldn't ask her to be my bride without asking Uncle Charlie and Aunt Mary and all of you for your blessing first. I would keep my badge and be there if Matt needed me, but the ranch or more pointedly, the horse breeding would become our focus. No, I wouldn't continue to be a deputy marshal, but would be deputized when necessary."

Annie smiled and tapped his knee like a child. "Perfect answer."

Steven grimaced. "You're not going to be henpecked, are you, Truet? We got enough of that weak man crap from Lee and Albert."

Albert grinned at his brother. "Well, now we know Nora's not in town. Steven's talking big boy talk again."

Lee narrowed his eyes while shaking his head. "That's like a hen accusing another hen of being a chicken."

William added, "Steven, roosters rule the roost, but you gotta straighten your spine and keep your head up, boy, if you're ever going to make your voice heard in your own home."

Steven laughed as his face reddened. "Can you believe this, Matt? I'm being ganged up on."

"You have to know when to open your mouth and when to keep it shut. You stuck your foot in it this time, buddy," Matt said with a smile.

Adam asked Matt, "I think we all want to know when you get married, do you think you'll still dress the same, or will you start wearing suits and shiny dancing shoes every day? I guess the real question is, are you going to start going to those high society balls and forgetting where you come from like Uncle Solomon, or do you think you'll be pretty normal still?"

Matt chuckled. "I think I'll be pretty common still. Christine has never been rich. She's a dancer and they dress and appear to be higher society, but the fact is she's a country girl in a hundred-dollar dress. She'll step out of the satin and into cotton as soon as we're married and her dancing days come to an end."

Steven commented quickly, "Any chance she

could give me a dress or two for Nora?"

"Probably."

"How is she doing?" Adam asked sincerely.

"Good," Matt answered.

"I'm going to see her tomorrow," Annie said. "I might even pick up a job dancing before I leave town."

Truet laughed. "They don't want cow crap on their floor, though."

Annie frowned. "That is a problem."

Matt offered, "I'll go over there with you and introduce you to Bella and Dave, so they'll know who you are. Otherwise, they probably wouldn't let you in to see her. They've become very protective over the ladies now."

"Can I raid her wardrobe since she's not wearing her fancy rich dresses right now?" she asked with a curious expression. "Even us country girls like to play dress-up once in a while."

"You could ask her."

"What about me?" Steven asked. "I've never seen dancing girls before. Any cute ones?"

William answered with a wink, "You bet!"

Adam shook his head. "Unfortunately, you'll be at the hardware store with me. The prettiest things you're going to be looking at tomorrow are stacks of lumber and bags of grain. Besides, you're married; you shouldn't even be curious to look at other women."

Steven scoffed, acting appalled. "Did you think I was talking about those women? No, I was asking about the dresses in Christine's wardrobe for my wife!"

"Right…" Lee said slowly.

"No men are allowed upstairs except for me. Annie's going to have to pick them out for you if Christine is willing to get rid of any," Matt explained.

Annie smiled wryly, "Oh, she'll be willing!" she nodded with certainty.

Chapter 22

John Gibbs stood behind the bar talking to Wes Wasson inside the Thirsty Toad Saloon. John had found out Wes was from the Sacramento, California area and asked about the railroad tycoon Louis Eckman who had claimed his daughter was missing and offered a large reward for her return that went unclaimed for three years. Marshal Matt Bannister had confirmed that Catherine Eckman and her husband had been murdered and burned in a cabin in the mountains. Then for reasons unknown, two conmen kidnapped a local dancer, thinking she was the real Catherine Eckman and invited Louis and Divinity to come to Branson and get her. The Eckman's private coach was robbed on the way to Branson and Louis Eckman was killed. Divinity came to Branson to get her daughter back and realized the kidnappers had taken the wrong woman. However, the real Catherine Eckman did finally come out of hiding and showed up to confront her mother. It was big news at the time.

Wes Wasson agreed it was big news in Sacramento as well. Wes told John that Catherine Eckman was a mystery and many people wondered where she had gone to, some even speculated, she was a victim of foul play. The news that she was alive was on the front-page in Sacramento.

John spoke in disbelief, "I knew her! I had a saloon up in a small logging community called Loveland and Cal and Nathan Pearce worked there. Nathan's wife was a beautiful blonde named Sarah, but she was the Eckman's daughter, Catherine. I found out a bit too late, because I would've turned her in faster than you could spit, for that reward! I knew she was something more than a lumberman's wife too. She wasn't like everyone else up there; she was proper and well educated. I always wondered why she was with a lumberman. Now I know. She was rich." He shook his head. "Missed opportunities, what can I tell you. Anyway, they live around here somewhere, but I couldn't tell you where."

"I can," Jack Sperry said. "That Nathan works on the Big Z Ranch outside of Willow Falls. I hear they have a house out there now."

John laughed. "I don't know where that is. But there's no reward now, so I guess it doesn't matter. But yeah, Sarah was special. It was odd, a bushman came into Loveland at the same time our bank was robbed and our sheriff hired the bushman to track the bank robbers. Cal and Nathan both went with the posse and our posse and the bank robbers were all killed except for Nathan, come to find out later. Some man around here killed the bushman. The rumor is the money is still up there somewhere under the tree the last bank robber hung himself on." He paused. "What never made sense to me though was Nathan's name was never in the paper when the story came out. He survived the posse being killed, but he was never even mentioned as being part of the posse. Strange."

Jack Sperry took a drink and looked at John. "The last bank robber did hang, but not up there. He didn't have the money, but he survived to get out of the mountains. You heard about the fellow who was hanging over the granite pit? That was him. Again, it was Adam Bannister that killed that bushman, as you call him. There's no treasure though, Adam took it back to the bank in Loveland. If you were there, you'd know that."

John looked a bit perplexed. "I was there. But I was moving here when it happened. I moved the next day."

"I heard you were part of the posse. That can't be true, either, or you'd be dead. I don't know Nathan, but I'll bet I could ask when I see him." Jack said. He was irritated about his friend Charlie Walker's death and it was coming out in his bitter countenance.

"You can ask him. Nathan knows me from Loveland. I was there just like I told you. I sold out and moved here. I couldn't go into a long hunt for the bank robbers when I was moving, although my friends might've survived if I had gone. I didn't like that bushman." He avoided mentioning the bank robbers were part of the Sperry-Helms Gang because he knew Jack was a Sperry and a member of the gang.

Jack shook his head. "They say the bushman as you call him was the Venetta Creek Killer. I don't think you would have made a difference at all. None of the bank robbers could have either. Adam Bannister? Yeah, it takes a monster to kill a monster and Adam's a monster of a man. I heard lots of stories about him. The only reason your old friend is alive is because Adam found him. I heard Adam took the top off one of the bank robber's head from two hundred yards away, and the man was in a hole exposing just that much of his head." He used his fingers to show about five inches. "That's how efficient and deadly Adam is. The lesson learned is, you don't miss when shooting at him."

John grimaced. "How would you hear something like that? They're all dead."

Jack looked at him. "Because they were my friends. And like I said, Pick told me, he was there in the gully with Deuce."

"Oh," John said as he saw the door opening and Chusi walking into the saloon with his red dog. "Chusi, no. I don't want the dog in here. It crapped on the floor the last time it was here."

Chusi nodded and led the dog back outside and closed the door. He came back in and ordered a drink at the bar.

Wes looked at him with a casual nod. "I'll pay for that. I owe you an apology, so we'll call it even, yeah?"

Chusi's eyes looked coldly at him. He nodded

in agreement as Wes moved down the bar closer to Chusi. He was weary of Wes's movements and his purpose for coming closer to him. Behind Wes were his friends, the white-haired Bruce Ellison, Bobby Alper, Ritchie Thorn and Jack Sperry. All of them Chusi knew and could expect some verbal harassment here and there, but seldom if ever had it become physical or overly personal. Wes, the older man with a weathered face and harsh eyes, had crossed lines that Chusi had never expected to back away from. If not for the vision of Omusa and her gentle soul, Wes would be dead for saying what he had about his family.

Wes stood next to Chusi. "John, two drinks. One for me, and one for the Indian here." He looked at Chusi in his aged brown eyes. "You don't mind me calling you an Indian, do you?"

Chusi shook his head while keeping eye contact. His reflexes were ready to jump if and when Wes tried to strike him.

Wes looked away and nodded. "Good, because I forgot your name. Well, here's to better and brighter days, huh?" He closed his eyes and said, "I do not have your wife's scalp. I was kidding about that. I'm sorry, it was a bad joke," he said and put his hand up to shake.

Chusi narrowed his eyes slightly irritated by the very idea of it. He was hesitant, but the vision of Omusa in the water as the flowers floated away came into his mind. He had promised himself that he would let the past go and focus on the pebble that was still in the stream. The love he and Omusa shared across the great divide between life and death. He shook the man's hand.

Wes grinned and chuckled wickedly as he refused to let go of Chusi's hand in a firm grip. He spoke softly so not to be overheard, "I sold the scalps of your wife and children for about fifty dollars. How does it feel to shake the man's hand that scalped your family and slit your wife open?" He laughed.

Chusi felt a rage that fired up through his soul like a volcano ready to explode with enough force to slaughter everyone who got in his way. His eyes hardened to stone, and his lips snarled as he tried to break free of Wes's grasp. Wes refused to let his hand go and squeezed harder the more Chusi tried to break free.

Wes continued, "You've probably been wondering for all these years what it was, it was a baby boy." His grin was wicked as he lightly snickered at Chusi.

Chusi's lips sneered into a fearful grimace and he yanked his hand out of Wes's grasp and threw a wide haymaker of a swing back towards Wes and caught his face in the crook of his arm. Chusi drove his arm around and downward, tossing Wes backward and driving his head down to the floor viciously. Chusi stomped on Wes's chest as hard as he could. Wes rolled to his stomach quickly to get up, but Chusi dropped a knee down into the center of Wes's back before sitting across his back. Chusi grabbed Wes's hair with his left hand and pulled his knife with his right hand.

Bruce Ellison and Bobby Alper grabbed Chusi

and pulled him off Wes while being careful of his knife not to be stabbed themselves.

Jack Sperry pulled his revolver and pointed it at Chusi but didn't pull the trigger only because Bobby was in the way.

"Chusi. Don't!" Bruce yelled, holding onto the arm that held the knife. He and Bobby were pushing him back towards the door. "Get out of here. Go!" They pushed the wild-eyed Indian out of the saloon and closed the door just as Wes stood up, feeling his head for any wounds and running forwards to catch Chusi. Bruce and Bobby stopped him. "Uncle Wes, stop it! Let him go!" Bruce yelled.

"He was going to scalp me!" Wes yelled furiously.

Bruce responded loudly, "What did you do? What did you say to him? You heard my Pa, you know you're supposed to leave him alone! If my Pa's hurt because of you, I'll never forgive you!"

"Shut up, Bruce! That old man couldn't hurt anybody."

"Well, he sure knocked you to the floor, didn't he? Now, what did you say to him?"

"Blind luck!" Wes spat out bitterly. "It will never happen again. Next time, I'll take his scalp and tack it to my wall!"

John Riggs shouted over the loud arguing, "Wes, come finish your drink."

Bobby Alper nervously said, "Come on, Wes, let him go and let's enjoy ourselves, huh?"

Ritchie Thorn sat at the bar watching. "I want to see Wes and Chusi fight."

Jack Sperry spoke, "I could've shot him if you

weren't in the way, Bobby."

Bobby grimaced. "Shot him for what? Did you not hear what Wes said to him? I would've stomped him to death if I was Chusi."

Bruce glared at his Uncle Wes. "What did you say to him?"

Wes glared out the window where he could see Chusi walking down Rose Street with his dog. "Nothing much."

"What did he say, Bobby?" Bruce asked.

Wes looked at Bobby with cold and threatening eyes. "I said nothing! The old man just hit me. Which is fine because before this night is through, I'll teach him a thing or two about hitting. I'm not even bleeding, you know. But I assure you all he will be!"

"No, you're not!" Bruce exclaimed. "It was fun at first, but not now. I had no idea my Pa, and you wiped out his family. If it weren't for Matt, that man would want to kill my Pa and maybe our whole family. Okay, it's not funny anymore! If you want to tangle with him, you go ahead but leave my family out of it. I've seen the way he moved when he fought Bobby, Ritchie, and me, and I remember him saying if he wanted us dead, we would be. I believe him! I've never seen my Pa worried about any man in my life until I saw the relief on his face when I got home from work tonight. I'm going to talk with Chusi and let him know; I have no part of this. I may have in the past, but not anymore. I love my parents too much to see them get hurt for something you did! Chusi is non-violent. He doesn't just hit anyone without reason. What did you say to him?"

Wes took a drink. He smiled. "Nothing. But you don't need to go chasing after him. He's a crazy old Indian and might scalp you just for the fun of it. Sit down and have a drink with us, Bruce."

Bruce shook his head. "No, I gotta go."

"Wait up; I'll come with you," Bobby said.

Wes stood at the bar and watched Bobby with his cold eyes. "Bobby, a word," He waved Bobby over to him. He put an arm around Bobby's shoulders to draw him close to his face blocking the view of the others with their bodies. Wes produced a steel blade from a sheath on his belt. "I said nothing at all. If I hear that I did, this will be in your heart and when you are scalped, they'll think it was the Indian. Understood?"

"Very," Bobby said, shocked by the sudden change in Wes's countenance.

"Good. Tell Bruce I said the Indian stinks and I warned you not to tell him." He finished with a wink as he put the knife back in the sheath as unnoticeably as he had withdrawn it. He laughed. "Okay, well, go have fun," he added with a quick and jovial grin.

Bobby stared at him, frightened and nodded as he stepped towards the door.

Outside, Bruce asked what was said. "Nothing," Bobby replied.

Bruce sighed irritably. "Bobby, I need to know so I can try to make things right. What did my uncle say to Chusi and then to you? He said something, I can tell."

Bobby shook his head. "Let's just say your uncle's crazy, okay? I don't want to say anything more."

"I'm figuring that out. You have to tell me, Bobby."

Bobby shook his head. "Look, he told Chusi he stinks, and he warned me not to tell you that. It's no big deal."

***

They saw Chusi's red dog tied to a post in front of Ugly John's Saloon. They went inside and found Chusi sitting alone, enduring the harassment of some of the men inside. Chusi's eyes narrowed in on Bruce as he walked toward the table and pulled out a chair and sat down with Bobby. Chusi held his glass of liquor to his lips and watched them with no emotion, except the hostility in his eyes.

Bruce spoke, "I just want you to know I have no part in what my Uncle Wes said to you. I am sorry for ever laughing at you and I will never bother you again. My pa told my uncle to leave you alone and he didn't. Granted, what he said wasn't as bad as what he said last time, but I'm glad you knocked him on his head."

Bobby Alper's eyes widened and he lowered his head. He cleared his throat quickly. "Bruce, I lied. What your uncle said to him was even worse than last time."

Bruce stared at Bobby in horror. "What? Why would you lie to me? You said Wes said he stank."

Bobbie's face turned red. "Your uncle threatened

185

to kill me if I told you what he said to Chusi."

"What?" Bruce raised his voice. He looked at Chusi, who was staring at him with a slight sneer on his lips. Bruce shook his head innocently. "Whatever he said to you, I have no part of, and either does my family. I am sorry. I want nothing to do with my uncle anymore."

Chusi looked sadly down the table. "Go home."

Bruce exhaled deeply. "Chusi, I just want to say I'm sorry. I'll never disrespect you again."

Bobby added, "Me neither."

Chusi nodded slowly. "Goodnight."

The sadness on his face was as deep as the ocean's depth. Bruce had never seen anyone look as broken as Chusi. Bruce stood up. "My pa's going to beat my uncle senseless when he finds out Uncle Wes said something to upset you."

Chusi's eyes rose to meet his, and it sent a chill down Bruce's spine to see the relentless murderous eyes glaring at him. "Leave now!"

Chusi watched the two young men leave and stared back down at his table. His breathing was slow and deep. His mind was on what Wes had said to him. If there was a touch of mercy for Bruce, it would be the fact that the trouble-making white-haired boy had no idea what was said to him. Had he been a part of it and laughed at him, he would die too. To forgive was a good thing, but to overlook a continuing threat was an impossibility. Bruce's father revealed sincere shame for what he had done; he admitted his wrong with tears in the jail. He showed great respect and relief when Chusi granted a truce. Chusi would keep his pledge of peace between the two of them and that included Frank's family. But he would not keep his oath for the man who held Chusi's hand and admitted to the heinous acts done to his family. Wes would pay for Omusa's and their children's blood with his own.

Chusi didn't know how long he had sat there in his thoughts or how deep his thoughts were until the owner, Big John Pederson, jarred his table. "Hey, Chusi, are you alright?" he asked with concern.

Chusi nodded. He stood up to leave. "Yes," he replied.

"Do you want another drink?"

"No." Chusi walked outside and noticed his dog was gone. He looked around and didn't see it anywhere. His first thought was Bruce and Bobby might've taken his dog, but then he heard the dog yipe in pain around the corner of the saloon. He stepped around the corner and was hit with a board in the stomach. He bent over from the unexpected blow and then was kicked behind the knee to knock him down. Boots began kicking him all over his body as three men wailed their feet upon him, stomping here and a swift kick there. He covered his face and head as best he could, but it was pointless as he was yanked up to his feet and being held upright by two strong men, each containing an arm. He was dazed by the blows and hurting when he focused on Wes Wasson, grinning at him.

Wes spoke, "So, you think you can hit a white man, huh? Not when I'm in town and you certainly never should've hit me!" He swung a hard-right fist that connected to Chusi's cheek. He hit him again in the face and then began punching him in the stomach. He hit him in the face until there was blood coming from a cut on Chusi's cheekbone and above his eye. "Drop him on the ground, boys; I'm taking his hair with me."

Chusi had no strength left to fight; it had been beaten out of him. Barely conscious, he felt the hard freezing crunch of the snow on his face as he fell and welcomed the coolness on his swelling face.

He was quickly flipped to his back and Wes sat across Chusi's chest with his knife in his hand. He grabbed Chusi's hair in one hand and leaned forward to speak over Chusi's face. "This reminds me of old times. Déjà vu, huh?" His two new friends, Ritchie Thorn and Jack Sperry cheered him on loudly.

Big John Pederson had been told of three men beating up an Indian outside of his saloon and knowing it had to be his friend, Chusi, John grabbed his shotgun from under the bar and stepped outside. He stepped around the corner and was enraged to see a stranger with a knife to Chusi's hairline. He shouted angrily, "Get your ass off him before I blow you to hell!" He was aiming the shotgun at Wes. "Now!"

Jack Sperry sighed. "John, it's me, Jack. Mind your own business."

"If you touch your gun, Jack, I'll blow you to hell too. Get off him. Now!"

Jack grimaced. "John, you don't want trouble with us."

"Shut up before I pull the trigger. Get off him. I won't repeat it!"

Wes sighed and shook his head, looking down at Chusi. "You're lucky for now. But I'll take your hair next time to hang on my wall." He patted Chusi's cheek and stood up, putting his knife away. He looked at John. "It seems to me that you should mind your own business like the barkeep at the Thirsty Toad."

John Pederson answered, "John Riggs squats when he pees, I stand like a man. Get out of my sight all of you!"

"We'll take our business elsewhere, then."

"Please do. And don't come back around here."

Wes spat down on Chusi. "Next time, you won't be so lucky." He looked at his two new friends, "Let's go back where we were."

When they had left, John helped Chusi up and took him inside and cleaned him up. He gave Chusi a glass of water and asked, "What's that all about, Chusi?"

Chusi spoke furiously in his native tongue.

"I don't speak your language."

Chusi smiled painfully as a tear fell down his cheek. He nodded his head with a sneer on his lips. Omusa's vision be damned; he had committed to seeking vengeance. "My dog?"

Before too long, John's employee brought in the dog. The dog was unharmed but cold and hungry.

Chusi ran his hand down her back lovingly and touched his hairline and then looked at the slight bit of blood on his fingertip. His jaw clenched in anger.

Chapter 23

Christine sat on her bed, reading her Bible. She hadn't been able to dance since being shot by Martin Ballenger and not being able to pull her weight around the dance hall like the other girls, made her feel worthless. She felt like a burden and depression set upon her like a heavy weight on her chest. She was used to being her usual optimistic self, but she couldn't pull herself out of the muck and mire that she could feel herself sinking in.

It was a mere four weeks ago when she was freshly courting Matt and looked at her future with the brightest of hopes. It seemed like only yesterday when Helen, Edith and her would laugh and play around in the hall corridor looking forward to another night of dancing. Edith had just found out she was with child and was engaged for one day to her beloved Paul Johnson. Then shockingly, Martin Ballenger ended Edith's life for no reason and put a bullet into Christine's abdomen as well.

The devastation was real. Edith was dead, Paul

was an emotional wreck, Helen Monroe was in a deep state of depression from losing her best friend and Christine endured hours of surgery to save her life. The recovery was taking more time than she could stand. In truth, she became exhausted and unstable if she stood for any length of time. Her abdomen muscles had been cut open all across her belly and they needed to mend. The best way for them to heal was to stay down and lift nothing for six weeks or so and then she would still have to take any lifting slowly. Granted, she felt better week by week, but the time spent in her room with nothing to do was eternally dull. A person could only knit for so long, read for so long and sleep for so long before they grew restless and bored. She could not go for a walk alone, so she was confined to the dance hall unless Matt was kind enough to rent a buggy to take her on drives around town. Even then, the roads were so rough the jarring of the carriage wheels going over the ruts were painful. The one thing that angered her most was there was no reason for any of it to happen. It made no sense to her why a young man like Martin would cause the heartache he had for so many lives. Even Martin's own mother and sister were paying the consequences for his needless and wicked actions.

You didn't have to read too far into the Bible to find wicked people or the heinous acts they committed. Unspeakable crimes were written in enough detail to know the evilness of the worst kinds had always been a part of human nature. Is it not why God flooded the earth in the time of

Noah? The first generation of human beings born of a woman and a man saw such an evil that it's still incomprehensible when it happens today; the murder of a man by his own brother. Envy seems like such a small word and for most folks, it goes no further than being a bit envious of someone or something. For Cain, it had become so embittering that he murdered his brother. Perhaps it was envy that had pushed Martin beyond rational reasoning. The word jealousy kept running through Christine's mind, but wasn't envy and jealousy the same? Martin had been rejected in public and maybe the bitterness of that mixed with envy had caused the anger and hatred that motivated him to kill Edith. Christine could read about the evil things people did in the Bible, but the mindset behind the reason for it, she could not comprehend. If Matt broke off their engagement and courted someone else, she would not kill him; she would let him go and move on herself. It would be painful because she loved him, but if he didn't love her, then why would she want to be with him? In time, someone would love her and that is what she would wait for. Fortunately, Matt was head over heels in love with her.

A knock on the door brought her out of her thoughts. "Come in, Bella," she said, recognizing Bella's knocking pattern.

The door opened, and Bella stuck her head inside. "Are you feeling well enough for visitors?"

"Who?"

"Your prince and his sister, Annie."

Christine's eyes widened. "Yes. I'll be right

down."

"Sorry, Sweetheart, but they're right here."

Matt stepped into her room with a smile followed by Annie. "How are you feeling today," he asked as he sat on the edge of the bed beside her.

She tilted her head. "I'm all right. I wish I could heal faster."

He smiled compassionately. "This is just temporary. You'll heal up and be as good as new before too long. Is there anything I can get you?"

"Yes, you can bring me a dozen pieces of the chocolate fudge from the Seventh Street Bakery. You know my favorite ones with walnuts on it?"

Matt laughed. "I'll do that. I brought Annie; she wants to raid your wardrobe for a new dress," he said, looking at Annie, who stood by the door respectfully.

"Oh, she does?" Christine asked with a smile.

Annie scoffed. "No. I came over to see you while I'm in town. How are you doing, girl?"

"I'm bored to death and restless to get out and start doing things again. But I'm doing fine. By the time my body heals, I probably will not fit into my dresses anymore. Especially if I keep sending Matt to the bakery for me." She laughed lightly. She looked at Matt, sincerely. "I am so bored, it's depressing."

Matt smiled softly. "Do you want me to get that fudge for you?"

She nodded with a slow smirk. "I would. Annie and I will go through the dresses while you're gone. Playing dress-up might make me feel better, at least."

"Alright, I'll be back."

When Matt left, Annie turned the chair at a small desk towards Christine and sat down. "Quit your faking and get to dancing! How is my brother ever supposed to get rich enough he can retire and work the ranch if you're not dancing your butt off to support his loafing out at the Big Z?"

Christine looked at her awkwardly and then smiled sadly. She knew Annie was teasing, but it was a sensitive subject.

"Well?" Annie asked sharply with a stern expression on her face.

"Annie, I know you're kidding, but I'm really not in the mood to play today." Her eyes filled with moisture.

Annie frowned. "Oh. Well, I wasn't kidding. How's Matt going to get drunk and lounge around out at my place if you're not supporting him?"

She smiled and wiped the small tears from her eyes. "I don't know. Maybe I can sell myself."

"That's what I was thinking. Good idea." Annie laughed. "No. I don't want him hanging out around my place. He'd teach my kids how to behave or something and I spend a lot of time encouraging them to be brats. It keeps Adam's wife, Hazel, busy that way. And she needs to stay busy."

Christine laughed lightly. "Why do I get the idea that you enjoy harassing people?"

Annie shrugged. "So what?"

"Would you like to try on some dresses?"

Annie laughed. "I would actually. I don't have

any really nice dresses. I have one green one I wear when I need to, but it is getting old. You probably know what that is like, right? Old dresses are so boring...right?" she emphasized. She added slowly, "Especially...if, you want me to be a bridesmaid."

Christine laughed loudly.

"What's so funny?" she asked with a confused shrug.

"Don't make me laugh, it hurts," Christine said through her laughter while holding her abdomen.

Annie stood up. "So, have you and Matt decided on a date for your wedding yet?"

"Not yet. We're thinking late Spring or early Summer."

Annie looked at her with a scowl. "Calving season? It's not a bad idea. We could work a wedding into the lunch hour of branding day. You won't mind changing out of your dress into some jeans and chaps, would you? You'll be able to lift up to a hundred pounds by then, right?"

"Sounds like a dream come true," Christine said as she slowly stood up. "Maybe we could just castrate the steers and toss those tasty treats in a cookpot for the reception guests."

Annie laughed loudly with an appreciative glance at Christine. "That is a good idea, but Uncle Charlie doesn't like giving up his jewels. He waits all year for that, you know."

"He can have them." She opened a built-in wardrobe full of dresses. Each one was pressed and cleaned. "Do you have a favored color, Annie?"

Annie furrowed her brow. "What color do you

think would look good on me? I don't know a whole lot about that stuff."

Christine smiled. She pulled down a copper-colored dress with faint yellow and green orchids in the pattern. "Try this one on."

There was a knock on the door and it opened. Helen Monroe stepped into the room. "I heard laughter and I could use some. Oh, am I interrupting?"

"No. Helen, this is Annie, Matt's sister. This is my very good friend, Helen."

As Helen and Annie shook hands, Christine explained, "I'm just going through my dresses with Annie. She doesn't have any nice ones."

"Oh. Well, Annie, I'm getting married on Valentine's Day and I won't be needing half of my dresses pretty soon. Let me go grab a few of my old ones for you to try on."

"Great!" Annie said agreeably.

Christine added, "Helen's marrying Sam."

Annie furrowed her brow in thought. "Sam... Troyer?"

"Yes. Do you know Sam?" Helen asked.

Christine spoke before Annie could answer, "Annie is the widow of Sam's friend, Kyle."

Helen's eyes widened. "Oh. I'm sorry."

Christine explained, "Helen was with us the night Kyle died."

Annie frowned with a touch of sadness, revealing itself in her eyes. "I've known Sam for a long time. Congratulations. And tell Sam I'd like to get an invitation."

Helen smiled comfortingly. "I'll do that. Let me go get those dresses and then we can talk some more."

Christine looked at Annie fondly. "I think we might make a lady out of you before you leave here today. Unfortunately for Matt, when he gets back, he's going to have to hand me the fudge and leave. Which reminds me, what size do you think Steven's wife wears? Between Helen and me and the other girls, I think we can find him a dress for his wife as well. We'll even bundle it up for him in a nice package for him to give her."

Annie chuckled, relieved to be on a brighter subject than what happened to Kyle Lenning. "You better put a fake receipt in there for him, too, because you know he's going to act like he spent a small fortune on her."

Christine smiled. "I can't do that to deceive her, but Helen would love to."

Annie's expression grew sincere. "Christine, thank you. Not just for the chance to have a dress or two, if they fit. But thank you for loving Matt. Thank you for agreeing to marry him, without me having to pay for it. I think we're going to get along well."

"You're welcome. I think we'll be good friends."

Annie shook her head slightly. "Sisters. Remember, you have a family now."

Christine's eyes filled up with thick watery tears and her bottom lip began to tremble. She hugged Annie and began to cry.

Annie held her and said, "But you better get used

to the idea of me harassing, teasing and picking on you whether you feel like it or not, because that's what I do. It's my job." Annie finished with a sniffle and a wipe of her eye before anyone would notice a runaway tear.

Chapter 24

Wes woke up in a large room filled with bunk beds. He and Jack Sperry had stayed up too late drinking to stumble back to the Ellison's house, so they rented beds at a bunkhouse designed for the men that came to town to spend their money on Rose Street. Wes sat up in his bottom bunk, opening and closing his hands. They ached from hitting Chusi. He smirked despite the queasiness that floated around in his head and the upset stomach. He wondered what Chusi looked like this morning. He wiped his face with his hands and then pulled his boots on and gathered his things. He looked at Jack, who was still sleeping on the top bunk. He decided not to wake him and left the Lucky Man's Bunkhouse Hotel and walked across town to his sister's house. He found the door locked and knocked on the door.

Florence asked who it was before she unlocked the door.

"Me. Come on, Florence, it's cold out here," he

said with a yawn.

The door opened and he stepped inside; she closed the door and locked it.

"Everyone at work?" he asked tiredly.

"Where have you been all night?" she asked curtly.

"There's a reason I never got married and that's one of them." He looked at her. "I like the freedom to do as I please without being asked where or what I've been doing."

"I've been worried that Indian got you."

Wes smirked with a quiet scoff. "Nope. He wanted peace. Remember?" He sat down on the davenport tiredly. "I drank way too much last night."

Florence sat down in her chair and looked at him harshly. "Yes, he wanted peace with Frank, and you had to destroy it, didn't you?"

"Huh?" he asked, confused with an irritated scowl.

"Bruce told us what you said to him. How could you risk our lives like that, Wesley? You sat right here when the Marshal brought that man here and you knew we had peace with him. The Marshal and Frank both told you to leave him alone, but you just couldn't do that, could you? Why do you like to terrorize people, Wesley? That man has lost everything and you just don't care about anyone but yourself. Because of your stupid mouth, you are going to get my husband killed! And Frank said if that Indian wanted to, he could take blood for blood, which means all of us, including me! Is that what you want? We never had any trouble until you came here!"

Wes shrugged with an innocent grin. "What are you talking about? I haven't done anything."

Florence's eyes hardened. "You know what you said! Don't play stupid. Bruce told us what you said to Bobby."

"Oh," Wes chuckled. "Yeah, I told the Indian he stinks. And yeah, he could use a bath."

"No. That's what you told Bobby to tell Bruce. What you asked the Indian was how did it feel to shake the hand of the man that... Did you mutilate his family? My lord, Wesley, how could you do what Frank said you did? That's monstrous!"

Wes sighed heavily. "He's a heathen. Nothing more."

Florence raised her voice, "He's a human being, Wesley! And you put my family at risk of his wrath. Do you understand that? Frank told me this man could be anywhere at any time and attack any of us! Do you have any idea how scary that is to live with? We could lock our doors and go to sleep and he could slide down the chimney of the fireplace or burn our house down. We are not safe and it's because of you and your damn mouth! Honestly, why do you have to be like that?"

"Florence, it's fine. You don't need to worry about him. I'll make sure of that. But if Frank is scared, tell him to take off your bloomers and put on his soldier's pants and get to work. He knows how to track him down."

Florence yelled, "Frank doesn't want to kill him

or anyone else! Frank wants to live in peace with him. And he can't if you're out there aggravating that man. You are lucky you didn't come back here last night because Frank was hot! I've never seen him so mad. And you better not be here when he gets home either. I'm sorry, Wes, but you need to leave and not come back. Maybe if we are lucky, that Indian will know Frank has nothing to do with you. Bruce went and apologized to that man after leaving you. Bruce said he had never seen that man looking so dangerous. We are scared and it's because of you! I need you to leave and stay away from my sons too."

Wes stared at her in disbelief. "You're kicking me out?"

"Yes! We don't want you here and we don't want you hanging out around town. You're going to get us killed with your stupidity. You have no right to talk to that man the way you do."

Wes chuckled defensively. "I'm a professional soldier. That is what I do. If you want to keep your family safe, then you might need me here."

She shook her head. "No. We don't need you here. Leave town while you can, Wes."

He sat in silence for a moment staring at the floor. "I came here to see you, Florence. You know we are getting older and time goes fast. If I leave, I may never see you again. You're my only sister and I'd hate to leave like this."

"Wesley, I love you, but you have to leave. Go back home and when that man leaves town or dies, I'll let you know."

He frowned deeply. "I don't have anything to go back to, Florence. I wanted to start over again here with my family."

"You can't. Not right now. If that Indian doesn't kill you, Frank will. You put his family at risk. And you're not going to stop, we all know that. You drink too much to stop talking and if it's not the Indian you're harassing it will be someone else." She stood up and said, "Wes, give me a hug, little brother. It's time for you to go."

"Sis, I'm sorry if I caused you all any trouble. I would never intentionally put you all in danger. I love you too much for that."

Her eyebrows raised. "But you did, Wes. And you are not welcome here anymore. Now please, leave town."

Wes hugged his sister and then picked up his saddlebags and rifle before walking out the door without another word.

Florence sat down in her chair and began to sob.

Chapter 25

Wes carried his rifle and saddlebags across town to the livery stable, paid his fee and saddled his horse. His own family had rejected him and it angered him. He did not consider leaving town. If he neutralized the threat, then his sister and her family could live in peace and they would welcome him back into their family again. Fear made people do crazy things and Florence was terrified. Wes found it odd that Frank would be so afraid over a single Indian. Wes had enough of the nonsense. He knew Chusi was hurting with possible broken facial bones and wherever he called home, is where he would find him licking his wounds. One-shot and it would be over and Wes would be back in the good graces of his family.

He asked around and discovered nobody knew where Chusi lived, but he found out Chusi always walked past the lumber mill on the other side of the Modoc River when he left town. Wes rode his horse across the two bridges of Premro Island

and past the sawmill where both Frank and Paul worked. Wes hoped neither of them would see him pass by. The last thing he wanted was to have a confrontation with Frank. He remembered clearly that morning when they attacked the village on Bear River how Frank had disappeared after the fight was over and came back to see the blood on Wes's hands. Frank was outraged. Many times, as sergeant over newer recruits, Frank was known for yelling, but Wes had never seen Frank go into such a furious rage. Wes had a feeling if he were to see Frank now, it might be a close second to what he had endured back then.

A half-mile past the sawmill, Wes noticed a smooth and flat trail in the packed snow, leaving the main road towards the east into the woods. Dog and one set of horse tracks were beside it. He turned his horse and followed the trail made by moccasins into the forest. He followed as far as he could with his horse, but when the low limbs and underbrush became too thick for his horse, he dismounted and tied the reins to a tree limb before starting on foot. The foliage made a tunnel of sorts that he ducked slightly under and followed the trail through the dark forest. He walked a long way and began to hear the sound of a creek up ahead and smell the faint scent of a fire coming from the bottom of the hill. He quietly chambered a round into his Henry rifle to have it ready. It would only take one shot to end the man's life and be done with him. Wes had no concern about the dog attacking him, but he did consider the dog smelling or hearing him before the Indian did. People knew their dogs and how the differing tones of barking warned of one thing or another. If the dog began barking and alerted Chusi to his presence and the man ran into the brush to hide, Wes had already decided he would leave while he could before he became the target. One thing he had learned was the element of surprise and catching someone off guard was far more effective than trying to fight a foe in his backyard. These woods were unmerciful with cover and shaded darkness within the trees. It would be hard to spot a man who knew how to hide behind fallen logs, rotting stumps and the thick underbrush. If that man had a good bow or a rifle, they could cut an intruder down without any warning or without ever being seen. Wes was quite aware of that as he slowly and carefully made his way along the trail leading down a slight hill towards the creek. There were no sounds other than the soothing sound of the creek and a few birds in the trees. He came to a large fallen tree with the roots standing upright. The trail led between the fallen tree roots and a standing tree, leaving a two-foot drop in the path. He placed his hand on the roots for support as he stepped down the two-foot step where the roots had once been. After he stepped down, he hid behind the exposed roots. He could not see anything just yet, but he was getting close and slowly continued forward. He rounded a bend in the trail and there was a large teepee set back from the creek a good twenty yards or so in a grove of young Birch trees that were about twenty feet tall. An old firepit was outside, but no smoke could be seen coming from it, but there was a hint of smoke coming from the top of the teepee. It was the only sign of life around the camp.

He moved closer quietly with his rifle, ready to be engaged. The elk skin hides of the teepee hid anyone that might've been inside. He knew if the dog were there, it would be barking by now and felt confident that Chusi wasn't in the camp. He flipped the entry flap open with the barrel of his rifle and glanced inside. It was empty except for a rack of dried fish and a bowl of roots, rolled up blankets and hides, some cookware and a bedroll laid out on the ground. There was nothing that interested him, except a bow with a quill of sharp metal-tipped arrows and a spear with feathers tied to the shaft and a large black obsidian hand chipped spearhead. He considered taking the spear as a trophy and breaking the bow and arrows but decided to leave them and leave no trace of his presence. The fire pit inside was warm and smoked a bit as it was burning out. He stepped outside of the teepee and looked for any sign of Chusi. He could not hear a dog and assumed Chusi had gone to town. He considered burning the teepee down to leave the man homeless, but he decided it was better to wait. He would come back early in the morning and catch Chusi by surprise and drag his body deep enough into the woods where it wouldn't be found. As he thought about where to place himself in the morning for the best shot, he let his eyes scan the hillside behind the teepee. The trees were close together and the underbrush created a wall of darkness that an entire tribe could hide within and no one would know they were there. He could feel the uncomfortable sensation of being watched that often follows such thoughts come over him. He knew it was his imagination getting the better of him and he walked back the way he had come and disappeared around the bend as he walked back uphill towards his horse.

***

Chusi Yellowbear had been coming back from checking his traps when he heard his dog growl as they neared his camp. He squatted down in the brush up the hill from his camp and watched. He held his dog's mouth closed just in case it barked. He watched Wes step out of his teepee and walk away after looking towards him blindly. Chusi had his rifle on him and could have killed the man, but he resisted. Chusi knew Wes would come back again at another time. Maybe first thing in the morning like they did when the soldiers massacred his tribe. Chusi decided to let him come again. He had an idea and he would make Wes sorry for what he had done. Wes would be sorry for the rest of his life if Chusi chose to let him live at all.

Chapter 26

Matt was in his small private office with the door closed, writing a letter to a friend of his from the Marshal's Office in Wyoming. The weight of Jed's death weighed heavily on his mind. He decided to go to the Sperry farm, not knowing if part of the Sperry-Helms Gang was there or all of them. Truet had asked on the way if Matt wanted to ask the Willow Fall's Sheriff, Tom Smith and his deputy to go with them. Having two more men might've saved Jed's life, or it might've gotten Matt's friend Tom or his deputy killed. There was no way of knowing. Jed had been an unexpected casualty none the less and Matt's leadership had cost him a friend and a family much more than he could ever repay or compensate them for. Truet was the only deputy that had any experience with a gunfight and using force when needed. Matt had hired two inexperienced young men and now one of them had a scarred face and limited to the office and the other, Nate, was still shocked by seeing his friend's chest blown away with a shotgun. Nate had yet to draw his weapon or fire it at a man. Matt needed tough, experienced men who could be reliable in a gunfight. He wasn't taking any more chances to lose another man if he could help it. He needed men who knew what they were doing and confidently so. He wrote to his old friend TJ Tolbert and offered him a job. He would send another letter to a deputy sheriff in New Mexico that he had met and was overly impressed with a few years ago as well.

The main office door opened, ringing the cowbell at the top of the door. Frank Ellison stepped inside straight from work dressed in his bib overalls. His son, Paul, was dressed the same as he followed his mother, Florence, inside. She dressed warmly for the walk to the Marshal's Office. Bruce Ellison had left work at the mine early as he too wore his filthy clothes from the silver mine. His face was covered with dirt and a smear of grease.

"We need to speak to the Marshal. Is he in?" Frank asked quickly.

Phillip nodded. "Give me one minute and I'll get him."

Matt followed Phillip out of his private office and seeing the Ellison family, he frowned. "Come on back and have a seat here at the table where we can talk. Can I get any of you some coffee?" He asked, walking towards the dining table with six chairs in the middle of the room near the woodstove. He stole the idea from the Prairieville Sheriff's Office.

They all sat down at the table as Matt got the three men a cup of coffee. "So, what's going on?"

Matt asked now that they were situated. He could read the anxiety on their faces.

Frank began, "You know we were good with Chusi, right? Well, I'll let Bruce tell you what happened last night."

Matt looked at Bruce seriously. "What's going on now?"

Bruce told him what Wes had said to Chusi in the saloon and then that Wes had threatened Bobby Alper not to tell Bruce what he said. Bruce went on to explain that at work, Ritchie Thorn shared the story with everyone that he, Jack Sperry and Wes had beat Chusi up outside of Ugly John's Saloon. Wes had pulled out his knife and was going to scalp Chusi and would have if Big John Pederson had not stopped it.

When Bruce had finished talking, Frank added, "Now I'm wondering if Chusi is holding me responsible, even a little bit for what Wes has done. I learned a long time ago, Wes is a troublemaker, but I don't want my family hurt or me either quite honestly. I've begged God to forgive me for what I've done and according to the Bible, he has, but I have the hardest time forgiving myself. And now… we just want Wes gone. He is not allowed at our house anymore, and Florence told him to leave town. I don't know if he has or not, but I don't want Chusi putting an arrow in me on my way to work either or slipping down through the chimney to kill us all while we sleep."

Matt took a deep breath. "How bad did they beat up, Chusi?" he asked Bruce.

He shrugged. "I don't know, but I'm guessing bad."

"Did your brother-in-law, do those things to Chusi's family?"

Frank nodded. "He hates Indians."

Matt narrowed his eyes with irritation. "Let me explain something to you, my best friend growing up was black and he was murdered because of his skin color and no other reason. That was one of the reasons I killed the Dobson Gang. They were bigots that hated black people. I have no patience or empathy for people like that. I'm part Indian myself and I've had to endure seeing the Indians killed, murdered, strangled, starved and herded like cattle onto reservations, including my relatives that live on the reservation now. I obviously live in the white man's world, that's where I was raised, but had it been different, I may not have been any different than Chusi. I've seen people look at me with scorn because I'd rather have Chusi at my house and as my friend than some of the most successful and respected men in this town. All of you work for two men I wouldn't have at my dinner table, Josh Slater and Travis McKnight. I have no use for either of them. Other people would rather lick the bottom of those two successful men's shoes than to help Chusi to stand up. And that's something that I don't understand. I look at the quality of the man, not what color or how successful he is. I wish more people would." He paused. "I'll go check on Chusi and make sure he's okay and make sure he knows you all have nothing to do with Wes. Is there anything else I can do for you?"

"Yeah," Frank said, "You can run Wes out of town and tell him never to come back."

Matt looked at him. "I'll do my best." He looked at Truet and said, "Truet, will you and Nate go to the livery stable and ask if Wes's horse is still there. Then if one of you would bring my horse back here for me and if Wes's horse is here, the other one of you needs to start checking the hotels or wherever else he may be staying. I want to know where Wes is if we need to find him." He looked at Frank, "Let me check on Chusi and I'll stop by on my way back to town. Misses Ellison," he said softly, "you folks came to me and I'm going to confront your brother. Sometimes that does not go so well. I just want you to know that."

She nodded quickly as she wiped her eyes dry. "I understand. My family is more important."

Matt nodded compassionately.

"Thank you, Marshal, we appreciate it. And if you could, run Wes out of town before he gets someone killed."

"I'll encourage him to leave town, you bet."

***

Matt rode his horse out of town and found a trail worn in the snow made by the flat-soled moccasins and beside it, multiple dog tracks. Fresh horse tracks covered the path leading to and back out of the woods. Matt followed the trail into the woods, concerned with what he would find at the end of the trail. He had no doubt the horse belonged to Wes because Truet had returned to the office to tell him that Wes's horse was still at the stable, but the stable owner had stated that Wes had taken the horse out for a ride and asked where to find Chusi. Matt dismounted where the brush grew too thick to continue on the horse. He moved through the silent dark forest cautiously and unhooked the hammer thong of his revolver out of habit when in uncomfortable situations.

He neared a large fallen tree's root mass standing vertically and was startled to see Chusi step out of the shadows from the other side of the roots with his bow pulled back and ready to release a deadly arrow aimed for Matt's chest. Quickly, Matt spun sideways and drew his revolver and pointed it at Chusi.

"Put it down, Chusi!" he shouted.

Chusi lowered the bow as he eased the tension off the bowstring and removed the arrow from the bow. "Why are you here?" he asked. He stepped up out of the natural pit where the tree roots once were and stood near Matt.

Matt could see Chusi's face was beaten black and blue and swollen. His left eye was nearly swollen shut and cut across the eyebrow and cheek. He looked to be in pain. "Why didn't you come to me so we can arrest the men who did this to you?"

Chusi barely shook his head with a sneer on his swollen and cut open lip. "No." He put his hand on Matt's shoulder. "Go home, my friend. Go home and do not come back."

Matt frowned curiously. "Wes Wasson came here today, didn't he? I saw the horse tracks."

Chusi shrugged. "Don't know."

"Let me help. I can arrest the men who did this to you and run Wes out of town and you'll never have to see him again."

Chusi's eyes hardened. "No. I don't want your help. Don't you understand, you must not interfere."

Matt holstered his revolver. "I have to interfere. It's my job."

"And it's my honor!" Chusi shouted angrily. "He came to me and he'll come again, let me do what I must do."

Matt narrowed his eyes. "I'm trying to help you."

"I do not want your help. I do not approach him; he approaches me. I did nothing and this is what they did!" he shouted while pointing at his face. "He wanted my hair while I still live! I don't want your help. I offered to forgive as your Jesus does and let the flowers flow down the creek as my Omusa showed me in my vision, but he pushes me and laughs about what he did. I offer no more mercy, but only wrath until his blood flows as my children's did. He wants my hair; I'll take his!" He lifted his hair to show Matt a faint line where Wes's knife began to cut at his hairline.

Matt looked at the knife mark and felt the anger rising within him. He took a deep breath. "If he comes out here, you can protect yourself. That is the law, but even so, you being Indian and him a white man, it will not go well with you in our court of law. Killing a white man even if you were in the

215

right, will lead to you being hung. If you kill him, it will end your life too. I'm asking you, let me handle this, okay?"

"Would he be hung if he took my scalp last night? He wanted me to live without my scalp. Would he have hung?" His eyes peered into Matt's angrily.

Matt shook his head. "Probably not. But he's white and you're not. It's not fair, I know, but that's how it is. That's why I would like to run him out of town before either of you get hurt."

"If he comes back here, I will take his hair."

Matt's eyes hardened angrily. "If he comes out here to hurt you, do what you must. But do not scalp him, Chusi! If you do, there will be nothing I can do to save you. There will be nothing I could say that would justify what you did. If you kill him to protect yourself is one thing, mutilating his body is another. Understand this, if you take his hair or mutilate his body in any way I will arrest you to face the consequences. Do you understand that?"

"I don't want your help!" Chusi spat out.

"I'm aware of that." He paused and spoke in a softer tone, "I wanted to let you know Frank Ellison and his family are very worried that you'll want to hurt them because of what Wes has done. They kicked Wes out of their house and wanted me to tell you they have nothing to do with him anymore."

Chusi answered, "I can see the torture in Frank's eyes. We are at peace, him and I."

Matt smiled slightly. "I'll let him know. Now, what about Wes?"

Chusi stared at him blankly. "We have already

spoken about him. I made peace; he breaks it. Leave us to settle the debt among ourselves. If he comes to kill me, I welcome him. I want to be with Omusa and my children again. I saw them and they are waiting. As your friend, I ask you, do not interfere with my fight. Give me a chance to be a warrior again and settle the debt owed to me with his blood."

Matt paused for a moment and then added sincerely, "Christine told you that your part of our family. We would like for you to be there when we get married and when we have children. I know he's guilty of many horrible things and you'd love to get your hands on him, but if you can let his flower from Omusa's vision go down the river and allow me to take care of him, you could enjoy many years ahead being a part of our family."

Chusi smiled sadly. "Leave my friend. And please don't come back, but if you do, go around the tree. Then I'll know it's you and not kill you on accident." He motioned around the front of the fallen tree. "I don't want to hurt you, so go around the tree."

"I can't stop this fight from happening, can I?" Matt asked simply.

Chusi shook his head. "He wants my scalp and I want his life. Leave us to our destiny. Now please leave." He put his hand out to shake. "Take care, my friend."

Matt shook his hand. "I'm going to talk to Wes and force him to get out of town. I know you want to fight him, but I cannot look the other way. I'm sorry, Chusi, but I like you far too much to lose another friend. I'm stepping in and stopping this now. Remember your vision and let the flower float downstream while you can."

Chusi smirked slightly with warm, appreciative eyes. "You talk to him. And I wish you success. Maybe we can avoid it all if he goes away."

Chapter 27

Wes Wasson tried to sleep on the bottom bunk of one of the many bunk beds in Lucky Man's Bunkhouse. It was merely an old single-story house that had been stripped out into one big room and filled with wooden bunkbeds that were rented out. The back half of the house had tables and chairs, a cookstove and cabinets with cooking wares. Some men stayed at the bunkhouse and worked in various places, others came to Branson for the weekend and stayed just long enough to spend their money on Rose Street. And some, like Wes, didn't have anywhere else to go.

Wes covered his head with his coat to make it dark enough and hoped to quiet the talking from the other men arriving for the weekend. He was tired and wanted to get a nap in before going to the saloon with his new friend, Jack Sperry. Jack was already playing a card game at the Thirsty Toad Saloon.

"Wes Wasson!" Matt yelled as he stepped into

the bunkhouse.

Wes yanked his coat off his head and yelled bitterly, "What!" It was then that he saw Matt Bannister walking towards him quickly. "What?" he asked a bit more concerned as Matt approached.

Matt grabbed Wes's shirt and yanked him up to his feet and then spun around and threw Wes across the floor without a word. Wes hitting the floor near the kitchen tables caught every man's attention, and they stood up and backed away from Matt and Wes.

"What's gotten into you, Marshal?" Wes asked as he started to stand.

Matt popped him in the face with an unexpected left jab as he stood and then followed it with a right cross that sent Wes down onto a tabletop and then rolled to the floor.

Wes wiped his mouth and spat out a touch of blood. He looked up at Matt just in time to see the bottom of Matt's moccasin slam into his face.

Matt grabbed Wes and lifted him back to his feet. Wes swung a hard-right fist, which Matt expected and ducked. Wes swung a wild left, which Matt evaded as well and then drove his right fist up into Wes's breadbasket knocking the wind out of him. Matt followed it with another right into the breadbasket again. He grabbed Wes's shirt and swung him around and drove him into a wall cabinet. Matt's hand went to Wes's throat as he held him there. His hardened eyes burned into Wes dangerously. His voice had a threatening tone as he warned, "Don't you say another word to

Chusi! Stay away from him, or I promise you will wish you had. I want you out of my county. Your family doesn't want you here anymore and neither do I. Get your crap packed up and get out of Jessup County!" Matt sneered as he let Wes go.

Wes bent over to catch his breath. "Marshal...I don't have to leave; I've done nothing wrong." He looked back up at Matt. "You can threaten me, but you can't make me leave. I know my rights, don't forget Marshal, I'm an American soldier."

Matt pulled his knife from the sheath on his gun belt and held it out by the blade out towards Wes to take by the handle. "I'm Nez Perce, why don't you try to scalp me? I won't even pull my gun."

He stared at Matt awkwardly. "If you're looking for a fight, I'm not taking it up with you. I don't believe in fighting lawmen. I'm not a criminal, Marshal."

"No, you're worse than a criminal, in my view. Get out of my county while you can."

Wes smiled well aware that other men were watching him in the room. He had to say something to save his pride among the men. "I might be staying longer than you like. I was invited to join up with the Sperry-Helms Gang, and I might just do that. It sounds like they need a man like me."

Matt smirked slowly. "A criminal. If you do join them, our paths will cross soon enough. Good luck with that. But I will tell you, leave Chusi alone, or you'll be dealing with me again much sooner."

He grinned mockingly. "Sure thing. I don't care about that Indian. I'll leave him alone."

"Good," Matt said pointedly. "Because I'd hate to have to tell your family that I found you dead."

"Is that a threat, Marshal?" he asked with a narrowing of his eyes.

Matt shook his head. "I know Chusi well enough to know buried down under that calm and docile man is a predator and you're nothing but prey. Leave him be for your own good. That's my warning."

Wes laughed. "That's like a hungry fox trying to kill a badger, isn't it? I'm not easy prey, Marshal. I'll kill him if he comes at me."

"That's what he says too. Leave him be."

Wes smiled uncomfortably. "He's not worth losing my family over, so I'll leave him alone from now on."

"That's a wise decision," Matt said and let the bunkhouse.

Wes looked at the other men that were staring at him. "It's never wise to fight a lawman on a Friday night. If it was Monday, I might've worked him over a bit, but no one wants to spend the weekend in jail. Am I right, fella's?"

Chapter 28

Wes Wasson rode his horse beside Jack Sperry's out to Slater's Mile to see Ritchie Thorn and Bobby Alper, who shared a cabin in the silver mine's employee housing community. They rode past a burned-down cabin as Jack led the way.

Wes pulled the reins to a stop near a hand pump well, where a blonde-haired lady was fetching a pail of water. He smiled. "Hello, Miss. This is my first time coming out here and if you don't mind my saying so, I wasn't expecting to find such a pretty lady out here. I don't want to sound forward, but it's like finding a diamond in the silver mine." He chuckled with a kind smile. "My name's Wes Wasson; What's your name?"

She glanced back behind her towards her cabin, uneasily.

"Wes, come on!" Jack yelled.

Wes smiled sympathetically at her. "Gotta go. Nice meeting you anyway." He rode forward to join up with Jack at Ritchie Thorn's cabin.

"All the women out here are married, bud. Leave them be; some of those husbands are pretty jealous roughnecks. They'll fight you for looking at their woman," Jack said as he knocked on the door.

"It doesn't hurt to say 'hi' to a pretty lady."

Ritchie Thorn opened the door. He had gotten off work for the day shortly before. "Jack, Wes, what are you two doing here? I was going to catch a nap before coming into town to see you two."

Wes asked, "Where's Bobby?"

"Right here. Hey, Bob."

Bobby Alper stepped to the door and was immediately grabbed by Wes and yanked out of the cabin and thrown onto the cold ground. Wes followed him quickly as Bobby rolled to a stop and kicked him in the face and then in the ribs. Wes kicked him in the face again and then in the stomach as Bobby rolled away from him. Wes jumped onto Bobby's chest and began to hit him with a repeating right fist. Bobby covered his head as best he could with his arms, but Wes hit any open area he could.

Jack Sperry laughed with excitement, "Hit him! Oh, buddy, you have to join the gang!"

Ritchie Thorn watched curiously and was soon joined by his older brother, Joe Thorn. "What's this about?" Joe asked.

Ritchie shrugged. "I don't know. The last I knew they were friends."

Wes hit him again and again until it became evident that Bobby did not have any fight left within him. Wes paused and looked down into Bobby's face and squeezed his cheeks tightly together, forcing

Bobby's mouth open. "I bet you're wondering why I beat you, huh? Think about it! The next time you open your mouth up to Bruce, I'll cut your tongue out!" he snarled viciously.

Blood seeped out of Bobby's nose and mouth.

Wes stood and smiled at Ritchie and Joe Thorn. He put out a bloody hand to shake. "Wes Wasson. You must be Ritchie's brother; you look like him."

Joe shook his hand. "Yeah, I'm Joe." He nodded at the sprawled-out body of Bobby. "Why were you beating up my friend?"

"Bobby needed to learn to keep his mouth shut. I think I taught him," he chuckled.

Joe nodded. "Looks like. I've never had a problem with Bobby talking, though."

"I did. But I think we're in good shape now. Joe, do you want to join us out on the town tonight?"

Joe rubbed his short black hair. He was in his mid to late thirties, a bit shorter than Ritchie with broader shoulders and muscular. He had a thick mustache on his oblong face. "Yeah, I might as well. It's Friday night. I can work tomorrow, hungover," he chuckled. He turned to face his cottage. He shouted, "Billy Jo, bring my coat, hat and money out here!"

The door opened, and the blonde lady popped her head outside. "What?"

A glimmer of animosity flickered in Joe's eyes. "You heard me. Bring my coat, hat and money out here. I'm going to town with the boys."

Her irritation reflected on her face as she disappeared inside.

Jack Sperry smiled. "Your woman caught Wes's attention coming over here. I had to tell him she's taken."

Joe looked at Wes and rolled his eyes with frustration. "Trust me; you wouldn't want her."

Wes replied, "She didn't say a word to me, but she sure is pretty."

Joe shook his head. "She's not pretty on her best day, but she does cook and wash my clothes," he said as Billy Jo carried out his things. He put on his coat and hat and put his money in his pocket. "I'll be back later," he said and nodded towards the house for her to go back in. She cast a nervous glance at Bobby as he slowly got to his feet and a glimpse at Wes before walking to the cottage to care for her and Joe's children.

"How long have you been married?" Wes asked Joe.

He grimaced. "I'll never be married. But we've been together for long enough. I've got her trained well these days. I'm not ready to trade her off yet anyway. She belongs to me, so you can forget about her."

Jack Sperry added, "You better watch yourself, Joe, Wes is going to become a bonafide member of the Sperry-Helms Gang and you know how it goes. If you mess with one of us, you get us all."

Joe looked at Jack skeptically. "Like Charlie? I could not believe the marshal put him up in front of his office like that. Talk about suicidal, huh? What did Morton say about that?"

Jack frowned. "In time. Right now, the marshal's

got our cousin Bo in his jail. But not for long, real soon I suspect he'll be getting a notice from Prairieville saying all the charges against Bo will be dropped. We got five hundred dollars out of the deal, so it worked out well. We might start doing that for a career if we can figure out a way of keep pulling the wool over the marshal's eyes." He laughed.

Joe scoffed bitterly. "That shouldn't be too hard. The marshal's not all that he's made out to be."

Jack asked, "Have you ever seen him shoot?"

"No."

"I did when he killed Charlie and I've never seen anyone faster or more deadly. You may think he's not much, but he's still alive for a reason and now I know why. He's fast and accurate. I wouldn't be stupid enough to go up against him alone, that's for sure."

Bobby Alper stood up finally and wiped his face, smearing the blood. Wes looked at him sincerely. "Hey Bobby, now that we got our situation taken care of, why not change your clothes and meet us in town for some fun? We're good to be friends again, right?"

Bobby shook his head. "I'm not up to it. Go ahead."

Wes smirked with disgust. "Are you a softy like my nephew? We're friends, still, right?" Bobby walked towards his cabin ignoring him. Wes shouted, "We're friends still, right?"

Bobby looked at him as his face swelled. "Yeah, we're friends."

"Glad to hear it, because I like you, Bobby. Now, change your clothes and meet us in town. If you don't, I'll come back here and beat you all the way into town." He chuckled. "We're going to play some cards and then go meet a few of the girls at the dance hall when they open. We're going to have a great time. You don't want to miss out, Bobby. You're only young once, my friend. Enjoy it."

Jack nodded. "Yeah, I've got my eyes on one named Bonnie. And if any of you try to dance with her, I'll bust your jaw. That reminds me, how is your jaw, Bobby?" he laughed.

Bobby looked at him scornfully, before entering the cabin and closing the door.

Chapter 29

Chusi Yellowbear had spent the day cautiously listening for any noises in the forest that indicated someone was nearing his camp and paying close attention to his dog for an early warning. Wes knew where Chusi's camp was and the terrain around it to plan his attack, but what Wes didn't realize was Chusi was expecting him. He knew the trail Wes would come down and where he would most likely take cover to attack him. Chusi had planned and prepared for most of the day and was ready and waiting.

Chusi's camp was located in a young birch tree grove along the creek. He looked at the trees and came up with a plan. He measured what rope he had and then cut his fishing nets into straight lengths and then tied the strands into lengths he could use. When he had enough cordage, he used his ax to cut a V-shaped notch on the backside of a larger birch tree. He then climbed up a smaller twenty-five-foot tall birch tree on the left side of the larger tree with a rope and tied a knot to the trunk near the top of it. He began rocking the top of the tree back and forth to untangle the limbs from other trees. When the branches were untangled, the top of the tree carrying his weight bowed over as he let go of the tree and held the rope until he reached the ground. He wrapped the rope around the V in the larger tree and tied the rope to hold the tree bowed downward. He took a seven-foot piece of cordage and tied a constrictor knot onto the main rope holding the tree so it wouldn't slip along the line. On the other end of the seven-foot piece of cordage, he tied a slip knot with a loop and let it hang near the ground. He repeated the same process to a birch tree on the right side of the larger birch that he anchored the two bowed over trees to. Each seven-foot piece of cordage had a slipknot hanging above the ground about five feet apart. All he had to do was cut the two main lines around the larger tree and both smaller birch trees would snap upwards like a snare. He had set a trap and expected to capture the former soldier alive. But if his trap failed, Chusi would be hidden in the forest with his bow and a rifle in case it became a bigger fight than he expected, which it could become if Wes brought his friends along.

Now that he was prepared, he ate the last of his dried fish and sat in the silence. There were only a few things left he wanted to do. He grabbed a rolled-up buffalo skin blanket that he had saved since his wedding day. It was special to him because it was a handmade wedding gift from his mother.

It was a large blanket with the thick fur on the top side and soft skin underneath. Though it would be time-consuming and challenging to do, his mother and other ladies had labored to sew beads along the edges. The base color of the beads was white about an inch wide surrounding the outside edge all around the blanket. Every six inches or so was a buffalo in blue beads, a child in red beads, a buffalo in yellow beads and then a child in blue beads interchanging colors with every figure sewn into the beadwork all around the blanket. It was given to Chusi and Omusa in the hopes it would help breed many healthy children. Chusi went back to the winter camp and found his teepee had been pulled down and burned away from where his teepee had been. His bedding was untouched and the blanket was intact and unharmed. He had rolled up the blanket to take it with him and was surprised to find a deer hide rolled up and tied tight that Omusa must have thrown under the blanket to keep her things safe. He had kept them both ever since. The blanket and the contents wrapped inside the deerskin were all he had left of his family.

His life was one of sorrow, persecution and unfairness if life could be called fair. He had seen the worst humanity had to offer and suffered outrages that no man should ever have to endure. But he had also experienced the best humankind has to offer as well. He was shown compassion and love by a Mormon family that took him into their home after the massacre. The Mormon family he stayed with for a few days had sat with him and read from the Bible and tried to give Chusi a reason to keep living. Of all the Bible stories he heard, the one that Chusi identified with was the story of Samson. The Philistines murdered Samson's wife and her family, and Samson went back for vengeance. Chusi understood that part better than any other part of the story. He wanted revenge, and he prayed to the Creator for the chance to do as Samson had done. The years passed and Chusi had seldom found anyone to be as friendly and loving to him as that Mormon family had been. Until he came to Branson and met the Fasana and Bannister families, they accepted him when no one else would. And then Matt showed up a year ago and had become a true friend that not only watched out for him but invited him into his family. The very idea of it made Chusi smile with a genuine heartfelt appreciation.

He grabbed the rolled-up buffalo blanket and his spear with the large carved obsidian tip and walked into Branson in the dark. It was getting late for guests, but he knocked on Matt's door. As always, Matt asked who was there, but then opened the door and invited him inside.

"Chusi, what's this? Did you come to spear me?" Matt asked with a friendly smile.

Chusi smiled a bit more than his usual smirk. "No. It's a gift for you. For all you've done for me." He handed the spear out for Matt to take. It was about six feet long and had a substantial chunk of black obsidian carved into a sharp point. The handle had a combination of beadwork and feathers attached to it. It was a beautiful spear.

Matt frowned. "Chusi, you don't have to give me anything. It's a beautiful spear. Did you make it?"

He nodded. "Yes. You keep it. Maybe you can show your children how to throw it someday."

Matt scoffed. "I don't even know if I could throw it effectively. Besides, it is a work of art. Are you sure you want me to have this?"

Chusi smirked pleased by Matt's appreciation of it. "Yes. And this." He pulled out a tied rolled deer hide from the blanket folds and set it on the floor. He unrolled the blanket halfway to show the beadwork. "This was given to me by my mother when I married Omusa. It blessed us with our four children. I want you and Christine to have it." He nodded. "Maybe you too will have four children or more."

Matt looked at him, quizzically. "Why are you giving me all of this? You're not planning on dying, are you?"

"No," he said with a grin.

"Then, why? This blanket should mean everything to you. Why are you giving it to me? Chusi, your mother made it for you, are you sure you want to give it away?"

Chusi stared at the floor for a moment. "I have no more family, except you and Christine. Please, take it and care for it."

Matt questioned, "Are you sure?"

Chusi nodded. "If that man kills me, he would either burn or take my things. I want to give them to you while I can. They are yours, anyway. Along with my bow, my knife, my teepee and my dog. If you will take her."

Matt shook his head. "I talked to Wes and told him to leave you alone and he said he would. I don't think he has any interest in pursuing a fight with you since his family doesn't want him around anymore. I don't think he's going to bother you again. You don't need to give your things away."

Chusi frowned. "You don't want them?"

"I love them, I do. I don't want you to regret giving away things that mean so much to you. I'll keep them safe, but if you ever want them back, just let me know, okay?" He could see the hurt in Chusi's expression.

"Thank you, Matt. I would like for you to have them."

"Thank you, Chusi. Do you want to sit down and visit for a while?"

He shook his head. "No, I must go." He looked at Matt momentarily. "You don't think Wes is coming in the morning?"

Matt shook his head. "No. Frank's family doesn't want anything to do with him anymore, not even Bruce, because of what he has been doing to you. I don't think it's worth it to him."

Chusi smiled with an appreciative grin. He waved at the blanket and spear. "These are for always being my friend. You're a good man, Matt."

"So are you, my friend."

Chusi grabbed the rolled-up deer hide and left Matt's house. He walked across town to Bella's Dance Hall. He had never been there before, but he knew Christine lived there. He walked up the steps and opened the door to the entry and closed the door behind him. He was met by a tall thin man with short brown hair and a friendly face, even though he looked at Chusi curiously.

"Hello," the man said. He didn't know what to think when he saw an Indian step into the dance hall dressed in dirty clothes, a deer hide coat and his tangled long hair and a beaten-up face under a floppy hat. He doubted any of the ladies would dance with him and questioned if he should allow the man into the dance hall or not.

Chusi glanced through the opened door into the ballroom and noticed all the men around the bar. He could hear the music and the sound of people dancing on the ballroom floor.

"Can I help you?" the man asked curiously.

"Christine? I'm here to see Christine," he answered.

The man shook his head. "No, Christine's not available."

"I need to see Christine, please. She's a friend of mine."

The man grimaced questionably and shook his head. "I'm sorry. You'll have to come back at another time. She's not available."

"I must see her. Can you tell her, Chusi Yellowbear is here? I'll leave if she can't see me, but would you ask, please?" his eyes pleaded desperately.

The man frowned. "Let me see." He stepped into the ballroom and waved at Bella. She came walking towards him with a glass of champagne. She smiled,

"What is it, Gaylon?"

"This man wants to speak with Christine. He seems persistent and wants me to ask if she would see him. He says he's her friend," Gaylon Dirks said uneasily. He was the new security guard for the dance hall.

Bella looked distastefully at Chusi. "What's your name?"

"Chusi Yellowbear, Ma'am. Christine and Matt are my friends."

Bella nodded. "Okay. Gaylon, would you go let Christine know Chusi is here to see her." She looked at Gaylon. "I do know he's her friend. Otherwise, the answer is always no. Okay?"

"Yes, Ma'am."

Bella looked at Chusi. "Wait here and she'll be down in a minute." She turned and walked into the ballroom.

After a few moments, Christine appeared at the top of the stairs with her long dark hair flowing naturally over her shoulders and down her back. She wore a long yellow dress without any shoes on. Chusi watched her coming down the stairs and noticed the hem of her long dress was longer than her legs and he stepped forward to help her if one of her feet got caught in the material. Four steps from the bottom, her foot landed on the hem of her dress and she tripped over the material. She fell forward without any control of her momentum. Chusi dropped the bundle in his arm and stepped forward quickly up on the first step and caught her, but the momentum of her falling bodyweight forced him to step back. He tripped over the bundle he had dropped to catch her. With a startled cry from Christine, they fell to the floor. He held onto her tight as he landed on his back; she landed on top of him.

He looked at her expression as she grimaced in pain and slowly rolled off him to lay on the floor. He got to his knees and leaned over her quickly. "Sorry, are you okay?"

"Oh, my gosh!" Galen exclaimed as he came forward. He hollered for Bella to come quickly as he also leaned over Christine.

Through a painful grimace, Christine said, "I'm fine." She held her stomach.

She held out a hand for Chusi to help her up, and he stood and took hold of her hand to pull her up when Bella and several men surrounded them. One of the men pushed Chusi back towards the door sharply to get him out of the way.

"Get your filthy hands off of her!" he shouted as he knelt beside Christine. Immediately, another man kicked his deerskin bundle across the entry wordlessly. Chusi stepped over to pick up his bundle.

"What happened?" Bella demanded and shot a wicked glare towards Chusi, not knowing if he had hit her. "What did you do to her!" she yelled with tears of anger filling her eyes.

Chusi shook his head, "She…"

Wes Wasson stepped quickly around the crowd of men and laid a hard-right fist into Chusi's cheek, knocking him to the floor. "Are you beating white women now? You piece of..." he grunted as he kicked Chusi in the ribs.

Christine grimaced in pain, the fall had hurt her stomach. She stood up gingerly with the help of a couple of gentlemen despite her urgency to stop Wes from hurting Chusi. She pointed at Wes while she remained bent over slightly. She spoke to Bella, "Stop him. Chusi caught me when I fell down the stairs."

Bella turned to her husband, Dave and Galen. "Stop him!"

Dave and two other men pulled Wes away from Chusi, while Galen helped Chusi up. Chusi stood with his fierce eyes burning into Wes.

Wes grinned daringly. "You better watch how you look at me and you know why!" He nodded slowly while smiling at Chusi.

Chusi looked at Christine and his eyes softened. "You're okay?"

She nodded, still showing some discomfort. "Thank you for catching me. Are you okay?" Christine asked him.

He nodded once. "I am fine. I brought you a gift."
"Oh?"

Wes could not stand to see Chusi talking to the most beautiful lady he had ever seen. "Darling," he spoke to Christine, "you don't want anything that heathen gives you. Fleas, ticks, bedbugs and maybe even leprosy is all he can give you. I'll buy you a ring though for a dance, how's that?" he asked with a flirtatious grin.

Christine looked at him with disgust. She held

up her engagement ring on her finger. "I already have one. No thanks. Chusi, follow me." She looked at Bella, "We're going into the reading room for a little while."

Bella frowned but nodded agreeably. She was not particularly fond of Indians herself, especially ones that looked like they hadn't bathed or washed their clothes in months walking through her business, but she wasn't about to tell Christine, no.

Christine led him through the ballroom to a room near the stage and turned up the lanterns inside to brighten the room. She closed the door to block out some of the noise. It was nothing more than a room with some padded chairs, davenports, tables with chairs and three bookshelves filled with books of various genres and catalogs. "Have a seat and let's talk," she said as she sat down in a padded chair across a small table from where she invited Chusi to sit.

He stood near the chair and unrolled the tanned hide and then unrolled a long light tan colored elk skin dress. It had beautiful solid blue beadwork about three inches wide running over the shoulders and down the outside of the arms to the elbows where the long tassels of four strings of elk hide each were beaded in blue all around the elbow's hem replacing the solid material. Four lines of blue beads, a half-inch wide, flowed from the inside of both elbows up the arms and across the upper chest dipping down at the neckline. Along the waistline was a two-inch band of blue beads going around the dress and just below that were upside down triangles of blue, white and red beads with a few tassels flowing down from each triangle spread out about every three inches all around the dress. The same upside-down triangle design was lower at the knees, but instead of being in a straight line, they were alternating in height and closer together at about every two inches apart. A little lower was another inch-wide band of blue beads that rolled like hills near the hem of the dress. At the bottom hem, tassels of the same design as the arms of the dress once again hung down around the feet.

Christine gasped. "That's beautiful!"

He smiled slightly. "It belonged to my Omusa. She wore it on our wedding day and special days. I want you to have it." He handed it over to her. Christine grinned appreciatively as she admired the beadwork and the intricate craftsmanship in creating such a beautiful dress.

"It's stunning. Thank you, Chusi. I can't believe how soft it is. Are you sure you want to give this away? It belonged to your wife."

He smiled sadly. "I can think of no one else who I want to have it. I hope it fits."

"I'm sure it will. I love it!"

He handed her the same pair of beaded moccasins that he had let her wear when he found her on Spider Creek in November. The moccasins were rabbit fur lined inside and had four blue horizontal lines running across the toe to a white square on top of the foot with a red flower in the center of it.

She grinned widely. "Chusi, did I ever tell you I loved wearing these? I didn't want to give them back." She laughed.

He grinned wider than she had ever seen him smile. "I want you to have them. And these are for your children someday." He unrolled a little dress with black, green and turquoise beadwork in the design of flowers going around the waist and three solid lines, one of each color ran up the arms and across the chest with a dipped neckline. The dress was the same type as the larger one with the tassels.

Christine gasped and was overwhelmed with emotion when she saw the little dress. "Was that your daughter's?"

He nodded. "Yes. Sitsi was beautiful like her mother." His lips lowered and Christine noticed his eyes mist over just a touch. "I remember her playing in the dirt in that dress. Omusa was not happy about it on her sister's wedding day." He smiled faintly.

"It's beautiful. Chusi, if Matt and I ever have a daughter, I'm going to put her in this dress and have a photograph done with you and her, okay? I wasn't lying to you when I said I wanted you to be a part of our family."

He smiled slightly but said nothing. He handed her another pair of moccasins, which matched the child's dress. The beadwork was of flowers on the top of the feet. He then gave her a small child's pair of moccasins for a toddler. They had red and blue beads, the left foot was a bow, and the right foot had a single arrow. "These were Chogun's when he was a little boy. I do not have anyone else to give them to, but if I did, I would still want you and Matt to have it all."

Christine picked up the small moccasins and held them in her hands. She looked at him emotionally. "I lost my daughter a few years ago when my husband and I were moving to Oregon. Her name was Carmen. She was a year and a half old. I know how much it hurts, but I could not imagine, no matter how hard I tried, how hard it must have been for you to see your whole family murdered. You've kept these for all these years and I know how much they mean to you because I still have things that belonged to my daughter too. I promise you; I will take care of these. I'll never get rid of them. Thank you for trusting me with your family heirlooms."

Chusi's brow furrowed. "I did not know you had a daughter."

She nodded, "Yes. She got sick and died while we were passing through Kansas. My husband was murdered in Colorado by a drunk man. That's how I met Bella. She helped me to get back on my feet and I thank God for that because I have no idea what I would've done without her."

Chusi sat down in the chair. "Your husband was killed?"

"Yes."

"You loved him?"

Christine nodded slowly. "Very much. He was my best friend."

"And now you marry, Matt?"

"Yes."

"Because you love him?"

"Yes, because I love him very much. You've never fallen in love again?"

He shook his head. "No one is as beautiful as Omusa. I never got a chance to love again. Omusa's family did not want me and I wanted to live free. The way I always had."

"Maybe you'll meet someone and get married again someday," she said, sounding hopeful.

He shook his head. "I'm old now." He stood up. "Goodnight, Angel."

She snickered. "You and my Grandfather are the only two people who have ever called me that. I have an idea; I am dying to try this dress on. Would you like to see if it fits me?"

His eyes opened slightly wider, and a slow smile appeared. "Yes. No one has put it on since Omusa last wore it."

"Come on out here and wait by the stairs and I'll grab Bella to help me put it on. I'll come downstairs and show you."

Chapter 30

Wes Wasson waited by the bar holding his drink, staring at the door he watched the beautiful Christine take Chusi through. He could not figure out for the life of him how she could be more interested in a dirty heathen more than himself. Wes was a decent looking man with a nice smile, and he bathed far more often than the Indian did. He wondered how many months it had been since Chusi had run a comb through his tangled hair. He had never seen Christine until moments before, but he was taken with her. He had questioned a couple of men about her and learned she was Matt's fiancé. She was a beautiful lady, but she had lousy taste, was the only conclusion Wes had come to. Why she was with Chusi or what they were doing behind the closed door was the most pressing thing upon his mind. No self-respecting white woman would have anything to do with the likes of a dirty Indian. Before too long, the door opened and Christine came out carrying an armload of buckskin clothing and moccasins. He saw a glimpse of the beadwork and assumed it was a dress. Christine went to Bella and asked for her help upstairs and then led Chusi to the bottom of the stairs to wait for her to reveal herself in heathen garments, Wes assumed. He wandered over to the doorway where the stairs were and leaned on the doorjamb, and glared at Chusi with his cold eyes.

"You don't belong here," he said to Chusi. "This is a white man's place, not a crib of pigs. The Chinese might accept your kind, but I don't."

Chusi ignored him.

Wes continued, "You should ask one of the ladies for a brush to straighten out that rat's nest. Last night, my blade was going to scrap your skull the same as it did your wife's and children's, but now that I got a better look at your rat's nest of hair, I don't want it."

Chusi ignored him and stared straight ahead towards the top of the stairs. He refused to react and miss seeing Omusa's dress being worn again. He would have his time to respond to Wes when the time came.

Wes narrowed his eyes and continued, "I don't like you, and I have no regrets for anything I have ever done. But I have better things to do than waste my time with you. I have family here and a future I like the looks of. You're lucky; I'm going to let you live. We're even."

Chusi could ignore him no longer. He looked at him with rage in his eyes. He nodded and spoke softly, "Just you and me when the time comes. It's coming soon."

Wes smirked. "Are you threatening me now? When I'm telling you that we're even? I'm sure I could have you kicked out of here for that and you'd miss seeing her in that dress."

Chusi looked back towards the stairs.

"Just go home and pet your dog. Don't cause trouble with me, Old Timer. I'm not going to ruin my future because of you."

Chusi nodded slowly once. "I have to use the privy as you call it."

"What?" Wes asked with a confused grimace.

Chusi looked at him. "I have to pee. I wish she would hurry so that I can go."

"Just go in your pants. I hear it wouldn't be the first time," Wes chuckled.

Chusi smirked slightly but said nothing.

Christine appeared at the top of the stairs in the buckskin dress and moccasins. She looked stunning. Her dark auburn hair had been put in a quick ponytail and for a moment, Chusi could've sworn he was looking at Omusa again, especially from behind when she turned around with her long hair falling down her back. His mouth opened as a wave of moisture blurred his vision and the emptiness of a vast hollow space ached in his chest.

"What do you think?" Christine asked Chusi from on top of the stairs.

Chusi could not speak. More than anything else, he longed to hold her and feel the dress with a body in it. The way it used to feel when Omusa wore it. He felt weak and his breathing grew heavier as he stared at her with tears thickening in his eyes. Through the lenses of moisture twisting his perception, he lost focus and he swore he could see Omusa standing at the top of the stairs. He gasped silently and began blinking to get his tears under control. He would happily give his life just to hold Omusa one last time.

Galen Dirks spoke, "Wow! That is gorgeous."

"Isn't it beautiful?" Bella asked from behind Christine.

Wes looked at Christine and shook his head. "Well, you're a hell of a lot better looking than the squaw that wore that dress was. I'd know, I got to see her real close." He looked over at Chusi. "Didn't I?" He chuckled.

Christine's excited expression changed to one of outrage and she was going to unleash her anger on Wes, but Chusi's calm voice got her attention.

"Christine, my friend, thank you. You are truly an angel. Have a good night." He looked at Wes with a cold glare. "I must pee now. . You remind me of a woman."

"What did you say to me?" Wes asked bitterly while he watched Chusi leave the dance hall.

Christine could hold back her anger no longer. "You are a deranged lunatic! I wish you would leave town and leave my friend alone!"

Bella gasped. "Christine, he is a customer," she said surprised, as Christine walked quickly towards her room.

Wes chuckled. He looked around for his friends and saw them all either dancing or engaged in a conversation. He grabbed his coat and put it on to follow Chusi. He debated about taking his gun belt, but only planned on beating the Indian while he was urinating, not killing him. He went outside and walked around the side street towards the back of the dance hall, where one of the public privies on Rose Street was located. He passed the backside of the dance hall and could see the lantern light inside of the public privy that was separated with a long bench seat with multiple holes on one side, and a long trough on the floor for urinating on the other side of a privacy wall in between. Wes walked towards it with a wicked sneer forming on his lips. Unexpectedly, Wes felt a driving foot collapsing his knee to the ground and he fell face forward into the packed frozen snow. He tried to stand but felt a sharp knife blade pressed against his throat. On his knees with a knife to his throat and a hand holding a fistful of hair, he heard Chusi's voice speaking in his ear.

"I knew you would follow me if I called you a woman. I could pee on your back right now and there's nothing you could do about it. I could take your scalp!" He hissed brutally under a lowered voice as he moved his knife up to Wes's hairline and dug the blade into Wes's skin, just a touch. "But I don't want your filthy scalp." He lowered his knife and turned the edge upwards and put it across Wes's upper lip at the base of his nose. "I want your pig snout of a nose!"

"Don't," Wes cried out in a shaken voice. "I said we were even."

Chusi shook his head bitterly with a snarled lip. "No, we're not!" he shouted and pulled the blade upwards, slicing through Wes's cartridge of his nose straight up almost to the bone.

Wes screamed in pain and grabbed his nose as blood flowed between his fingers.

Chusi, still holding his hair, lowered his head to Wes's ear and said, "I'll see you soon. It's not over!" He shoved Wes's head down and kicked him forward with a hard push.

Wes stood up and looked around, but Chusi was already gone in the darkness. "I'll kill you!" he screamed. "I'm going to kill you!"

Chapter 31

The front door flew open and Joe Thorn shouted, "Billy Jo, get your ass up and get your sewing kit! We need your sewing needles!"

Billy Jo Fasana opened her bedroom door irritated. "The kids are sleeping and so was I."

Joe pointed at her warningly. "You better change your attitude, or I'll change it for you. Do you hear me?"

"Yes," she resigned and then grimaced when she saw Ritchie walk into the house with Wes Wasson. Blood had drenched the front of his shirt and dripped continuously from his nose. "Did William break his nose too?" she asked.

Ritchie glared at her. "No! That crazy old Indian slit him open."

Joe continued, "We need you to sew him back up. Here is a bottle of whiskey for the pain, and I have to get to bed. I must get up in a few hours and get to work. Can you do this on your own?" he asked sharply.

She grimaced. "You have to work on Saturday?"

"We are this weekend!" he snarled bitterly with an irritated scowl.

"Oh. Let me get my sewing kit and some rags. Ritchie, could you fill this pail with water for me?"

He shook his head. "No, I have to get to bed too."

Joe shot an angry glance at Billy Joe. "You can get your own water. His horse is outside, so he can go when you get done." He looked at Wes. "You can sleep in the chair over there or leave, but if you stay here, you have to leave when I do in the morning. Billy Jo will get you fixed up before you go, though. Goodnight."

Billy Jo looked at Wes, holding a towel over his nose. "Let me see what you have there."

He moved the towel, the three points of contact of his nostrils on his upper lip were sliced back to the bridge of his nose. "Oh, my... Okay. Let me clear the table and you lay down. I'll go get some water first."

Wes laid on his back on the dining room table with his head flat, as Billy Jo leaned over him with her sewing needle and white thread. She had washed his face clean of dried blood and grimaced. "I'm going to put one stitch in all three parts of your nostrils just to hold them in place before I finish it up. I'll do my best, but you really should see the doctor tomorrow. This is going to hurt," she said, looking down at him sympathetically.

"I can take the pain as long as I can look at you," Wes said with a painful grin.

"Shhh!" she said with an annoyed look. She

glanced at her bedroom door and whispered, "Don't talk like that, please."

"Fine," he spoke lower. "But it's true."

"Mister Wasson, your nose was nearly cut off and that's what you're thinking of?" she asked as she pushed the needle into the edge of his nostril and watched him grimace as she pushed the needle through his nostril and then down into the flesh of his upper lip and back out again and tied a knot.

He exhaled, turning a grimace into a slight grin. "Yeah. The Indian got me good, but it might've been a blessing in disguise because I could never get tired of this view," he said and added a friendly wink.

"You're incorrigible."

He chuckled slightly. "I may be a little drunk too, but I know what I like. And I'm not too far off, because you remembered my name, right?"

She looked at him with a coy smile and then grabbed his face to maneuver it where she could get the best angle for stitching the middle cartilage of his nostril. He grimaced as she pushed her needle through the severed tissue and into the flesh over his upper lip. "I told you it was going to hurt," she said as tears slipped out of his eyes.

He chuckled. "Pain's temporary. I can handle the pain. Like I said before, the view is worth the pain."

She smiled uncomfortably. "Oh, stop it. Joe's in the next room and if he heard you, he'd make you leave before I'm done. And you don't want to go walking around with half of your nose flapping around in the wind, do you?"

"No, I suppose I don't. He should be sleeping by now, right?"

"He should be, but you never know. I've never had a man lying on my table before," she whispered nervously, "He gets pretty protective over me."

"As he should be. If I had a beautiful lady living with me, I'd be careful of someone like me stealing her away too. But I'm not going to win your heart tonight, am I?" he asked with a grin.

"No. I'm Joe's woman. Now hold still," she said as she pushed the needle into the left nostril and connected it to his face. When she finished, she said, "I can sew the two outsides, but I can't get the middle of your nose. You'll have to have the doctor do that tomorrow, okay?"

"Yeah, I'll do that. I don't want a crooked nose. It might ruin my good looks."

"It might. You should be glad he left a nose to sew back on."

"Ahh, that's true," he said as she positioned herself to start sewing the remainder of his nostril together. "You do think I'm kind of handsome then, huh?"

Billy Jo shook her head with a humored grin. "You're okay. I have seen better. Are you going to tell me why someone cut your nose like this?"

"It's a long story. I'll be taking care of him in the morning, though. I'm a nice guy, but I'm not going to let this go. You know what I mean?"

"You sound like my cousin, Matt. He always says he's a nice guy, too. But he wasn't so nice the last time I spoke to him. He doesn't like Joe and was mad at me for moving back out here with him."

"Why is that?"

"Because he doesn't like Joe. None of my family does, so it kind of separates us from family functions a bit. Joe won't go. He has no use for my family at all."

"Why don't they like Joe?" He grimaced as she pushed the needle into his nostril to make another stitch.

"They just don't. They think he's mean to the kids and me," she explained as she focused on the stitch she was doing.

"Is he?"

She shrugged slowly with a sad frown coming to her lips. "No. Joe is just tired when he comes home and the kids are loud, and he can get irritated. It's the same as anywhere."

"Where'd you live before you moved out here?"

"My house. My father bought me and the kids a little house in town, but kids need their father and Joe didn't want to walk three miles to work every day, so we moved out here with him."

"Are you renting your house out to anyone?" he asked curiously.

"No. It's there if I need it."

When Billy Jo had finished, Wes sat up and looked at his nose in the mirror. It was better, but it was not perfect by any means. He would have to get to the doctor early enough to have it sewn up right. "Thank you," he said, sitting on the table.

"You're welcome. Now, if you don't mind, I have to get some sleep. I have to get up when Joe does to make him some lunch."

"I understand. You got me curious though, do you have any interest at all in renting your house out to me? I'm new in town and need a place to call home. And if you ever want to move back in, I'll either move out or share it with you and your kids. What do you say?" he asked as he put his coat on.

"Let me think about it."

"Deal. Billy Jo, it's been my honor to meet you. And I don't care if Joe hears me or not. I have yet to meet the man that can scare me. But you are one incredibly beautiful woman. If you ever want a man that will treat you right, because you deserve better than this," he nodded towards the bedroom. "You just let me know."

She looked surprised and uncomfortable all at once. "Thank you. Now goodnight, Mister Wasson."

He shook his head. "After all we have gone through tonight, I think we qualify as friends. Call me, Wes."

"Wes. Goodnight, Wes."

He put on his hat and nodded. "My dear, I think I could get used to calling you that. Until then."

When he left, Billy Jo took a deep breath and locked the door. She peeked out the window as she watched Wes ride away in the darkness.

Chapter 32

Wes didn't sleep. He had gone back to the bunkhouse where he was staying and laid down, but his nose throbbed painfully. His mind was on Chusi and his determination to take the man's scalp and tie it to his saddle for slicing his nose. He had decided to not cause any more trouble with the Indian to save the relationship with his family. The idea of joining up with the Sperry-Helms Gang had a certain appeal and sounded a bit more exciting than throwing bags of grain for a couple of dollars a day. There was a future he wanted to pursue in Branson: he liked the town and his new friends. He loved his family. The Indian wasn't worth losing all that he could have. The court of law might have condemned him for scalping an Indian, but they would not condemn him now that Chusi had attacked him. Despite the fury he had for Chusi, gentler thoughts of Billy Jo also ran through his mind. Granted, Billy Jo wasn't as pretty as the ladies in the dance hall, but for whatever the reason, she had captured his attention. He was attracted to her in every way possible at the moment, anyway. It was not hard to see she feared Joe Thorn, and he treated her poorly. One evening spent in Joe's company and Wes new Billy Jo meant little to him. A man either speaks highly of his woman or poorly and Joe found talking about her an annoyance, which spoke far more than his words did.

At first light and the sound of a bird chirping, Wes climbed out of bed and checked his weapons. He kept his horse tied out front all night and walked outside to put his rifle in its scabbard. He climbed into the saddle and moved through the fading darkness of town. He wanted to hit Chusi early before he disappeared or had a chance to walk to town. He rode to his brother-in-law, Frank's house and waited outside. He wondered if he should knock and say good morning or not. He knew he wasn't welcome, but when Chusi was dead for slicing his nose, there would no longer be a reason for them to fear. It would be justified on his part and Frank would be free of his past. The town was waking up and he could see the lantern light inside the house. Wes wanted to go inside and have a cup of coffee with his family and let them know everything was going to be alright but decided against it. The worst they could do was refuse him but being rejected by family was a painful thing that he didn't want to go through.

The front door opened and Bruce Ellison came walking out with his lunch pail and heavy coat. He stopped when he saw his uncle sitting on his horse, strangely staring at the house. "Uncle Wes?" he questioned awkwardly. He was surprised to see him so early.

Wes smirked. "Do you want a ride to work? You could hop on the back."

Bruce shook his head. "No. I enjoy the morning walk. What's wrong with your nose?" he asked curiously.

Wes grinned painfully. "Shaving mishap. Keep your razor pointed down when you sneeze, alright?"

"Sure, I'll remember that," he replied, knowing it was a lie. Wes had a mustache and goatee. "You should go in and say good morning, if you want to. I'll talk to you later."

"Take care, kid." He watched his nephew walk towards the main road that led past the sawmill and out to the mine. A sneer came to his face knowing it was Chusi who had placed the wedge of distance and acceptance between him and his family. He would win them back; he just wished he could make amends. He had time to wait for the sun to rise a bit higher to cast some light into the dark forest before he went into it. He waited until the door opened again and Frank and Paul Ellison came walking out.

Frank looked at Wes severely. "What do you want?"

Wes shook his head. "Nothing."

"If you're waiting for me to leave so you can talk to Florence, you're out of luck. She doesn't want to see you either. What kind of trouble did you get into to get your nose all messed up?" Frank asked sharply.

Wes grinned and lowered his head before raising it. "None. It was a shaving accident."

"Bull. Are you leaving? Did you come by to say goodbye?"

Wes nodded. "Yeah, that's what I'm doing. I didn't think you worked Saturdays." He could not help but feel the sadness that came over him by the reception he was getting.

Frank nodded. "Normally not, but we have a shipment going out today heading east, so we need to load about four wagons. Well, you can say goodbye to Florence if you want. She might appreciate it, but Paul and I have to go."

He shook his head. "No, it's better this way. Besides, I'll see her again. I think I'll just ride out of town with you and Paul. I'm heading south anyway." He looked at the sky and the sun was rising over the town. He walked his horse beside Frank and Paul as they walked across Premro Island and paused outside of the sawmill.

Frank faced him. "Well, maybe we'll see you again someday. Take care, Wes." He shook Wes's hand.

Wes smirked. "I will." He paused. "I didn't mean to cause you all any trouble. I mean that."

Frank sneered. "But you did. Goodbye, Wes."

He nodded sadly. "I'll see you, boys, later," he said and rode out of town towards the silver mine.

Frank grew suspicious when he noticed there was no bedroll on the back of the saddle. Wes' bedroll was left tucked under the table by the davenport in the Ellison's family room. A man wouldn't forget to tie his bedroll to his saddle before departing into the wilderness, especially a seasoned soldier like Wes. It was a very good indicator that Wes wasn't leaving town like he implied. Frank stepped towards the sawmill and then turned to watch Wes continue to ride forward. "Oh no..." he said quietly with concern on his face. He watched Wes disappear around a curve in the road. A sense of panic froze his soul.

"What is it, Pa?" Paul asked, noticing the strange expression on his father's face.

"Paul, go get started loading those wagon beds. You'll find the order list on the top of my desk. I'll be back," he said anxiously.

"Where are you going?"

"Paul, just get working and stay here! I'll be back."

"Where else am I going to go?" Paul asked innocently, as he watched his father walk quickly back towards town.

Frank walked quickly through town, wishing he was young and had better feet so he could run, but he walked as fast as he could towards Matt Bannister's house. He knew it was too early on a Saturday morning for anyone to be in the Marshal's Office. He found the single-story brick house on Franklyn Street and from a distance, he heard gunshots. "Oh, my Lord, please be with my stupid brother-in-law." He anxiously banged on the door. More shots were fired. He banged on the door again, but harder. "Marshal!" he yelled.

"Who's there?" Truet yelled through the door. He was irritated by the loud banging.

"Frank Ellison, open up I have to talk to the Marshal."

"Matt!" Truet yelled in the house as he opened the door cautiously. "Come in."

Frank stepped into the cold house with Truet standing in his long johns. "Where's Matt?"

"What's going on?" Truet asked with a yawn.

Matt came out of his room wearing a pair of pants over his long johns. His hair was loose and fell over his shoulders. For the first time, Frank realized how Indian Matt did look when his hair was loose. "What's wrong, Frank?" he asked immediately.

"I just said goodbye to Wes. He said he was leaving town, but he was going south without his bedroll. I just heard shots! By out where Chusi lives, I think."

Matt spoke urgently, "Frank, will you do me a favor and run down to the livery stable and tell them to saddle Truet's, mine and Nate's horses right now. We'll be there soon. We'll go check on Chusi." He pointed his finger at Frank with a stern expression. "I warned your brother-in-law! I warned him to leave Chusi alone."

Chapter 33

Wes tied his horse to a tree in the dark forest, pulled his rifle from its scabbard, and slowly continued on foot down the narrow brushy path towards Chusi's camp. He stayed as quiet as he could and stepped lightly, not to alert Chusi's dog. It would ruin the element of surprise if his dog began barking and revealed Wes's position. He took a few slow steps and paused to listen, but so far, all he heard were the birds chirping. He stepped further down the trail with his rifle ready to shoot in his hands. When he came to the steepest part of the hill, he stepped carefully, not to lose his footing and slip and fall. He came alongside the large fallen tree with the upright roots and paused. He knew once he crossed beyond the roots and around a bend, Chusi's camp would be in sight. He could hear the creek running and there was no scent of smoke in the air. The dog had not noticed him and he bet his last dollar that Chusi was still sleeping. He went to the upright roots and stepped down into the hole created by the roots, but his foot dropped through the snow-covered ground that was supposed there. He glanced down just in time to see a white cloth had been placed over a hole and covered by a thin layer of sprinkled snow. Below the fabric was a pit about two feet deep creating a near four foot drop with broken arrows shoved into the ground with their metal sharp arrowheads pointing upwards.

He dropped downward with all of his weight on his right foot onto the arrows. He came to a jolting stop and screamed loudly from the pain that consumed his foot. He quickly fell forward throwing his rifle as he fell and began to crawl as fast as he could to pull his foot out of the trap that had been set for him. He rolled to his back to stare in horror at two arrows stuck in his foot. One arrow penetrated the heel of his boot, driving the tip deep into his heel, while the other arrow penetrated his boot and went through the flesh of his mid-foot; the arrow exited out of the top of his boot. The arrow shafts had been broken and buried in about three inches deep in the soil. He laid on the ground screaming in anger for not recognizing the trap on one hand, but the pain that burned through his foot and the fear of being handicapped in the enemy's camp all combined to create the animalistic rage buried in the screams that his lungs bellowed out. He knew exactly how cruel and cunning Indians could be, and he was suddenly the wounded prey.

He heard Chusi's quiet laughter in the brush behind him somewhere and panic began to fill him. Sweat began to bead on his forehead as the adrenaline pumped through his veins. He reached for his rifle, but it was out of arms reach. His heart raced and his breathing became heavy as fear began to overtake him. He pulled his revolver and looked for any sign of the man that he expected to come running out the brush at any minute.

Chusi stood behind a tree above his camp with his rifle at hand. He could have shot the ex-soldier at any time, and still could but he chose not to. He waited a moment to see if Wes had come alone or brought a friend or two. He had broken some of his arrows to create his pit trap and placed the shafts precisely where Wes's boot print had stepped down on the snow the day before as a guide to where to set the arrows. To hold the arrows upright when weight was applied to them, Chusi had added just enough water to the bottom of the pit for the night's temperature to freeze the arrows solidly in place. He had watched Wes walk down towards the camp and was pleased to see his trap work perfectly. Convinced Wes had come alone, he picked up a stick and tossed it into the brush near the injured man. Wes pointed his revolver quickly in reaction and fired two shots in panic into the brush.

"You missed," Chusi said with a haunting chuckle. Three more shots were fired towards him. He chuckled loudly to let Wes know he was finding humor in Wes's torment. He picked up a river rock he had stacked by the tree and threw it in the brush. Wes swung his revolver around in alertness, the fear showed on his face, but he didn't fire his last shot.

"Come out here and fight like a man!" Wes yelled. "I'm crippled, you coward, the least you could do is come out here and fight me!"

"I will," Chusi said and gently tossed another rock that arched up in the air over the brush and came downward, landing on Wes's chest with a hard thump.

He cried out painfully. "I'm going to kill you!"

"I'm here," Chusi said as he tossed another rock that arched and fell barely missing Wes's abdomen. "I have lots of rocks."

Wes grimaced in anger and swung the revolver towards the sound of Chusi's voice and pulled the trigger. He immediately opened the cylinder and began to eject the spent shell casings to reload. He heard Chusi running down through the brush towards him and knew he didn't have time to reload his revolver. He reached for his rifle and began crawling as fast as he could towards it. He got his hand on it and started to pull it towards him when he saw a worn moccasin stomp on it. He looked up and Chusi was staring straight down at him, holding a river rock about the size of a fist over Wes's face at waist level. Chusi released the rock and it fell and bounced off Wes's nose.

Wes released his grip on the rifle and grabbed his nose painfully crying out as the rock hit the bone and flattening the cartridge, ripping the stitches through the flesh of his nose. He rolled back and forth, squirming in pain as the blood flowed from his nose and split skin. Chusi tossed the rifle away and sat down on Wes's chest. Wes began to fight for his life as Chusi tried to pin Wes's arms under his knees. Wes refused to surrender and physically fought to keep his arms free. He had a knife in its sheath on his gun belt, but he could not take a moment to try to grab it without losing control of Chusi's right arm. Wes held one wrist of Chusi's and Chusi held the other wrist of Wes's, neither man was willing to let go and both strained desperately to get control of the other man. Wes was the much stronger of the two, younger and more accustomed to fighting, but he was limited to what he could do. He would have liked to have bridged up on his feet and rolled Chusi off him, but he could barely move his right foot without being paralyzed by the pain.

Chusi saw an opening and head-butted Wes's face, causing his already fractured nose to break. The severity of the pain loosened Wes's grip and brought his arms automatically nearer to his face to protect it. Chusi, expecting that reaction, was ready to maneuver his knees to trap Wes's arms under his knees and control him. Chusi pulled his knife out of the sheath with his right hand and swung it back behind him to jab it into the top muscle of Wes's left thigh. He twisted the blade to cause more damage and bring more pain. It made it harder for Wes to use his good leg to push off while trying to dislodge Chusi. With that done, Chusi grabbed Wes's hair with his left hand and held Wes's head firmly in place.

Wes's watering eyes widened as he stared at Chusi. His voice pleaded with desperation, "Please, don't do it! Please..."

Chusi moved his blade to the hairline and with a wide swath, he drove the blade downward and ripped Wes's scalp off. Wes screamed in agonizing pain and began sobbing.

Chusi stood up and walked away for a moment and then came back and grabbed Wes's arms and drug him into his camp over between the two bowed trees he had tied off on a larger birch tree. Chusi slipped one of the slip knots tied to one tree over Wes's left wrist and the other slip knot he placed over his right wrist. He picked Wes up to stand on his left foot. He was groaning and physically faint from the level of pain he was enduring.

"Just kill me," Wes said softly.

Chusi looked at him mercilessly. "You'll wish for me to very soon."

Chusi stepped over to the larger birch tree and cut one of the ropes causing the young tree to spring upwards, yanking Wes up sharply with it and dislocating his shoulder. Chusi cut the other rope and the other tree sprang upward, yanking Wes two feet off the ground sharply dislocating his other shoulder as well. Wes screamed in pain and began sobbing while begging Chusi to kill him.

Chusi stood in front of him and smirked. Wes's scalp was gone and blood covered his face as it dripped consistently onto his clothing. His nose was deformed and one nostril flapped in and out as he breathed. Blood dripped from his boot off the arrow shafts and he would never look the same, walk the same or be the same again. "Look at me," Chusi said, getting Wes's attention. "I wanted your blood and I have it. I will not kill you; you will kill yourself, or you will live to be old and always look as hideous as you are. That is my revenge for what you have done to my people." He smiled with pleasure. "Your scalp is mine. Forget me not, as I was unable to forget my wife and children. Today vengeance is mine."

"You'll hang for this," he mumbled.

Chusi smirked with pleasure. "Death does not scare me. I lived for this day and the day has come. If I hang, I will still smile when I think of you. I see you now and my heart is joyful, like a fawn in the meadow. Yes, I am pleased."

Wes began weeping as he spat out some blood he was choking on from his nose.

"You must be cold. Let me make a fire." Chusi said and began stacking wood up under where Wes's feet hung above the ground.

Wes began kicking his feet and screaming in a panic to stop Chusi from making a fire underneath him. Every moment and movement he made was agonizing under the weight of hanging by his dislocated shoulders. However, the thought of his feet being roasted over a fire was too much to bear. He kicked and begged through his panic-stricken tears to stop the unimaginable torture of being burned alive.

Chusi laughed. "I'm tricking you. That's funny, yeah?"

"Let me go, please," he mumbled through his heavy breathing.

Chusi shook his head. "No. You deserve no

mercy. Hang there and consider the harm you've brought to others. The families you destroyed and the money you collected off the death of others. My people are no different than you. You, me, do we not both love our families equally? You bleed when your scalp is taken, the same as my family and all you have taken. You cry and scream the same as my people did! You will face the same creator as I will. I've done wrong, and I ask forgiveness from my Creator, but you have done more wrong! Men like you call my people heathens, but when have I ever done what you have done? I could kill you, but the worst I could do is let you live and so I will. Sooner or later, they will come to find you. If not, you can crawl like a slug leaving a trail of blood back to town."

Chapter 34

They collected their horses and woke up Nate Robertson to take him along with them out to Chusi's camp. Matt led the way and turned off the road onto the trail to Chusi's. They rode through the forest and found Wes's horse tied to a limb. They dismounted and tied their horses, and Matt led the way down the path. They could hear groaning as they got closer and knew someone was hurt but didn't know what they would find. Matt motioned for everyone to be quiet and wondered where Chusi's dog was and why it had not started barking yet. He came to the big fallen tree and remembered Chusi's words to go around it, but it would cause too much noise and invite an ambush if one was so inclined. He went to the roots and saw the pit with three arrows sticking upwards. He now understood why Chusi was acting so differently the day before and warned Matt to go around the tree. He hopped over the pit, making sure Truet and Nate saw it as well. He could see spots of blood in the snow and where a scuffle had taken place before the apparent trail of someone being dragged into the camp. Matt had no doubt it was Wes that had been dragged.

"Chusi, I'm coming in!" Matt yelled as he stepped around a curve along the creek and entered the camp. Matt's eyes went to Wes, who was covered in blood and hanging by two tall young trees by his wrists. He was barely conscious. He was horrified to see Wes in the condition he was in. Matt was filled with fury when he saw Wes's scalp setting on a larger river rock for Wes to look at as he hung there. "Chusi!" Matt yelled. He could see faint blue smoke coming out of the top of the teepee and figured Chusi was in there. He wasn't afraid of Chusi attacking him and his men, but he was cautious.

"Oh, Lord..." Truet said, appalled.

Nate stared in horror and began breathing harder.

Matt pointed towards Wes and spoke to Truet softly, "Let's get him down and back to town. Keep your eyes open for Chusi coming out of that teepee with a weapon. Nate, help Truet get Wes on his horse and then I want you to run into town and warn the doctors he's coming. Tell them to be ready!" Matt lifted Wes's chin and to look at his eyes. "We're going to get you to the doctors as fast as we can, Wes. Your scalp's over there and Lord willing, the doctors can sew that back on for you. Okay? This is going to hurt a lot, but we have to move you. Try to grit your teeth and bear it."

Wes mumbled something unintelligible. He was

near unconsciousness.

Matt pointed at the removed scalp. "Nate, take that scalp to Doctor Ryland and don't you forget it! Maybe they can sew that back on!" He looked back at Wes and shook his head. "Chusi!" he yelled loudly. "Oh, forget it, I'll take care of him in a minute, let's get Wes down and to the doctors." He helped his two deputies cut Wes down. Once he was laid on the ground softly, Truet and Nate found it nearly impossible to carry him by the shoulders and knees due to his crying out in pain from his shoulder's being dislocated. Matt and Nate stood Wes upright and held him as Truet wrapped his arms around Wes's waist and lifted him over Truet's shoulder.

"Are you going to be able to carry him out like that?" Matt asked. "I can grab a blanket from the teepee probably, to lay him on if that would be easier."

Truet shook his head. "No, it would be too clumsy for either of us to walk backwards up that hill. He's heavy, but I can get him up there to his horse."

Matt watched as Truet carried Wes around the corner, followed by Nate with the scalp and their rifles. Wes groaned and wept as they did so. With Wes being taken care of, Matt put his attention on finding Chusi.

Matt pulled his revolver and walked to the front of the teepee, where he heard the dog whine inside. He stood back and lifted the elk hide cover to peek inside. Chusi was sitting near a small fire cross-legged with the dog's head on his lap while he petted it.

Chusi looked up at Matt. "Sit with me, my friend."

A blanket had been spread across the ground for him to sit on. Matt stepped inside and shook his head. "You took his hair; you're under arrest."

Chusi smiled contently. "Yes. I knew you would come before too long. He would have taken mine if I had not taken his. I see no crime in that. Please sit with me for a moment."

"There is a crime in that!" Matt exclaimed heatedly. "I told you if you protected yourself it was one thing, but taking his hair and hanging him like a dead deer to freeze out there isn't acceptable to the law. We don't live by the codes of the Shoshone; what you did is a brutal crime!"

Chusi grinned sadly. "I offered to make him a fire to keep his feet warm."

Matt was not humored. "I saw that. The pit trap would have been enough. He has two arrows through his foot. That should have been enough," Matt stated severely.

Chusi shook his head contently. "No. Now it is enough. He will live forever, scaring women and children with the hideous of his flesh being as hideous as his soul. I did not kill him for that reason. Long after I am gone, he will still remember me. Just as I had to remember my Omusa and children without their hair." His eyes had gone dark.

Matt sighed. "The doctors can sew his scalp back on and he will heal. All you have done is guarantee that you'll be found guilty. I didn't want to have to arrest you," Matt said with a heavy heart. He knew the court of law in Branson would not give him a fair trial nor seek justice, only punishment. "I told you not to take his hair. I might have been able to help you, but there's nothing I can do now, except take you in."

Chusi pet his dog lovingly. "I gave Omusa's dress and moccasins to Christine last night after I left you. She is beautiful in it, you will see." He looked at Matt. "I knew you would come and take me with you. I am not sorry for what I've done. You told me he would not come here. He told me we were even himself at Christine's. So I ambushed him and cut his nose to bring him here to me today. He had no chance. You would have no chance either if I wanted to kill you and your deputies."

Matt looked at him, harshly, but chose to ignore his last sentence. "That explains why Wes is here. You set him up."

Chusi smiled and nodded. "I did. He ran into the trap as blindly as a rabbit. I was very pleased." They could hear Wes scream from up the hill. "I still am."

"Congratulations. You have guaranteed yourself a one-way trip to the hangman's platform."

Chusi shrugged uncaringly. "I am old and ready to see Omusa and our children again. I will not fight you, my friend. I will not fight the court or the end they give me. But if they do not give a good end, I will make a good end happen."

Matt said, "These are your last few moments of being free. Is there anything you want to do or say?"

Chusi looked around his teepee. "This is all

yours now. Keep it and use it someday; my rifle, my traps, my skins, my bow and arrows. I do not have much, but what I do have is yours. Come take this teepee down and store it until you use it. My dog is yours too."

Matt raised his eyebrows distastefully. "Your dog is a nightmare."

Chusi looked at him sincerely. "Can I keep my dog in jail with me?"

Matt shook his head. "Not this time."

Chusi untied his knife sheath from his waist and handed it to Matt. "For you. May it cut swiftly for all time." It was a deer horn handle over a steel blade.

"Thank you. I think you're too good of a man to end like this."

He nodded sadly. "Sit with me and enjoy the fire for a little while, Matt. It's the last one I'll be able to see."

Matt frowned and sat down. "You know I'm a Christian because we've talked about that before. Do you know anything about the Bible or what it says?"

Chusi frowned and responded. "The old days were good. Until the good became bad. Today I collected the blood owed to me. Today is a good day. We can leave when you are ready. I am happy to leave here and be with my family again."

"We'll leave after we have a conversation. Do you know anything about the Bible?"

Chusi looked at him. "After the soldiers attacked our camp, the Mormons helped us. One man read to me from the Bible. The story of a strong warrior named Samson, his wife and her family was killed too and Samson got his vengeance by killing many men for their crimes. I wanted Wes's blood and I have it."

Matt stared at him awkwardly. "Yes, you did and you're going to pay for it with your life. It wasn't worth it."

Chusi smirked slightly. "To me, it is. It was to Samson too."

"Was it? Do you know what happened to Samson?"

"He got revenge."

Matt nodded. "Yes, he did. But there's more to the story than that. God gave Samson supernatural strength, but there were three rules he had to keep; no alcohol, no touching a rotting corpse and he could never cut his hair. The Philistines would not allow the Israelites to have any weapons so that they couldn't rebel and win their country back. Samson never used any weapon other than his hands or what he could find on the ground. The only weapon the Bible mentions is a fresh jawbone from a donkey and he killed hundreds of men with that in a big battle. Samson was undoubtedly the greatest warrior that ever lived. He was unbeatable. But Samson had one significant weakness, beautiful Philistine women. He has a reputation now for being a fool, perhaps even a stupid man, I think he was just a human being and gave into temptation like many of us do. The Bible says *he saw* a beautiful woman two or three times. One was the woman he wanted to marry; unfortunately, she married Samson's best man, because he had left the wedding party angry over losing a bet. He went to get what he owed and was gone long enough that her father gave her to Samson's friend. Samson came back much later and discovered his beloved belonged to someone else. To get even, he burned all the wheat fields that belonged to the Philistines. He hoped to starve them out of his land. The Philistines thought Samson was burning the fields because of what the woman's father did to him, so they killed Samson's beloved woman along with her father and their family by burning them alive in their house. What they hoped would appease Samson brought him back for revenge and he killed the Philistines responsible for killing her.

"The most important beautiful woman he saw was a prostitute named Delilah. The Bible says he loved her. We do know he spent the night with her a lot and the Philistines knew that too. So, they offered Delilah a lot of money to find out the secret to where his unnatural strength comes from. Three times she tried to prod it out of him and he'd lie. He would make something up and in the morning, his hands were tied with whatever he said, or his hair was weaved in a loom as he said. Delilah would wake him up by saying, 'The Philistines are here,' and he'd jump out of bed and break the binds she tied him with. It had become a joke, a fun little playful joke that he didn't take seriously. Finally, she used her tears to make him feel guilty for saying he loved her, but not trusting her enough to be honest with her. The Bible says he opened his heart up to her and told her everything. That night she sent word to the Philistines to bring her money and arrest him in the morning because she knew Samson had told her the truth. While he slept, she cut his hair off. In the morning, all of the joking the times before had come back to haunt him. This time the Philistines were there and his strength was gone. The Bible says, 'God's spirit had left him' and he was no stronger or more significant than anyone else. The Philistines had suffered many defeats because of Samson and they were excited to have him in their jail. So excited that they burned his eyes out and turned him into a blind slave. He was blind because *he saw* a beautiful woman that he should never have loved and she betrayed him for money. She was a prostitute."

"Worse, than just becoming a blind slave though, the Philistines mocked the very man God had set apart to lead his Nation. Samson was once a great warrior and a man the Philistines feared, but he had become a circus freak if you will. They made him dance and laughed at him, and who knows what other humiliating things they said and did to God's chosen leader. He was born a Nazarite and that is an extraordinary privilege. He was meant to free Israel from the Philistines, but he broke all three rules given to him and failed big time. Samson had his days of vengeance, but in the end, he had nothing except shame, humiliation and unmerciful regret. One day the Philistines were having a big celebration in a stadium and brought Samson out to entertain the crowd. They wanted to laugh at him, mock him and say, look at the great warrior now. While the Philistines in the stadium were laughing at God's chosen servant, Samson asked a servant boy, most likely a Jewish slave boy, to place his hands on the support pillars. Samson prayed for God to restore his strength one last time to end his life and the lives of the enemy of God's people. Immediately, God filled Samson with probably more power than he ever had before. While the Philistines were laughing, he destroyed the stadium they were in and killed them all, including himself. How do we know it happened, because that Jewish slave boy was probably told by Samson to run before he brought it all down. There's always more to the Bible than meets the eye at first glance. That is the story of Samson in a quick lesson because it's about much more than just vengeance. When I think of Samson, I think of God's grace. Samson sinned and broke every rule God told him not to break. He failed to live the life God had set out for him to live, but even so, God never left Samson. When the time was right, God answered that prayer and took Samson home. In the book of Hebrews, there is a list of people known for their great faith and Samson is listed there as an honored man. We could look at Samson's life and say what an idiot he was, but the truth is, are we so different? Samson failed to serve God the way he was meant to and so do we. God still made sure Samson's name was honored for the life he lived because of his faith. You see, Samson put his faith in God and not into his own strength. He knew without God; he was nothing at all. Neither are we."

Matt continued, "Every day we sin and sin is like falling into the cesspool under the privy behind the dance hall. Let's say you fell through the rotting floor of the privy into eight feet of crap and that stinking filth covered you from head to toe, would Christine let you walk into her house on her perfectly white rug and sit on her white chairs to eat dinner?"

Chusi shook his head. "No."

"You already know that, huh? It's the same thing with heaven, Chusi. We cannot go into heaven with sin on us. God sent his Son, Jesus, into the world with limited powers so he could feel everything we feel and live as we do. Jesus got hungry, so he ate, tired, so he slept and when his heart was broken, he wept. Jesus never sinned though, so he had no filth on him. He had more supernatural power than anyone on this earth ever had or will have and could have done just about anything to spare himself from being crucified on the cross. He could have blinded everyone as the angels did in Sodom, he could have called down a bunch of Angels to save himself from the pain and the suffering he was to endure. But all of us would be lost for eternity if he had because we have all sinned and no sin is allowed in heaven. However, Jesus allowed himself to be tortured, mocked, beaten and willingly went through the suffering and excruciating pain of being crucified. What you did out there to Wes is nothing compared to what Jesus went through and he endured it because he loves us. He died for our sins and gave us the gift of salvation through him to be with him in heaven when we die. Jesus paid for the consequences for our sins on the cross so that we can be free of sin and able to walk and sit on those white rugs and chairs in heaven. Jesus was resurrected and is very much alive and well today. Jesus is God and he wants to forgive our sins and have a personal relationship with us. The Creator of everything, even the stars, wants us to talk to him like a friend, like a father and he loves us enough never to leave us, just like he never left Samson. The more we pick up our Bibles and read it, the more we will live for him and his will in our lives. We are helpless to ever get to heaven without accepting Jesus as our Lord and Savior and that starts by simply inviting Jesus to be your Savior. The Bible says, 'For God so loved the world that he gave his only begotten son for whoever believes upon him, shall have eternal life.' That's called the Gospel, and it is good news because it can change your life. Accepting Jesus and asking Him to forgive your sins can lead to a changed heart and a life of more peace. When we die, we either go to heaven or go to hell. With Jesus as our Lord and Savior, we go to heaven. It's a promise."

Matt took a breath and looked at Chusi, "I want to see you in heaven someday and be friends for eternity. You need to decide on accepting Jesus and I hope you do before it's too late."

Chusi looked at Matt with a small smile. "That would be a good end for us, my friend."

Chapter 35

Matt led his horse by the reins as he walked beside
Chusi on the road back to town. He knew there
would be outrage when the townspeople heard
what Chusi had done. The townspeople would
have no knowledge of why Chusi did what he did,
but they would condemn him, and if allowed, they
would take Chusi by force and hang him the same
way they lynched Martin Ballenger. Indians were
not part of the white society and Chusi's reputation
as the town drunk, a vagrant, and unwholesome
character had already led many to prejudge him
as human filth. The news of him doing the most
hideous of things to a white man for no apparent
reason would be looked at as an act of war. There
was no other justice for an act of war than death.
Matt's heart grew heavier with each step towards
town. He expected a group of vigilantes to come
riding out of town to find them at any minute. He
would protect Chusi with his life to give him his
day in court, even though Matt knew the outcome

of that day already.

As they walked in silence, Chusi asked, "When you take the angel, Christine, as your bride, maybe she could wear Omusa's dress?"

Matt raised his eyebrows. "Maybe. That is up to Christine."

"You wouldn't mind her wearing a Shoshone dress?"

Matt smiled sadly. "I wouldn't mind at all. If Christine likes it, she can wear it. Do you want her to wear it?"

Chusi nodded. "Omusa was the most beautiful woman in the world to me. The world was a beautiful place. The first time I saw her in her marriage dress, I knew my life would be a paradise from that day forward. And it was. Now that dress is all the world has left of her." He looked at Matt with tears in his eyes. "When I saw Christine in Omusa's dress, it was as if Omusa was alive again. Yes, it would be good for that memory of her to become beautiful again when she marries you."

Matt looked at his friend, appreciatively. "I'll let her know that."

They walked in silence once more when Chusi spoke, "I have never scalped anyone before. I do not like it. I never wanted to kill him. I have never wanted to hurt anyone. If Wes had never said a word to me, I would never have known. I wish it were like that."

"What about Frank Ellison? Would you have recognized him eventually?"

Chusi paused. "I have seen him in town before. I

looked at him and wondered, but I could not say for sure if he was the one. I will not harm an innocent man for the blood he did not cause. After Wes spoke to me that night, then I knew. And I wanted to spill their blood until they had not a drop left to give. Rage filled me. Now, as we walk the last walk into town, I think of Samson. The blood I longed for only satisfied for a moment. Maybe instead of my eyes being blinded out, they've been opened to my wrongs. I should not have scalped him. I could've smiled again with your children someday."

Matt's eyes filled with thick tears. He squeezed his lips together tightly. "We would've liked that."

"I could have seen Christine in Omusa's dress again and celebrated with you and her. Maybe I could have learned to smile without a drink and laugh as easily as I once did if I had a new family to share it with. Maybe I would not be made fun of like Samson, but stronger as a man. Maybe people would respect me again as my people did years ago. Maybe I'd go back to my people and let them see a man of strength again."

Matt remained quiet to let Chusi talk. They had walked a little way in silence when Chusi said, "I wish I would have listened to you. My rage would not allow it, though; the words Wes would say made the memory of my family run through my mind. I was afraid he would not come back to my camp if I did not mark his nose last night. I should not have done that."

Matt wanted to agree, but it was pointless to say when a man already knew he was wrong. He walked casually and waited for Chusi to continue.

"Death comes for me soon and now I see the time wasted. Now I see what Truet tried to tell me. Christine's husband was killed too and now she loves you. Truet loves your sister and I wasted twenty-one years on an angry memory and even now, with the man's blood on my hands, I feel worse than I did before. And Omusa and my children are still nowhere to be found."

Matt took a deep breath as they got closer to town. The lumberyard of the sawmill was in view and the town was just beyond the mill. Matt spoke, "Don't be surprised if vigilantes come for you. If that happens, stay behind me. I won't let them take you."

"If too many come, you only have six bullets in your gun. You may not be able to save me, so do not try. Let them take me to my grave. Christine needs you alive, not dying to save an old man like me."

Matt smiled sadly. "I think they'll back off if they come at all. As we go through town, stay close," he said. They would be in Branson in a matter of ten minutes if they walked at the same slow casual pace.

"I'll not worry. I know you'll keep me safe," Chusi said with a wry smile at his friend.

"I'll do my…" A shot rang out and a bullet ripped into Chusi's chest, knocking him to his back on the road.

Matt pulled his revolver and quickly ducked under and around his horse's neck and aimed over the saddle towards the lumberyard. He saw Frank

Ellison standing upright while raising his carbine rifle above his head to surrender from behind a stack of boards.

Frank stepped out from behind a stack of boards with his rifle still held up in his right hand. "Don't shoot, Marshal! I'm the only one here." He walked towards Matt.

Matt kept his revolver on Frank as he maneuvered back behind his horse and knelt beside Chusi, who was taking his last breaths. He yelled forcefully at Frank, "Throw your rifle over there and sit down! If you move, I'll fill you up with lead!" Frank did as he was ordered. Matt put his attention back on Chusi. The bullet was of a higher caliber and had torn through Chusi's lungs. He could barely breathe and gasped for air with droplets of blood coming out of his mouth. Chusi looked at Matt with water in his eyes. Matt spoke quickly, "Be like Sampson and ask Jesus to forgive you now while you can. It's not too late while you still have a breath." Matt's chest heaved with emotion as he watched his friend dying.

"Al...ready did," he struggled to say. His lips turned upwards into a slight smile. "Like ... Samson."

Matt tried to smile comfortingly, but his eyes filled with tears and his lips twitched from hearing Chusi's words. "You'll be okay, my friend."

Chusi's eyes appeared to focus on something above him and a peaceful expression came over his face. "I...see..." he gasped and breathed his last. Blood came out of his mouth. Matt looked upwards and sighed as he fought to control the water in his eyes. His tears slipped out and ran down his face despite his effort to restrain them. He stood up and took a few deep breaths to regain control of himself. He holstered his revolver.

Frank stood up and spoke carefully, "I'm sorry, Matt. But I couldn't let him get away with what he did to Wes. I saw Wes when Truet brought him by. The man needed to die for what he did. I wasn't going to take a chance of him doing that to me or any of my family members! No, sir, he deserved to die, so I shot him!"

Matt looked at Frank with a snarl on his lips. Matt drew his revolver and pointed it at Frank. He yelled, "By that logic, I should kill you! He didn't kill Wes, but he certainly could have if he wanted to! Wes went there to kill him; it was self-defense! You know that because you told me about it! Wes comes back hurt and you killed Chusi because you are what? Seeking vengeance or scared? He was in my custody and would pay for what he had done, but you robbed him of his day in court. You robbed him of ever telling a jury what you and your brother-in-law had done to him. And now you killed him too. Let me ask you, Frank, how does it feel to murder an entire family that never meant you any harm?" He pointed down at Chusi's body. "He had the decency to forgive you. He had the decency to spare Wes's life when Wes went to his camp to kill him. But you killed him without saying a word! Who's the damn savage, Frank? Because it sure as hell isn't him!" Matt yelled.

Frank looked down at the ground and then back up at Matt. "At least, we don't have to worry about him coming after us anymore."

Matt holstered his revolver and quickly stepped towards Frank.

Frank sputtered, "I'm not going to fight you, Marshal! Arrest me if you want to, but I'm not fighting you!"

"He was no threat to you!" Matt shouted and swung a hard-right fist that connected to Frank's face sending him down to the ground.

Frank shook his head and wiped a bit of blood from his nose. He looked up at Matt and said, "You know as well as I do that he deserved to die. He hurt my family, so I got even."

Matt shook his head in disbelief. "You're like the servant in the Bible who was forgiven millions of dollars and then threw a man in prison for not paying you the two bits he owed you. Except you murdered him. Stand up. You are under arrest for the murder of Chusi Yellowbear. A prisoner who was in my custody and my friend."

Chapter 36

Once again, for reasons he did not understand, Matt was summoned to the courthouse unexpectedly at five o clock with the requirement of bringing Frank Ellison with him. He entered the courtroom with Frank's hands shackled in front of him, and they sat down on a courtroom bench to wait. The District Attorney, named Jackson Weathers, stopped by Matt's office earlier and requested the neccesary reports of the day's events and the arrest report for Frank Ellison. It was Saturday and the request was quite unusual. Matt had an emotional morning and then had to write reports about Wes Wasson, Chusi Yellowbear and the murder of Chusi by Frank Ellison. The reports were long, detailed, based on facts without any emotional input. When he was finished, it was near three o'clock, when he gave the report to Jackson. It wasn't too uncommon for the District Attorney to read through any arrest reports and set bail or release the prisoners before the weekend came if the offense wasn't too serious on a Friday. However, being summoned to the courthouse with a First-Degree Murder suspect after closing time on a Saturday when the courthouse was closed was unheard of and irritated Matt greatly.

Matt furrowed his brow curiously when he noticed a long table set up in front of Judge Jacoby's bench with William Slater and his son, Josh, sitting at the table. Standing in front of them, Wu-Pen Tseng petitioned the City Council to allow the Chinese Benevolence Society to join the Branson Business Association. Matt shook his head with disgust because it was not a formal City Council meeting; it was a ruse. Josh Slater wasn't on the City Council and no other City Council members were there except for William Slater. Wu Pen was explaining why he wanted his organization to become a part of the business association and how the Chinese community could help serve the city in several ways.

William Slater cut Wu-Pen off uncaringly, "Chinese are not Americans and no, we're not about to let some foreigners pretend like they are. You people are only here until the railroad is completed and then you're gone. We'll run you all out of here just as fast as we can. We don't need your cooks, doctors, laundrymen, or whatever else you have up your dingy sleeves. You people are cheap labor and that's all. Your petition is denied. Good day," he said with finality and stood up to leave. Almost as soon as Josh and William R. Slater walked out of the courtroom, Sheriff Tim Wright and one of his deputies removed the table and two chairs.

Wu-Pen appeared to be irritated and deep in thought as he walked between the two rows of court benches. He looked at Matt curiously and motioned for his two guards, Bing Jue and Uang Young, to remain seated. He smiled at Matt and sat down himself. He spoke in Chinese to his guards to settle their curiosity.

The District Attorney, Jackson Weathers, took his place behind the Prosecutors table on the right side of the courtroom and waited for Judge Jacoby to start the procedures. Judge Jacoby looked at Matt. "Marshal Bannister, do you want to bring the accused to the defendant's chair, please."

Matt furrowed his brow. It was most irregular, and he had never had anything in court happen like this without some legal notification, at least. There was no jury nor anyone else in the courtroom except Frank's family and Wu-Pen and his two guards. Matt led Frank across from the District Attorney and waited. The District Attorney read the report from Matt and then read the doctor's report on the wounds of Wes Wasson and the doctor's cause of death report of Chusi. When he had finished, the District Attorney, Jackson Weathers, said, "This is the indictment hearing of Franklyn Dean Ellison. He is accused of First-Degree Murder in the preplanned assassination of the deceased, Chusi Yellowbear, on Silver Road near the sawmill's lumberyard this morning at around nine-thirty. I have had a chance to go over all the documents from the Marshal's Office, Medical reports and the cause of death report as well. There is no need for an autopsy. There is no doubt that the accused did pull the trigger and intentionally did kill, Mister Yellowbear. It was quite intentional as told by the accused to the Marshal at the time of the incident, your Honor. We have no reason to doubt that. What we have not heard is the defendant's testimony to know if the killing was justifiable or not."

Judge Jacoby looked at Frank. "Mister Ellison, do you have anything to add? An explanation, perhaps?"

Frank stood next to Matt. He nodded. "I do. I was a sergeant in the California Volunteer Calvary in 1863. On the morning of January 29th, we were ordered to attack the winter camp of the Shoshone tribe. We massacred them. Men, women and children, God forgive me. I killed Chusi Yellowbear's family, his wife and three children. I remember them. I had him in my sights too, but I was out of bullets. He barely missed me with an arrow. I remember that too. My brother-in-law, Wes Wasson, was there as well. He mentioned it to Chusi and our lives have been threatened ever since. The Marshal had arrested Chusi for acting like a madman and I went and asked Chusi for his forgiveness. He told me that he wanted blood for blood. In Indian terms, that meant he intended to kill my wife, my two boys, myself and Wes too. A life for a life. This morning, I watched Wes ride out towards Chusi's and I knew he was going there to end the threats. I went and got the Marshal, but he got there too late. Mister Weathers read what the

Marshal found when he got there. Well, I work in the lumberyard as a supervisor and we had wagons to load, so I watched as Deputy Marshal, Truet Davis brought my brother-in-law back to town. He was a bloody mess. I know him and I know how tough he is, he was in so much pain that he was whimpering. I saw the depth of depravity that Chusi did to Wes and it scared me. I didn't know if Chusi had killed the Marshal or what was taking so long, so I ran home and got my rifle. Please understand, I could not afford for Chusi to escape from the Marshal's supervision and ambush my family in the middle of the night. I could not take that chance, so when he came into view, I shot him. Your Honor, my brother-in-law, was scalped clean of his hair! His arms don't work; he has arrows through his foot. His nose is nearly gone. He's lucky to be alive and if Matt hadn't gotten there, he wouldn't be! Wes isn't the one who killed his wife and children. I am! Just imagine what he would do to my wife or my sons. That is what I was thinking about when I aimed and pulled the trigger today. I was protecting my family, plain and simple."

Matt offered, "Just so the court remembers, I'm not a lawyer and Frank Ellison does not have any legal representation nor from my knowledge has he spoken to anyone except his family. Also, I will state for the record, Chusi was in my custody when he was executed. Because that's what it was, an execution. Chusi had no intention of harming Mister Ellison or his family and Frank knows that because Chusi asked me to take him to the Ellison's home, so he could forgive Mister Ellison. He gave his word and he would have kept it because he knew Frank was sincerely sorry for what he had done. And quite frankly, Chusi had more honor to his word than most people do."

Jackson Weathers asked, "Mister Ellison, was Chusi shackled when he was in the Marshal's custody?"

"No, sir. His hands were as free as yours."

"But, your hands are shackled for the walk of four blocks to here?"

"Yes, Sir."

Jackson looked at the Judge. "It seems the Marshal knew exactly how dangerous the deceased could be since he found Wes Wasson in the condition he was in, but did not think the deceased was dangerous enough to shackle when he arrested him. But surely, Mister Ellison is shackled even as we stand here."

Judge Jacoby asked, "Marshal, can you explain why Mister Yellowbear was not restrained for the walk into town? He could have overcome you and escaped if I understand correctly. And then Mister Ellison would be correct to have reason to fear."

Matt shook his head. "Chusi was my friend. He was coming along willingly."

"That doesn't answer my question."

Matt narrowed his eyes with irritation. "I didn't have time to grab my shackles when Frank came over this morning."

Jackson Weathers spoke quickly, "Your honor, I find it questionable at best that because the deceased was his friend, the Marshal didn't find it 'necessary to follow basic safety procedures of a lawman. On the contrary, the character of Frank Ellison is questioned by the shackles still upon his wrists in the courtroom. Frank Ellison has always been an outstanding citizen of our community, a responsible foreman at the sawmill, he was a sergeant at the time of the massacre but was promoted to a Lieutenant in the California Volunteer Cavalry and served our country with honor. He is a military officer, a good husband and a good father, a Christian and a respected man in all ways. Chusi Yellowbear, by contrast, was a drunkard, often passing out in the alleyways on Rose Street. He begged for money to drink with, never bathed, and was a...how should I put this, a vagrant and blemish to our city's reputation as a family community. Chusi was just arrested this week for wildly and uncontrollably brandishing a knife and, in the Marshal's own words, could have killed somebody in his drunken fit of rage."

"Therefore, as the Jessup County District Attorney, I do not doubt that Mister Ellison had reason to fear for his own and his family's lives and acted reasonably to protect his home. I recommend the court drops all charges against Lieutenant Frank Dean Ellison. I believe that self-preservation is a legitimate cause for justifiable homicide. I recommend the court allow the accused to be released and allowed to go home to his family immediately. The family has a long road ahead to heal the only real victim of today's events, Wes Wasson."

Matt shook his head irritated; He knew it was coming.

Judge Jacoby spoke, "Marshal, please release the prisoner. Mister Ellison, all charges against you are dismissed. You are free to leave."

Matt released the shackles and watched Frank hug his wife and leave with his family.

"Matt," the District Attorney Jackson Weathers said, handing him an envelope. "This came to my office today. It's a wire from the Aurora County District Attorney."

Matt took it without looking at it. "Do you argue with yourself in the mirror, Jack? I'm not sure if you were a District Attorney or a defense lawyer today."

"I'm just doing my job, Matt. If a man has a justifiable reason, I'm not going to prosecute him. You should know that."

"And Chusi?"

Jackson shrugged. "Reread your reports and you tell me. He was a threat and there are no two ways about that. And there's no reason for Frank to stay in jail all weekend either and that's why we're here today. Like you, I serve this community, too. Have a great weekend, Matt."

"So, it has nothing to do with his being your personal friend, huh?" Matt asked. He had heard Jackson Weathers and the Ellison family were good friends. It explained how and why Jackson could arrange the indictment hearing within hours on a Saturday.

Jackson nodded with a smirk. "That too, yep. Take care, Marshal."

Matt opened the envelope and read the wire and shook his head. "Are you kidding me?" he asked loudly. It was a notice stating that all the charges against Bo Crowe had been dropped. He was to be released from jail immediately.

"Unbelievable," Matt said with disgust.

He could see Wu-Pen waiting to talk to him.

"Marshal, my upmost sincerity for the loss of your friend, Chusi. I will have another dessert made for you. If there is anything I can do, please let me know," Wu-Pen said.

"Thank you. William Slater wouldn't let you join their club, huh?" Matt asked about the business association.

Wu-Pen made a sad exaggerated expression. "No. But they will. It just takes time for them to see the benefits of the Chinese. Everything will be good. Good evening, Marshal," he said and left the courtroom with his two guards.

Wu-Pen looked at Bing Jue and spoke in Chinese, "Go find every man of ours that works in the silver mine and tell them to meet me in the Temple in one hour without delay. We have much to discuss and plan."

***

Matt stepped into his office and went into the jail cell. Bo Crowe was lying on his bed and looked at Matt. "Shouldn't you be out dancing or whatever you do for fun, Marshal?"

Matt nodded. "Yeah. Well, I got a message

from Aurora County. It seems your accusers have changed their mind all of a sudden. You're out of here."

Bo chuckled and slowly sat up to put his boots on. "Well, that's a...big surprise, isn't it?" he said with a knowing grin.

Matt raised his eyebrows and nodded as he unlocked the cell door. "Yeah, it is. I wasn't expecting that. But you're free to go."

"Oh, Marshal, I need my weapons. You wouldn't want me leaving town without them, would you?" he asked sarcastically.

"You'll get them."

After Matt returned his gun belt to him, Bo put it on and looked at Matt with a slight grin. "Hey, let your brother know I don't appreciate what he did. It's not forgiven."

Matt smirked. "Let me tell you something, your brothers might be able to intimidate the townspeople in Aurora County, but not here in Jessup County. You and your brothers, cousins, or whoever else, will get your heads broke open or yourselves killed if you try intimidating anyone here. My brother is not concerned about you or your family period. Nor am I. If you want to feel important, go back home."

Bo grinned. "We'll see ya."

"You bet," Matt said and watched Bo walk out of the office.

Chapter 37

By Monday, Wes Wasson was in severe pain. He laid on a bed placed in the Ellison's family room with his foot wrapped in a bandage and elevated with a soft pillow under it. His thigh was stitched and wrapped up as well. His face and head were covered in white bandages that needed to be changed periodically from the bleeding. His shoulders had been put back in the socket but hurt far too much to use them. He had said extraordinarily little since coming to the Ellison home. He was morose and on a consistent dosage of morphine for the pain level to be kept under control. To use the privy was an impossibility, so a chair with a cut out wooden seat and bucket placed under it was next to the bed, it was his deepest humiliation, except for using a bedpan if there was no one there to help him to the chair. He didn't want to read and he spoke very little, he merely laid on the bed and slept or stared at the wall in his own thoughts. The bandage over his head hid where he had been scalped. The good news was Matt had sent his removed piece of scalp with Nate to the doctor who had sanitized it and was able to sew it back onto Wes's head. If it healed correctly, it would leave scars that could be hidden by his hair and only a scar at the hairline would be visible, but that was the best scenario. The worst scenario was it wouldn't heal and would have to be removed. The next best thing they could do then was to use an awl and puncture through the top layer of the skull into the bone marrow, which would form new skin over the skull bone as it filled in. It would be a long process taking about two years and would develop as scar tissue so that no hair would grow. The prayer of the Ellison's was the scalp would heal. The anxiety Wes felt about his appearance and the coming days of finding out if his skin would attach or not, was overwhelming to him. Of course, Doctor Ryland had done much of the suturing the scalp back on and the straightening and re-stitching of the three lobes of his broken nose, so the hopes were high that it would all turn out well.

Florence did her best to be his nurse and assist him as needed, but he was often indifferent and infuriated by his humiliation of having his sister care for him while he could not do so himself effectively yet.

A knock on the door brought Florence out of the kitchen and she opened it with questionable surprise. She spoke with an unknown female for a few moments and then she invited the unknown woman inside. Wes looked up and furrowed his brow with a slight smile forming on his lips as he watched Billy Jo Fasana walk into the family room carrying a pie.

"Hi, I heard what happened and wanted to drop off a pie I made. I hope you like apple pie," she said, standing in the middle of the room.

He nodded slowly. "I do," he said, watching her appreciatively.

Florence spoke, "Well, let me grab that from you. Wes, would you like a piece of this pie, right now?" She explained to Billy Jo, "He just had lunch a little while ago."

"I would," he said lightly. When Florence left the room, he continued, "I don't look my best right now."

Billy Joe waved a hand. "It's only temporary. Heck, I've looked my worst many times. I looked terrible when I met you."

"No. You're beautiful. And I appreciate the pie. You were thinking of me?"

She nodded. "I heard what happened and thought the pie would be a nice gesture. I'm glad you survived such an awful experience."

He frowned. "I wasn't so sure about that until now. If my hair does not stick back on, then I'm going to be awfully ugly. The kids will be calling me a monster everywhere I go with half my skull sticking out of my head."

Billy Jo frowned sympathetically. "I'm sure it will heal, and you'll never know it was taken off. You have to think positive about it. When you're all healed up, you'll be whooping it up with the ladies again!"

He smiled slightly. "I hope so. And maybe you'll promise to whoop it up with me?"

She grimaced. "I'm with Joe and he'd be mad, so I can't promise that."

"Yeah...but you're here and not at home. Does Joe know you're here or even know that you made me a pie? He seems like a controlling kind of guy to me."

Her face reddened as Florence came back into the room with two plates with a piece of pie on them. "Sit down, Billy Jo and have a piece of pie with my baby brother."

"Thank you. Wes mentioned it and if I could ask you both not to tell anyone, I was here. Because if my man finds out, I was here, I'll be in trouble. So, if anyone asks, someone else made the pie, okay? And I was never here, okay?" she asked with an anxious expression.

Florence frowned. "Well, my dear, we don't want you getting into any trouble. We don't need to tell anyone where the pie came from. I'll just say I made it."

"Thank you," Billy Jo said with relief.

Wes explained, "Her man works with Bruce."

"Oh? Do I know him?" Florence asked.

Billy Jo sighed. "Probably, most folks know of him anyway. Joe Thorn."

"Oh, Sweetheart, he's a brute! You should leave him and find yourself a man that will treat you right, like Frank, my husband," she explained. "I wouldn't change my husband for anything in this world. And that's what you need."

She lowered her head in shame. "I know…"

Wes smirked as he watched her. "She will when I'm healed up and back on my feet. Won't you, Darling?"

Billy Jo laughed. "No! But I wanted to tell you that you could rent my house when you can."

"Oh…We'll start there then."

Florence smiled. "I'll leave you two to talk and do not worry; no one else will know you were here."

"Thank you."

"Where are your children?" Wes asked.

"At my friend, Lucille Barton's. She's watching them for me today. I need to get back home and make dinner before Joe gets home. You take care, Wes."

"I will. Thank you for the pie and for coming over. You can always come back, you know. I would like the company."

"Okay, I'll arrange it soon enough."

After Billy Jo left, Florence came into the family room and sat down in her chair. "Wes, how did you meet her?"

"Through Bruce's friends. She's Ritchie Thorn's sister-in-law, but she says she's not married. She sutured my nose back together."

Florence took a deep breath. "Wes, Joe Thorn is a terrible man. He is dangerous from what I understand. Ask Bruce about him when he gets home, but do not get mixed up with her. She seems very sweet and is a good cook, obviously, but we don't want you getting into any more trouble, and that's all there will be with Joe Thorn if you pursue this lady."

Wes smirked. "Florence, I don't know what she does to me, but for whatever the reason, I want her. I'm hooked, and I don't even know why. Probably one out of fifty men would say she's beautiful but to me...she's stunning." He added, "And she's treated poorly. She deserves better."

"Wesley, you're not the marrying kind and I doubt you ever will be. So, don't ruin what little of a good home that girl has if you're not going to see a relationship through. She deserves better than to have high hopes just to be let down when it gets boring or hard for you."

"I'll keep that in mind, Sis. How about another piece of pie?" he asked, holding his plate out for her to take and refill.

"I think that's a good idea."

Chapter 38

A week later, Matt stood alone in the cemetery holding Chusi's dog on a rope leash. It was snowing heavily as another cold front had dropped down from the north, bringing a lot more snow with it. He was watching his uncle Luther Fasana and one of his employees place Chusi's tombstone on his grave. Matt had volunteered to pay for the granite marker like he had Jed's, but Luther refused to accept payment and made the tombstone free of charge due to his close friendship with Chusi.

Luther compressed the soil down around the bottom of the memorial with his foot, where they had dug out to bury the bottom of it. He looked at Matt when he had finished and smiled comfortingly. "Well, there it is. He'll never be forgotten now. It turned out alright, yeah?"

It was a piece of granite about two and a half feet tall and four inches thick. It was engraved with the utmost perfection. It stated:

Here lies Chusi Yellowbear

Shoshone Warrior, husband, father,
Survivor of Bear River Massacre,
The heart of a good man. Our friend.
Murdered 1884 – age 59 years

Matt nodded his head, approvingly. "It's perfect, Uncle Luther."

Luther stood beside Matt, looking at his craftsmanship, "Thank you. I've been making too many of these lately for people that I know. Chusi was a good man. Jed was a good man too. I hate engraving the names of good men into stone."

"I hate seeing them go."

"You just make sure it's not your name next," Luther said pointedly. "Don't you think it's time to retire that badge, Matt?"

Matt shook his head. "You've been on me about that since I came back a year ago. Uncle Luther, are you fulfilled by the work you do? I mean, is it a part of who you are?"

Luther nodded. "It's my company, of course, it is."

"Yeah, but is it satisfying? What do you get out of it that keeps you doing it besides money?"

"I enjoy it. And I get to make beautiful memorials that will last forever and I think that's important to the families that are suffering a loss of a loved one. Three generations from now, people will be able to come here and find their ancestors and I think that means something. Why? Are you looking for a new career?"

Matt shook his head. "No. It's the same thing for

me. I love what I do even with all the bad that goes with it. I've seen too much death; those I have killed, those killed by others and my friends dying too. All the violence, all the evil. When I was in Wyoming and on the hunt for bad men, I often knew it would end badly, so I expected it and partook in it. When I came here, I thought it would be easy and calm. There is constantly stuff going on here and it just doesn't end when you want to mourn a friend. It comes in piles, Uncle Luther, one after the other. I love my profession and no, I am far from retiring, but it does weigh on me. It's hard to push some things aside to focus on another and then that issue becomes harder than the one before it."

Luther frowned. "You're going to grow old before your time, Matt. Your beard is going to turn white like mine and then your hair, all by time your fifty if you keep it up. Worse, you'll lose your laughter. You don't laugh much as it is and you're still in your mid-thirties. What are you going to be like at fifty if you live that long? Our county is not wild, but you still have criminal elements, dangerous men and enough stuff to keep weighing you down. I wish you'd lay that badge down and come work for me. You're going to be married before too long, Christine will sleep easier and gray slower if she knows your engraving stone instead of chasing outlaws."

Matt smiled slowly. "I'm just not ready for that. Despite the horrors and heartbreaks, I love helping the innocent. I love the idea of law and order and bringing people to justice. I like the idea that my community is safer because of what I do. I love doing what's right and making a difference. And I know me, I'd be the first one to grab my guns and go after a criminal whether I had a badge or not. It's who I am and what I believe in." He looked at his uncle. "I'm where I'm supposed to be."

"Do you want to come over to the house and sit down and talk for a while?" Luther asked caringly.

"Not today, but I will soon. Before Chusi died, he asked me to ask you to take his dog and love it like your own. So, here is your gift from Chusi." He held out the rope for Luther.

Luther grimaced. "You're lying, right?"

Matt rolled his eyes as he explained, "Oh, I am desperately lying. I never wanted the dog, but I've had it for a week. It's made a mess out of my house and I don't have time for a dog. She's a good girl and she grows on you like a fungus. I like her, but I can't spend the time with her that she needs. You can take her to work with you like you used to do with your dogs, I can't. Do you want her?"

Luther nodded. "I'll take her. Does she have a name?"

Matt shrugged. "Just dog. It's a red tick hound."

Luther took the rope. "Yeah, I think she and I will get along well. She looks cold, so I think I'll take her home. Matt, you take care."

"I will, Uncle Luther and thank you again. Chusi's memorial is perfect."

Luther nodded. "He was a good man."

Matt nodded in agreement. When Luther had left Matt knelt and read the marker again. His eyes filled with moisture and he sniffled in the cold air. "I'll never forget you, my friend. Until we meet again."

Chapter 39

It had been over a week since Jed and Chusi were killed and Christine had mourned with Matt for the loss of their two friends. Christine was tired of staying in the dance hall doing nothing all weekend, so she asked Matt to rent a buggy and drive her to his house rather than walking clear across town in the cold and snow. He did so and she had spent the day cleaning his house while he and Truet were at the office. Neither of the two men were terribly sloppy, but the home needed a woman's touch in many ways and not just the cleanliness. There were no decorations, no home appeal and nothing made the beautiful home inviting except for when either of the men said, "Come in." Rather than sitting in her room, she decided to take it upon herself to clean their home, organize the kitchen and family room into an inviting environment that had more to offer than gun oil and dirty rags on the table and muddy boots on the floor. If she were feeling better and could move around like she used to, she would go to different shops in town and purchase paintings, knick-knacks and flowers to liven up the drab atmosphere. Some new drapes and add some color to create a warmer feeling, but she worked with what she could, and that wasn't too much. At lunchtime, she fed the men a simple lunch with what little they had and gave Matt a long list to buy for a dinner she was going to make. He wasn't too pleased about shopping, but when he returned, she sent him back to work while she began preparing dinner. He, like always, was more concerned about her wearing herself out needlessly far more than he was about creating a home out of his house.

She had prepared baked chicken with mash potatoes, gravy, some biscuits and green beans for dinner with a pitcher of fresh milk to drink with dinner. The house was clean and smelled of some good home cooking when the men came home. They were respectful enough to take their boots off at the door and not spread mud around on her clean floor. The dining table was set and ready for them to sit at the table and eat together. Matt and Truet were pleasantly surprised to have a good meal waiting for them when they came home.

Matt sat at the table and looked at her caringly. "The house looks wonderful and so does this meal. You worked hard, that's for sure. As much as we appreciate it, how are you feeling?"

She smiled with tight lips. "I'm a little sore, but I'm doing okay. You two just need to keep things cleaner from now on."

Truet grinned his handsome smile. "It's Matt;

he's a pig. Just ask Annie, she'll tell you."

Christine chuckled. "Oh, I know she'd tell me. But I'm telling you, you both are to blame. Let's say grace and have some dinner," she said and held her hands out for each one of them to take hold while they prayed.

Matt closed his eyes. "Father, Thank you for Christine and her work to make our home a better place and for this meal before us. I want to thank you for her presence here and your blessing on the life we are planning together. Thank you for Truet and the friendship we have made. He's been a blessing as well and I pray you'll watch over him and keep him safe, I ask that you'll keep all of my deputies safe and myself as well. This has been a terrible time for us recently, with the loss of our friends Chusi and Jed." He paused and then continued, "There are some things I will never understand, Jesus, but I'm aware that evil exists and evil people do evil things far out of your will. It may seem like you don't care sometimes, but I know nothing is unseen or forgotten by you. And those who are evil will be held accountable for all they've done. Everyone wants to take vengeance for wrongs done to them, myself included sometimes and I'll do my best to remember that you said, vengeance is yours. And your vengeance is justice. Justice will come to everyone. I ask that we can bring as many people into the Kingdom of heaven as we can with your help. May it be my life's goal to share the gospel and your love, hope, and grace with everyone I meet. Though I am a bad example of you, I ask that your light will shine through me despite my shortcomings. Jesus, let your peace and comfort fill Jed's home and I ask that you'll hold them close and tight. Thank you for Chusi's and Jed's life crossing with ours. Thank you for the blessings you pour on our lives even when we don't see it. In Jesus' name. Amen."

As they ate, there was a knock on the door.

Matt got up and went to the door. "Who is it?"

"Wu-Pen."

"Wu-Pen?" Matt questioned as he opened the door with a curious expression. "Wu-Pen, this is quite a surprise. Would you and the fella's like to come in?"

"Yes, that would be nice," he said with a smile.

Matt smiled at both Uang Yang and Bing Jue as they entered. They politely nodded back with a slight smile.

Christine Knapp stood up at the table politely. "Oh! I thought it might be William. He always seems to show up when there's food."

Matt laughed lightly. "Christine, this is Wu-Pen and his two friends Uang and Bing. This is Christine, my fiancé and you know Truet, of course," Matt explained.

"Hi, Wu-Pen, it's nice to meet you, gentlemen." She stepped forward to shake his hand.

Wu-Pen handed a box to Matt and put his attention on Christine. "My, what a beautiful lady. It's my pleasure to meet you finally. I heard about the horrible thing that happened to you and I am so happy you are okay."

She grinned pleasantly. "Thank you." She looked at Uang and put her hand out to shake, "I'm Christine, what's your name?"

Uang smiled and bowed politely but didn't say anything. Bing also bowed respectfully.

Wu-Pen spoke, "I'm sorry, but they do not speak English. I am sure they are pleased to meet you, though." He spoke in Chinese, and both men answered shortly. "Yes, they are pleased to meet you. And because of what happened to you, if ever needed, they offer their protection for a friend's beautiful fiancé." He looked at Matt. "Because of your enemies, if ever you are concerned for her safety, let me know and these men will give their lives to keep her safe, I promise you."

Matt furrowed his brow, not quite knowing how to take the statement. "Thank you."

Wu-Pen smiled and then frowned. "I am sorry to hear about your friend Chusi. I had some more Chongyang Gao made for you. I understand you enjoyed it last time, yes?"

"I did. It's very good."

"Excellent. As I explained before, it is a customary dessert to mourn a loved one."

Christine's mouth opened. "A dessert? That is so nice. I made these men dinner, but I didn't make a dessert. Thank you, Wu-Pen." She took the box from Matt and walked into the kitchen.

Wu-Pen asked Matt, "I must ask, does William Slater not like you?"

Matt furrowed his brow again, not expecting such a random question. "I don't think he does.

Why do you ask?"

"In the courtroom, he looked at you with a despiteful eye. I think he does not like you. Nor me. Why does he not like you?" Wu Pen asked.

"I'm not the puppet he wanted me to be."

Wu-Pen nodded understandably with a small smile. "He is not a good man, is he?"

"I don't like him, but I don't have to like him. I just try to do whatever is right, whether he likes it or not. Sometimes he doesn't."

"I understand. I do not mean to interrupt your dinner. It does smell delicious. Oh, and Lady Christine," he called into the kitchen. He continued when she walked back into the family room. "Would you be so kind as to honor my friends and me with an invitation to your wedding? If not, I understand, we Chinese are not welcomed by many Americans. But I will get you a gift anyway."

Christine answered sincerely, "As of the moment, we don't have a date set. But when we do, we will go through the guest list and see if we have room in the church. I do not mean to sound rude, but Matt has a big family and we have lots of close friends. So, there may not be room, so I can't promise. But do know, I don't care that you're Chinese, it would not bother me at all to have you and your friends celebrating with us. And if there is room, I certainly will invite you. Are you married, Wu-Pen?"

He smiled pleased with her honest answer. "I am not. I understand about having room perfectly, and I appreciate your honesty. Thank you. Have a good evening, my friends. We must get back as you know, we Chinese are not supposed to be out after dark."

Christine spoke, "I didn't make a whole lot for dinner, but would you and your friends like a piece of chicken to eat on the way home?"

Wu-Pen looked at her kindly. "If it would not be too much trouble or leave you short."

"You brought us dessert when we did not have one; I should return the favor. Let me grab some for you and your friends."

He looked at Matt. "Your fiancé is wonderful. You have the world in your arms, my friend. I like her very much."

Matt smiled. "Me too. Thank you for the dessert."

"It's the least I could do. Thank you, Lady Christine," he said as she handed him and the other two gentlemen a piece of chicken. Uang and Bing were surprised and bowed with friendly smiles of appreciation. It was the first time Matt had ever seen either of them grin.

When they left, Christine put her arms around Matt and kissed him. "I heard what he said, you do have the world in your arms, you know," she said with a deep sincere gaze into his eyes.

Matt looked into her eyes and the thought of Jed's wife and children who were mourning deeply for their husband and father who left with a smile one morning and never came home. Their lives would never be the same and the pain would ripple through their lifetimes with the hollowness that would never be filled completely again. Matt thought of Chusi, who lived in hopeless despair for so long after losing his wife and children. Life is a limited time opportunity to enjoy and cherish those you love while you have them. For Matt, he had his family back after fifteen years and his father back as well. He had found love with Christine and knew he would never betray her, abuse her, or let her slip away. He had everything that a man can dream of. Matt looked into Christine's eyes and smiled slowly. "I do indeed, " he said and kissed her gently.

Take a look at
A Winding Trail to Justice by Reg Quist

———

AWARD WINNING AUTHOR OF THE MAC'S WAY INTRODUCES BOOK TWO OF A NEW WHOLESOME WESTERN SERIES!

Zac Trimbell has found himself in Las Vegas, New Mexico where a troubled lady, Claire Maddison, arrives at his ranch seeking help. Claire's sister and brother-in-law are missing, and all their cattle has been stolen. The sheriff advised Claire that if Zac can't help, no one can. Trig Mason pushes his way into the search and together the three set out to solve the mystery and return the cattle.

The sister and her husband are located wounded and weary. They are taken back to the ranch while Zac and the others look for the lost cattle. A long ride following the churned up, grassy trail takes them back to the gold country of Colorado.

While Zac continues to struggle with his post-Civil War PTSD, he makes it his mission to help where he is needed and see that justice is done.

Now it's time for the age-old question, *"Is it still well with your soul?"*

AVAILABLE NOW

About the Author

Ken Pratt and his wife, Cathy, have been married for 22 years and are blessed with five children and six grandchildren. They live on the Oregon Coast where they are raising the youngest of their children. Ken Pratt grew up in the small farming community of Dayton, Oregon.

Ken worked to make a living, but his passion has always been writing. Having a busy family, the only "free" time he had to write was late at night getting no more than five hours of sleep a night. He has penned several novels that are being published along with several children stories as well.